──────────── ★ ────────────

## I WAS LYING ON
## A BRICK FLOOR

No bones seemed to be broken, but I had a welt on my head the size of a corncob.

I turned on the cold water, splashed some on my face. I glanced around the bathroom and noticed, for the first time, that the toilet was pink, the same shade as the towel. So were the sink and the bathtub and the bathmat atop the blue tiled floor. The translucent plastic shower curtain was printed with a bright blue floral pattern, and it was pulled shut.

But not all the way, because a flat-soled woman's shoe was jutting out from one end, and there was a foot in it.

──────────── ★ ────────────

# WALL OF GLASS

## Walter Satterthwait

**WORLDWIDE**

TORONTO • NEW YORK • LONDON
AMSTERDAM • PARIS • SYDNEY • HAMBURG
STOCKHOLM • ATHENS • TOKYO • MILAN
MADRID • WARSAW • BUDAPEST • AUCKLAND

Second edition December 1993

**WALL OF GLASS**

A Worldwide Mystery/September 1989

First published by St. Martin's Press, Incorporated.

ISBN 0-373-83265-6

For their encouragement, for their help,
or for the information they provided,
I would like to thank the following people:
Charles Baldonado, Alan Ball, Dick Beddow,
Gene Bonner, Chuck Fair and Office Incorporated,
Claudia Jessup, Jon Richards, B.E. Kitsman,
Jane Magan, Nick, Jeanne Satterthwait,
and Gary Wolfe.

For their patience,
I would like to thank my editor,
Tom Dunne, and my agent,
Dominick Abel.

# ONE

IT WAS A FRIDAY in mid-April, warm and clear and spectacularly sunny, and a blizzard was due by midnight. Weather like this happens every spring in the New Mexico mountains, and it produces one of our famous annual events, the Death of the Apple Blossoms. Tomorrow all the pink-white petals in the courtyard would be buried beneath a foot of snow. In another few days, the snow would be gone and the petals would be littering the ground in sodden drifts, like fans of debris left behind by a storm tide. And in another few months, when fall rolled around, there would be no apples on the trees. If the Garden of Eden had been planted here, Adam and Eve might still be working things out.

I was sitting with the chair swiveled toward the window, my feet hooked on the sill, watching the clouds pile up black and bloated above the ski basin and wondering what the weather was doing in Tahiti, or Sri Lanka, or Bali. Wondering if I could ever persuade Rita to share a week or two, or a year or two, on a soft warm beach somewhere, listening to the waves curl and slap against the sand.

When I heard the door open, I swung my legs down off the sill and wheeled the chair around. The man in the doorway looked at me and frowned. "Sign on the door says Mondragón Agency."

A point in his favor. Some of our clients can't read. "That's right," I told him. "I'm Joshua Croft."

He nodded. "Reckoned you didn't look like no Mondragón."

He was short and muscular, and he moved across the office with a quick alert strut, a bantam swagger, like someone who might take offense at the word "Napoleon." He wore dusty Western boots, faded jeans, a tight-fitting denim shirt, and a gray Stetson with the sides of its brim curled up. His face was sun-reddened and his eyes had the prairie squint. This being Santa Fe, he could've been exactly what he looked like. A real live cowboy.

On the other hand, this being Santa Fe, he could've been a stockbroker.

He didn't introduce himself or offer his hand or take off his hat. Which probably eliminated stockbroker. He plopped down into the client's chair, stretched out his legs, and crossed them at the ankles. Lacing his fingers together atop his chest, he said, "I got what you call a hypothetical situation." Which probably eliminated cowboy.

"And what might that be?"

"Well now. Let's say I got this friend who's got a friend."

I nodded. "A friend of a friend." Wonderful.

He grinned, as though to congratulate me for catching on so quickly. "Exactly right, bro. And let's say this friend of a friend, he knows where he can put his hands on a piece of hot property. Some jewelry, let's say."

"Let's not say."

He frowned. "How's that again?"

"I'm licensed by the state. In exchange for the license, they want me to report any little peccadilloes I run across. They'd be real pleased to hear about grand theft."

He grinned. "Peccadilloes," he said, and nodded appreciatively. "Good one, bro." He made his face go serious. "But now, s'pose this guy'd be willin' to make it worth your while?"

"He might be willing, but he wouldn't be able."

"What's that mean?"

"It means farewell. *Adios*."

"We're talkin' some good money here, bro."

"We're talking goodbye."

"Now listen here, bro," he said amiably, sitting forward, drawing in his legs, and tucking his feet under the chair. "Won't take but a minute for me to lay the whole thing out for you. You decide you don't want a piece, you just say so and I'm gone, I'm history, and no hard feelings. And you wanna report anything, you go right ahead and do it. I wasn't even in town when the thing was lifted. And this friend of a friend wasn't neither."

I glanced at the clock. Four-thirty. I could afford to kill half an hour. I'd been killing them, one by one, all day. "What was it we were saying was lifted?"

"Piece of jewelry. And let's say the insurance company already paid out on it. A hundred thousand bucks. One hundred large ones, bro. Now don't you reckon they'd come up with a few thousand more to get the thing back?"

"A finder's fee."

"Exactly right," he grinned, opening up his hands to show me his palms. He sat back, stretching out his legs again and crossing them. "A finder's fee. A simple little business proposition. You reckon they'd go for a dealy like that?"

"Depends."

His face remained friendly, but his eyes narrowed. "Depends on what, bro?"

"On the company, for one thing. Some of them don't do it."

The tightness left his eyes and he nodded. "But some do, you're sayin'."

"Some do," I admitted. The police aren't too fond of the idea, but the police don't have profit and loss statements to worry about.

"And what you reckon they'd pay for somethin' worth a hundred thousand?"

I shook my head. "It's not worth a hundred thousand. Not unless whoever received the claim on it, the former owner, wants it back badly enough to return the money. If he doesn't, the company has to offer the thing on the open market, as salvage, and take whatever it can get. They might be able to make a third of its insured value. A half, maybe, if they're lucky. When was it stolen?"

He smiled. "While ago."

"One year? Two years? Seven?"

The smile became a grin. "You're thinkin' statute of limitations, ain't you, bro?"

I had been, but I said, "Inflation. The real value of the thing could've gone up against its insured value."

He shook his head. "Nope. Not that long a while."

"What kind of jewels are involved? What kind of stones?"

He grinned. "Now how come you wanna know a thing like that?"

I shrugged. "Some stones would be easier for the company to move," I said. Improvising.

"That right?" he said, and grinned again. "Sounds to me like you're tryin' to shit a shitter. No wisdom in that, bro. No profit, neither."

"Let me just get a pen," I said, "and jot that down."

Another grin. "Hey there, bro. No need to get riled. Just givin' you a little free advice is all. The benefit of my experience, you might say."

"I'm not riled. As a matter of fact, I'm delighted to get the benefit of your experience. But what is it, exactly, you want from me?"

Languidly he uncrossed his legs, then languidly recrossed them. "Well now, this friend of a friend, he's a shy kinda guy. Likes his privacy, you know what I mean?

What he wants is to be a sorta silent partner-type. And we figured, the two of us did, that maybe you'd like to be the one who went to the insurance company with the deal. Handled all the details, if you follow me."

"Acted as middleman."

Smiling, he nodded his head in a quick cocking movement that signaled admiration. "I could tell, bro, soon's I walked in the door, that you were one sharp dude. So what would you say to maybe ten percent, right off the top?"

"I'd say no."

He nodded, nonplussed. "Uh-huh. You got a counter-offer?"

"A third."

He nodded again. "And that don't strike you as maybe a little bit excessive?"

"I'd be the one doing the negotiating. I'd be the one with my head on the line."

"Just how much you plan to be negotiating for?"

"Depends."

"On the stuff you said before."

"On the stuff I said before."

"You got a ballpark figure?"

"As little as five thousand, as much as thirty."

"Meanin' your share could be ten grand."

"If we're lucky."

"Ten grand just for doin' some talkin'."

I shrugged. "I don't remember putting an ad in the paper asking you to drop by."

He grinned again, slapped his thigh, and pointed his index finger at my forehead. His cocked thumb came down against the finger like the hammer on a pistol. Pow. "Awright, bro, you got it. I like your style. I gotta talk to the other guy, o'course, and square it with him. But my money's on you." He stood, hitched up his belt, adjusted his Stetson. "I'll be in touch directly."

I said, "I don't suppose you want to leave a name."

He grinned again. "You got that one right, bro. See you." And he turned and swaggered from the room. For a moment I imagined I could hear spurs go jingle jangle jingle.

AFTER I FINISHED swimming my mile at the municipal pool, I drove up the Ski Basin Road to Rita's house. Maria told me that Mrs. Mondragón was out back on the patio.

Rita had rolled the wheelchair up to the balustrade overlooking the Douglas firs that swept down the mountainside till they met the piñon and juniper growing outside the town. From where she sat she could see all of Santa Fe, mostly brown adobe buildings in a sprawl that made it seem larger, and more important, than it was. Directly overhead, the sky was black now; but it was still bright blue off to the east, beyond the town, past the rolling hills and the invisible Rio Grande, over there where the sun was sliding slowly toward the crouching purple slopes of the Jemez range.

On Rita's right was the easel, on her left was a small table holding a cordless telephone receiver, three or four tubes of oil paint, a pitcher of what looked like lemonade, and two drinking glasses, one full and one empty.

She turned to me and smiled. "Hello." Palette in her left hand, paint brush in her right.

"Hi," I said. The air always seemed clearer around her; and yet, at the same time, somehow seemed to be gathering density and substance, as though it were crystallizing. "How's it going?"

She looked at the canvas and frowned. "I can't get the light," she said. "The light is everything."

"It looks fine to me, Rita." It did, a view of the mountains, spare and uncluttered; but I would've said the same thing if it had been a yellow Happy Face, and she knew it.

She smiled again. "So speaks the Northrop Frye of Santa Fe."

Her hair was thick and black, exactly the color and sheen of ravens' wings, and it tumbled down below her shoulders. She had high cheekbones and very dark brown eyes so large they were sometimes difficult to meet. Her mouth was broad and full, set between finely drawn smile lines, ironic parentheses. She was wearing a heavy white wool cardigan sweater over a white silk blouse and a white skirt sashed at the waist with a band of red. The skirt, like all the skirts she wore since the bullet had smashed her spine, reached to her ankles.

"Lemonade?" she asked me, and set palette and brush down on the table.

"No thanks," I told her. I sat down against the balustrade. "It's a little early for me."

She smiled. "For lemonade?"

"A little early in the year. I'll wait for the Fourth of July. By then the temperature may be up into the fifties."

Some exasperation crept into the corners of her smile; I had complained before about the weather. "It's not that cold, Joshua."

I blew a puff of air from my mouth and pointed to the plume of white vapor. Up here we were at least a thousand feet higher than the town, and the approaching storm was adding its chill to air that was already cool.

"You could've gone to Los Angeles this week," she said. "You had the chance."

"No tan," I said. "You don't have a tan that reaches under your eyelids, they won't let you in. They make you go to Anaheim and hang out with Mickey Mouse."

She smiled. "I should think that'd be right up your alley."

I ignored that. "But speaking of L.A., Norman called this morning. He has a line on the Sherman girl." We sometimes got work that required a warm body in L.A., and usually we subcontracted it to Ed Norman's agency in Burbank.

"Is she all right?"

"Probably not, Rita. Norman thinks she's running with some bad people out there."

She frowned. "Drugs."

"And maybe prostitution."

"She's only fourteen, Joshua."

"In some circles, that's considered over the hill."

"Will he be able to get her out?"

"Probably."

She sensed the reservation behind the word. "But?"

I shrugged. "You know what the *but* is. Even if he does, even if he gets her back here, there's nothing to stop her running away again."

She nodded. "We'll worry about that later, if we have to. I'll call him tonight. Did anything else come up?"

"As a matter of fact, something did. We got an offer to fence some stolen jewelry."

"Oh?" Smiling, she sat back in the chair. "Tell me about it."

I did. When I was finished, she said, "And what do you think?"

I said, "I think he was fishing. Trying to find out what his options were. I don't think we'll ever see him again."

She nodded. I could never tell, from the way she nodded, whether she was agreeing with or merely placating me. She said, "Do you think he actually has access to the jewelry?"

"I think so, yeah."

"He claims he had nothing to do with the theft?" She lifted her glass of lemonade, took a sip.

"He said he was out of town when the thing was stolen. Even if that's the truth, it doesn't mean he didn't know about it."

"You feel he was involved."

"Sure. He's real short, Rita. And short people are capable of anything."

She made a face. "Joshua."

"And this is a guy who knows about the statute of limitations."

"So does everyone who's ever watched a 'Perry Mason' rerun."

"Yeah, but they don't all show up at the office offering a hundred thousand dollars worth of hot jewelry."

"He didn't say what kind of jewelry it was?"

"No. On the whole, he wasn't very forthcoming."

"But you were, apparently." Another sip of lemonade. "He knows enough now to contact the insurance company by himself."

"It was all part of this clever ploy, see. Cunningly designed to make him spill the beans."

"Ah," she said, and sipped at her lemonade.

I shrugged. "Sometimes these clever ploys don't work so well. Maybe I should've picked him up and put his head through the ceiling. Forget the subtlety shit, right?"

She smiled. "I'm not sure that the physical approach would have been any more fruitful."

"Yeah. He probably would've punched me in the kneecap."

"Or shot you."

"You know me, Rita. Nothing bothers me but kryptonite."

"Be still my heart."

I laughed. "Do you think we should go to the cops about this guy?"

She considered this. I considered, in the meantime, the curve of her throat. After a moment she said, "We can give Hector a call." Hector Ramirez was a friend on the Santa Fe P.D. "But I don't think the police'll be able to do anything productive. He doesn't sound, from what you've said, like someone who'd go to pieces if they turned up on his doorstep." She smiled. "Assuming they could find his doorstep. And after all, it's only your word against his." She frowned. "But I wonder why no one's tried to move that jewelry before this. If the claim's been paid, the jewelry was stolen some time ago. Insurance companies don't hand over a hundred thousand dollars without an investigation, and that takes time."

"Maybe he couldn't find a fence who'd take an item that big."

"Then why steal it in the first place?"

"Maybe he was waiting for things to cool down."

"And why is he willing to deal with the insurance company now, instead of a fence?"

"Maybe he saw it on a 'Perry Mason' rerun."

She smiled.

"Listen," I said. "There's a new Rohmer movie playing downtown."

Her smile was affectionate but weary. "You don't give up, do you, Joshua?"

"I think of it as a selling point."

"I think of it as stubbornness."

"And that's something you'd know about, Rita."

"It's not stubbornness."

"Pride, then."

"If you like. Joshua, we've been over this a hundred times. I'll go downtown when I can walk downtown."

The doctors had said she would probably never walk again. Rita said she would, no probably about it. I tended to put my faith in Rita, but it had been almost two years.

"How's the therapy?" I asked.

"Fine."

I didn't ask if there was any improvement. She would've told me if there had.

"Why don't you ask Clair?" she said. "To the Rohmer movie. Are you still seeing her?"

"Clair thinks a Rohmer is a guy who never goes home."

"I thought you liked her."

"I like her. She's a peach. She's not you, though, Rita."

"Neither am I, Joshua." The words crisp, her face blank and unreadable.

"Rita—"

"You won't forget to call Hector?"

I sighed. "I'll call him tomorrow morning. Am I being sent home?"

"It's time for the pool. I'll see you on Monday."

As it turned out, I saw her before Monday. The next day, Saturday, there was an article in the morning paper about the man who'd come to the office. It gave his name, Frank Biddle, and said that he was a former rodeo star. It had a nice picture of Frank, beaming and holding up a big bronze trophy. He wasn't wearing his cowboy hat; maybe he'd lost it riding the bull. The article said that his body had been found late on Friday night, with four bullet holes in it and two bullets.

# TWO

"THEY MEANT four entry and two exit wounds," said Hector Ramirez. "Two of the slugs stayed inside. All thirty-eight's, and probably from the same gun. According to the preliminary autopsy report, one lodged in his spine and the other rattled around in his rib cage before it tore his heart apart. We dug up the other two slugs from the far side of the arroyo."

We were sitting, Hector and I, in his cubicle at the Santa Fe police station. I'd called him earlier, after speaking to Rita, and he'd asked me down to make a statement. I'd made it, taped it into Hector's cassette recorder, and in a day or two, after one of the secretaries had transcribed it, I'd come back to sign it.

A sergeant in the Violent Crimes Unit, Hector was short and beefy. The beefiness was deceptive; he ran five miles a day and he could bench press two hundred and fifty pounds, which is fifty more than I weigh and a hundred more than I'd care to think about moving, even with a fork lift. His eyes were dark and half-hooded, giving him the bored sleepy air of someone who's seen it all, twice. He had thick black hair and a thick black mustache that dropped over the corners of his mouth and made him look a bit like the Frito Bandito. Which was something, however, that I'd never had occasion to bring to his attention. Today he was wearing a pale blue pinstriped shirt with a white collar. The collar was open, the knot of his navy blue tie was pulled down to the third shirt button, and his cuffs were rolled back.

I said, "So he was shot there. At the arroyo."

"Oh yeah," he said. "Blood all over." He laced his fingers together behind his neck and leaned back in the chair, away from the desk, so that his head was nearly brushing against the pale green wall. "His car was parked up on the road. That's why Johnson, the officer driving the unit, stopped to check it out. This was in the middle of the storm, and he thought a motorist might be stranded."

"Any tracks? Footprints? Another car?"

"Not in the snow. And the ground underneath is hard-packed soil."

"So he was killed before the snow started last night. Before eleven o'clock." It had begun then, just a few soft fat flakes spiraling down in the darkness. In fifteen minutes it had become so dense, whipped and whirled by the wind, that you couldn't see twenty feet ahead of you. Johnson had been lucky to spot the car at all.

"Yeah," Hector said. "Except for the blood, the ground beneath him was dry. From body temperature, the M.E. thinks he was only lying there a couple of hours. Figure the time of death at around ten o'clock."

"So someone shoots Biddle at ten, then drives away. Or walks away."

"Drives, we figure. The keys to Biddle's car were in the ignition. If the guy didn't have his own car, he could've taken Biddle's. And the arroyo is maybe two miles from town. Long walk when a blizzard's due."

"No one saw anything? Heard anything?"

"Nope."

"It was Friday night, a lot of traffic. No one passed by?"

"Not any who told us about it."

"You have any suspects?"

He smiled. "Besides you, you mean?"

"The world lost a great humorist when you became a cop, Hector."

His elbows winged slightly outward as he shrugged his thick shoulders. "Far as we know, you were the last one to see him alive."

"Next to last," I said.

He nodded. "Why'd he pick you?"

"Biddle? He didn't. He just walked into the first P.I.'s office he came to."

"Only a coincidence that it was yours."

"Yep."

"You still have that thirty-eight?"

"Why? You want to borrow it?"

"You still have it?"

"I still have it. I don't carry it."

Hector nodded again, his square face expressionless. "Biddle didn't mention any names?"

"Nope. I said so in the statement."

"And he said jewelry."

"A piece of jewelry, yeah."

"He didn't mention any particular piece?"

"I told you, Hector, no. You're sure asking a lot of questions."

"Hey," he said, and shrugged elaborately. "I'm a cop. Wanna see my handcuffs?"

"I don't think so. Have you tied Biddle to a particular piece of jewelry?"

"They're real nice. They're chrome."

"Well," I said, "maybe just a peak."

He grinned and slipped his hands away from the back of his neck, put them along the arms of his chair. "Could be. You know Derek Leighton?"

"Of him. Money. He builds things."

"Biddle used to work for him. Gardener. Handyman. Leighton fired him last year, beginning of October. Biddle went down to Amarillo for a couple of months. A week or so after he leaves, someone breaks into the Leightons' house, ransacks the wife's bedroom. Takes off with some money, a gun, and a diamond necklace. The necklace was insured for a hundred thousand dollars."

"But Biddle was in Amarillo."

"Biddle had a friend. Stacey Killebrew."

I frowned. "I thought Stacey was off making license plates."

"He only did eighteen months. They let him out early last year. Good behavior."

"Must've changed some."

"He got rehabilitated, they tell me."

"That's a real tribute to the system, Hector. You should be proud."

"Oh yeah," he said. "Pleased as punch."

"Was he alibied for the time of the burglary?"

"Playing poker, he said. Three of his friends corroborated. But for ten bucks apiece, those three would alibi John Wilkes Booth. For another ten, they'd hold his horse while he took in the show."

"Why did Burglary like Biddle for the snatch?"

"Nolan was handling the case. He found out that Biddle had been running a number with Leighton's wife. Turns out she's one of those women who like rough trade. Nolan figured that Leighton realized what was happening and dumped Biddle, and that Biddle decided to get even by setting up the snatch with Killebrew."

"But Nolan wasn't able to nail Biddle. Or Killebrew."

"No."

"Is Killebrew alibied for last night?"

He nodded. "Another poker game."

"Same people?"

"Yeah."

"How much money was taken from the Leightons?"

"Couple hundred. Pin money for them."

"And the gun. It belonged to the wife?"

"Yeah. A thirty-eight. Police Special."

"Pretty heavy armament for a housewife."

Ramirez shrugged again. "Women's lib. Some of these housewives got bazookas now, I hear. Tanks, even."

"The gun never showed?"

He shook his head. "And neither did the necklace." His eyes narrowed. "You know why I'm giving you all this?"

"Sure. You're angling for an invitation to the prom."

"Besides that."

"Why?"

"So you've got everything we've got, and you don't start snooping on your own, maybe try to pick up a finder's fee on that necklace. This is a homicide now, Josh, not just a burglary. You've always been straight with me, and I respect that. I want your word you'll stay out of this."

"I'm a little overwhelmed, Hector."

"Do I have it?"

"Sure."

He nodded and sat back in his chair.

"Am I excused now?" I said.

"Yeah. How's Rita doing?"

I felt the small private stab that always came whenever anyone mentioned her name.

"The same."

He nodded. "Give her my love. Tell her we miss her."

OUTSIDE THE police station the air was bitter and the sunlight that glared off the bright white snow was blinding. The snow blanketed the ground four inches deep and lay like lacework in the trees. It might have been pretty if I'd been looking at it from behind a double-glazed picture window with a fire roaring and popping beside me, instead of standing in it while it slowly seeped into my boots.

But everyone seemed to be enjoying it just fine. To my left, two young boys were hurling snowballs and shrieks at each other. To my right, two young girls, giggling, were pushing a much larger snowball across the station's patch of lawn. The base, presumably, for a snowman. Maybe this division of labor said something profound about an inherent difference between the sexes.

Then again, maybe it just said that children, at least, could still take pleasure from what would probably be the last snowfall of the season.

Their pleasure, unfortunately, would soon be gone, along with its source. By midday the thin mountain air would finally begin to warm up and the snow would begin to melt. Already it had turned to a slurry in the street. As I watched, a Chevy Blazer drove by, tires spraying gray fans of it off to the side as the car splashed toward the Plaza.

I crossed the street, stepping around the water and over the drifts and ridges of blackening slush. I tramped into the public library, stomped most of the snow off onto the welcome mat, and called Rita on the pay phone while the rest of the stuff dribbled down my boots and puddled out along the tile floor. I told her what, in general, had gone on with Hector. She asked me to stop by her house later in the day, and I said I would and offered to cook dinner. Ginger beef. She said that would be splendid, and that she'd provide the wine.

WHEN I ARRIVED, at six, there was one set of tire tracks in the snow atop Rita's driveway. Which meant that Maria had driven into town or that someone else had come visiting. This is what we detectives call a deduction.

The gravel beneath the snow had turned to muck, and I had to put the Subaru into four-wheel to get up to the house. I saw that Maria's car, a Volkswagen Beetle, was gone. Score one for the deductive process.

Hefting my grocery bag, I wrestled my way out of the wagon and proceeded, with more caution than grace, down the flagstones. The snow that had melted earlier in the day was freezing over again as the sun went down, and the walkway was slick as glass. I thumbed the doorbell.

After a moment, Rita opened the door. Smiling, she rolled back the wheelchair to let me in.

"Hi," I said, wiping my feet on the mat. "I hope you're hungry."

"Starving," she said. She was wearing a black skirt and a black silk blouse, a strand of pearls around her neck.

"Good." I passed through the foyer and crossed the living room, Rita following behind, the motor of her chair giving off a soft electric whirr.

In the kitchen I set the groceries down on the island in the center of the room, the brown grocery bag crackling as I did, a homey and vaguely comforting sound.

I began hauling out the food. "Snowpeas," I said. "Green peppers. Ginger root. Chicken stock á la Campbell. And look at this." I unwrapped the butcher paper. "Is this a handsome piece of beef or what?"

"Lovely." She smiled. "But are you sure it'll be enough? After all, there *are* two of us."

"Don't get sarcastic with the chef. It's only a pound and a half. And I had to take out a bank loan to get it." I turned back to the bag, rummaged inside. "Where's the cornstarch?"

"I've got cornstarch," she said. "You left it here when you made the hot and sour soup."

"Well, now you've got some more. A body can never have too much cornstarch."

"I've got rice, too," she said as I set the box of Uncle Ben's on the countertop.

"A body can never have too much rice. Where's the knife?"

"Same place it always is."

"Ah."

I turned and plucked a paring knife from the rack on the wall, set it down on the counter.

"You have your choice of wines," Rita said. "There's a Zinfandel and a retsina."

I opened a cupboard door, lifted out a colander. "Retsina is the Greek stuff that tastes like turpentine?" I dumped the snowpeas into the colander and turned on the faucet.

"This is a different brand than that last bottle you had. Better. I thought it would go well with ginger beef."

Rinsing off the peas, I said, "Then retsina it is."

"Do you want some now?"

"Sure. Where is it?"

"I'll get it," she said. Naturally. Rita never needed any help.

She rolled to the refrigerator, opened the door, and leaned forward to take out the bottle of straw-colored wine. She put the bottle on the countertop, swiveled the chair around and rolled it to the cabinet, searched through the middle drawer and plucked out a corkscrew. I busied myself shaking water from the snowpeas.

The wineglasses were in the cabinet below the island's counter. Rita took out two glasses, set them beside the wine bottle, then lifted the bottle and went at it with the corkscrew. It was a standard restaurant model, the kind with a lever that folds so the thing can fit neatly into a waiter's vest, and on my best days, at the peak of my strength, it can reduce me to a babbling idiot. Turning aside, I got the butcher block chopping board down off the wall and began to slice snowpeas into two-inch-long sections with meticulous attention, as though I were the sous chef at the Peking Hilton.

I heard a dull pop behind me as the cork left the bottle, then the gurgle and splash of pouring wine. I didn't turn around. No big deal. Millions of people were opening wine bottles all over the country, right this very minute. And maybe a few of them were even doing it in wheelchairs.

"I got a phone call today," she said. "From Allan Romero."

I turned to her, taking the glass of wine she held out. "Thanks. And who might that be?"

"Head of the claims department for Atco Insurance."

"About the necklace?" I sipped the wine. It tasted like turpentine. "Atco was the insurer?"

"Yes."

"He's a quick worker."

"He read about Biddle in the paper and called Nolan, in Burglary, this afternoon. Nolan told him about your statement to Hector. Do you like the wine?"

"It's great. So what did Allan Romero have on his mind?" I set down the glass and went back to the snow-peas. I was fairly certain I already knew what Allan Romero had had on his mind.

"He was curious whether you knew anything more than you told Hector."

"Hector was curious about the same thing. You think my puckish charm is beginning to fade?" The snowpeas were done, all sliced into neat sections cut on the bias. I opened a cabinet door, located the stack of plates, slipped one off the top.

Rita said, "And he's willing to offer a finder's fee for the necklace's return."

"I gave Hector my word, Rita." I dumped the cut snowpeas onto the plate and picked up the green pepper. "And a man's gotta stand by his word. Code of the West."

"You were born in Scarsdale."

"*West* Scarsdale." I rinsed the green pepper off under the faucet.

"You gave him your word that you wouldn't go out looking for the necklace on your own. You didn't say anything about accepting, or not accepting, a valid offer volunteered to you by the insurance company."

I sliced off the top of the green pepper with the paring knife. "Are you sure you haven't spent any time with the Jesuits?"

"If Hector said it was all right, would you be willing to work on the case?"

I turned to her. "Suddenly I have this feeling that I'm about to be sandbagged. You already talked to Hector, right?"

She smiled. "About half an hour before you got here."

I sipped at the wine again. It tasted better this time. Maybe I was developing a taste for turpentine. "And he said?"

"He said he'd be delighted for you to do so."

"In exactly those words?"

Another smile. "I'm giving you the gist of it."

"Be a different gist if *I'd* been the one to talk to him."

She nodded. "Which is why I did."

"What's Romero willing to pay?"

"We left it open. You've got an appointment with him tomorrow, at two. You can negotiate then."

"On Sunday? Claims people don't work on Sunday."

"Romero does."

"I don't think I'm going to like this guy."

"I called Paul and had him put together a contract." Paul Gallegos was our attorney. "You can pick it up before you see Romero."

"You've had a busy day."

She smiled. "Idle hands are the devil's tools."

"And a stitch in time saves nine."

"Romero will offer five percent of appraised value. You can ask for fifteen and a per diem. He won't go for the per diem, but I'm pretty sure he'll settle for ten."

"Uh-huh." I could feel my lips moving into a frown.

Still smiling, Rita narrowed her eyes. "Is it possible that you're just a little bit miffed?"

"Miffed? No, not me. Vexed, maybe, but not miffed."

"We don't have to take the case. I told Romero that acceptance was contingent upon the approval of my associate."

"Very nicely put."

"You *are* miffed."

"I thought we were going to talk together before we committed ourselves to any particular case."

"We are talking together."

"Seems like you've already got the thing wrapped up."

"I tried calling you, Joshua. I couldn't reach you."

I'd been at the pool all afternoon. "Right," I said. The word sounded stupid and pouty, even to me, so I turned around and began slicing at the green pepper. It didn't seem, under the circumstances, an entirely appropriate sort of behavior, but nothing else did either.

Behind me, the silence started growing.

At last Rita sighed. She said, "Joshua, it seems to me that we have a number of choices at the moment. You can keep sulking and hacking at those green peppers and probably amputate your thumb. You can take back your snowpeas and your green pepper and go sulk in the privacy of your own home. Or we can talk about this and decide whether we want to work on the case."

I took a deep breath, and then a deep swallow of wine, emptying the glass. I turned to her. "You know," I said, "one day that sweet reason of yours is going to get you into a lot of trouble."

She smiled at me. "But not today."

I smiled back. "You think Romero would spring for a retainer?"

She shook her head. "I don't imagine he'll go for anything but a straight spec contract. But it's not as though we're overloaded right now. I thought we'd give it a week, no more. What do you think?"

"Okay," I said. "A week."

She nodded. "Do you want some more wine?"

"Yeah. You got another bottle of that stuff?"

# THREE

ATCO INSURANCE was on Washington Street and occupied the whole of a large remodeled adobe house near the Bank of Santa Fe. It was a convenient location. Lackeys could haul the premium money over to the vaults without working up a sweat.

Not all the money went into the bank, however. A good percentage of it had been spent fitting out Allan Romero's office. Thick pile carpeting, padded leather furniture, oil paintings of Southwest scenes on the walls, everything oversized and everything, including the paintings, color coordinated in browns and beiges. Romero's desk was mahogany, and you could've strung a net down its center and played a mean game of volleyball on its top, so long as you didn't mind skidding around on the polish.

Romero himself had probably never given a moment's thought to the idea of desktop volleyball. One of the new breed of Hispanics who spoke English without a trace of accent, emphasis, or humor, he was somewhere between thirty-five and fifty. It was difficult to tell because the thin lines that ran down along the sides of his thin and narrow mouth might have been there when he was born. His face was thin too, and so was his mustache, which was as black as his slicked-back hair and looked as if it had been drawn on with an eyebrow pencil.

He was wearing a dark gray three-piece suit with subdued pinstriping, a white silk shirt with a gold collar pin, and a striped silk regimental tie. I don't know what regiment the tie came from, but maybe Romero did. He looked like the kind of person who would, and who'd be happy to tell you about it, at length, if you asked him. I never did.

He set the contract down and flattened it carefully against the desktop with fingers that were thin and very nicely manicured. Something that might have been a smile flickered briefly on his mouth, but vanished so quickly I couldn't be sure. "I believe I detect," he said, nodding to the contract, "the fine Italian hand of Mrs. Mondragón. I particularly admire the stipulation that payment of the fee be contingent only upon the necklace's recovery, and not upon its return to Atco."

"The thing's going to be confiscated by the police," I said. "You know that as well as we do. It's evidence in a homicide. But Atco is the owner of record. You'll get it back."

He raised his left eyebrow, a trick I've always envied. "But when? In six months? A year? If the person responsible for the theft is also responsible for the death of this Biddle, and the police manage to apprehend him, then the necklace will be held until after the trial. And Lord knows when that might take place. With appeals and whatnot, do you know how much time a good lawyer can waste? And throughout it all, Atco will be unable to recoup its claim payment. Its money will be lying dormant."

"Maybe you'll be lucky," I said, "and we won't find the thing. Then all you'll have to do is raise your rates."

Another flicker. "You have, I think, an oversimplified view of how an insurance company operates."

"Probably. I'm an oversimplified kind of guy."

"Putting aside," he said, "just for a moment, the payment of the finder's fee, let's discuss the fee itself. I've spoken with the Home Office, and in view of the size of this particular claim, they are, of course, quite anxious to retrieve the necklace. They've authorized me to make what

I think is a very generous offer of five percent of insured value."

I doubted very much that he'd spoken to anyone. Romero might work on a weekend, but everyone in the Home Office was probably out bruising tennis balls or down in the basement counting Krugerands. "Well," I said, "I've spoken to Mrs. Mondragón, and in view of the difficulty of this particular case, she's authorized me to propose a fee of fifteen percent of insured value, plus a retainer of one percent, and naturally, a per diem of one hundred dollars."

The smile flickered back to his lips and this time it stayed for a while. "An admirable woman, Mrs. Mondragón."

"I've always thought so."

"But you realize, of course, that my hands are tied. I can do nothing without a go-ahead from the Home Office, and I'm afraid they'd never agree to such a proposal. They might very well direct me to contact another detective agency."

"They've had six months to contact another agency."

"Ah, but that was before Biddle appeared, offering the necklace."

"Biddle's dead, and I'm the one he offered the necklace to. Even if you hire another agency, in the end you'll still be dealing with me."

He pursed his lips. "Are you suggesting you know more about its whereabouts than you've so far revealed to the police?"

"I'm suggesting the same thing to you that I suggested to Biddle, two days ago. You called me. I didn't call you."

Something new flickered across his lips, something that might have been a frown. He eyed me for a moment. At last, with a small crisp nod, he said, "Perhaps you and I can come to an agreement without my further involving the Home Office. But naturally you understand that a retainer and a per diem are simply out of the question."

After that, it was just a matter of horse trading. The two of us dickered for a bit, Romero occasionally flicking his cool quick smile in my direction, and finally we agreed to what Rita had said we would. A simple speculation contract, no retainer, no per diem, ten percent to be paid to the Mondragón agency upon recovery. We both signed the contract, I slipped my copy into the inside pocket of my jacket, Romero folded his and put it into his desk drawer.

I took out my notebook and my Erasermate. "Suppose you tell me," I said, "how the necklace got stolen."

His elbows on the arms of the chair, Romero sat back and locked his fingers together atop his vest. "It happened in October of last year. On the sixteenth, a Friday. Mr. and Mrs. Leighton had gone to Albuquerque and stayed overnight. Mrs. Leighton returned on Saturday morning and discovered that the house had been burgled, the necklace taken. She notified the police, and, later that day, our claims office."

"The husband didn't come back to town with her?"

"No. Mr. Leighton was planning to play golf later that day and then fly back."

"His own plane?" There are no commercial flights between Albuquerque and Santa Fe.

"The plane of his host in Albuquerque, a Mr. John Dupree. As I recall, the plan was for Mr. Dupree and Mr. Leighton to golf that afternoon, and then for Mr. Dupree to fly Mr. Leighton back to Santa Fe."

"Is that what happened?"

He shook his head. "Mrs. Leighton called the Dupree house at eleven and informed Mr. Leighton of the theft. Mr. Dupree flew Mr. Leighton to Santa Fe. They both arrived at the Leighton house at two."

"That's three hours later. The trip only takes an hour by car, and a lot less in a private plane. Did they slip in a quick nine holes before they left?"

Romero shrugged. "Something to do with the plane. A preflight check of some sort."

"And when did you people get involved?"

"That day. Saturday. We have an emergency claims number, and this was the number that Mrs. Leighton called. The agent who took the call notified me immediately."

"Is that standard procedure?"

"In the case of claims exceeding a certain amount, yes."

"What amount?"

He frowned slightly, to make it clear the answer wasn't really any of my business, then said, "Twenty thousand dollars."

"And what time did you arrive at the house?"

"A little after two, shortly after Mr. Leighton and Mr. Dupree arrived."

"What time did Mrs. Leighton call the emergency number?"

"One-thirty."

"Why did she wait so long to call?"

"She had been dealing with the police for several hours. It was on their advice, very properly given, that she called us."

"The police were still there when you arrived?"

"No. I spoke with Detective Sergeant Nolan later, at his office."

"Were you and Nolan both satisfied that this was a genuine burglary?"

"Of course." He showed me his eyebrow trick again. "You're not suggesting, I hope, that the Leightons themselves were somehow responsible?"

"The thought never crossed my mind."

"We've been handling the Leightons' account for nearly twenty years."

I nodded. "Was the necklace included in a general policy, or did it have its own?"

"All of Mrs. Leighton's jewelry was on a rider attached to their general homeowner's policy."

"What kind of premiums were they paying?"

Another quick frown. "Twelve thousand."

"What part of that represented coverage on the necklace?"

"Five thousand."

"For a total coverage of one hundred thousand."

He nodded.

I said, "I thought that whenever something that valuable was being insured, the insurance company usually farmed out part of the coverage to other agencies."

He frowned again and gave me a small quick nod. "That is, yes, our usual policy. The agent who wrote the coverage, however, chose to do otherwise. And the supervisor at the time accepted it."

Both of them hot, presumably, for the larger premiums to be had if Atco carried the necklace by itself. I wondered what'd happened to those two after the necklace had been stolen. They'd probably been assigned to the office in Minsk. "The necklace," I said. "Where was it kept?"

"Normally, as I understand it, in their safe-deposit box at the bank, with the rest of her jewelry."

"Where was it that Friday night?"

"In the drawer of her dresser. In her bedroom."

"Why?"

"Mrs. Leighton had worn it that week to some social function."

"Was anyone in the house at the time of the burglary?"

"No. They have two children, teenagers, but both were sleeping over with friends."

"Alarm system?"

"Yes. A Cartwright."

"Interior and perimeter?"

"Interior only. And it wasn't armed. Apparently their son forgot to turn it on before he left the house."

The Cartwright's a decent system, infra-red, motion-sensitive. You punch a number code onto a keyboard before you leave the house. If anything moves in there before you disarm the system, an externally mounted siren goes off and a phone call is automatically made to the local Cartwright monitoring office in town. From there, someone telephones the police department. But, like any other system, it doesn't work very well if it's not turned on.

"Were the phone lines cut?"

"Yes."

"They have a leased line?"

"No. But it hardly matters in this instance, since, as I say, the alarm wasn't activated."

When the alarm is set, a leased line, also called a balanced line, will automatically notify the monitoring service if it's been cut or tampered with. But the phone company charges about thirty bucks a month for one, and some people can't see their way to spending the extra money.

I asked him, "What about the wires to the siren?"

"They were untouched."

"The house is isolated," I said.

He nodded. "Yes."

Disabling the phone lines to an empty house is one of the first things a competent professional burglar would do. With an armed Cartwright, and with most other systems, cutting the lines will sound the siren, but a burglar's not going to worry about that if the house is out in the boonies. And if the house is out in the boonies, even a leased line isn't going to be much help. A good man can get in and out of the average private residence in less than twenty minutes, and he'll be carrying a police scanner with him. By the time the cops arrive, if they ever do, he'll be long gone.

I said, "The son was there after they left?"

"Yes, with some friends. They all left shortly after nine o'clock."

"No possibility that he or his friends were involved?"

"None."

"And the other kid?"

"A daughter. She'd left earlier in the day."

I sat back in my chair, the leather whispering against me. "Sergeant Nolan felt that Biddle masterminded the burglary, using a friend named Killebrew to do the actual work. Did you agree with him?"

"Yes, I did. Unfortunately, as perhaps you know, we were never able to substantiate our belief."

I nodded. "I'll have to talk to the Leightons."

He showed me his quick flicker of a smile once more. "I've anticipated you in that regard. I spoke with Mr. Leighton this morning. He's willing to see you this afternoon at four."

THE SUN was shining and the temperature back up into the sixties as I turned off Old Santa Fe Trail onto the rutted and muddy dirt road. For a moment, before I eased up on the gas, the front of the Subaru slewed in the muck and the steering wheel jerked against my hands.

In any other American city this size, the road would have been paved. But in Santa Fe, raw earth is as chic as raw fish. The wealthier locals like it especially in the winter, when they can hop into their four-wheel-drive vehicles and feel like cowboys as they go whizzing down the mudslides into town. I put the Subaru into four-wheel drive, and felt pretty much like a cowboy myself.

On either side of me were gently rolling hills dotted with scrub pine and gullied by arroyos, deep open wounds in the reddish earth. For most of the year these were dry, but now their rocky bottoms were covered with brown meltwater, gurgling and gleaming as it sluiced down toward the far-off Rio Grande. The snow had vanished, all of it except for a few dispirited clumps huddling in the shade beneath the piñon. The houses here were set back from the road and hidden behind stands of juniper and walls of adobe.

The driveway I wanted was maybe two miles from the main road, and marked by a large wooden gate with the name "Leighton" branded in rustic letters on the frame overhead. The compound itself, I saw when I reached it, was like the others, walled round in brown adobe, and there were enough cars outside to start a small but exclusive dealership. I had a choice of parking the wagon beside a Mercedes 450SL, a Saab Turbo, a Maxda RX7, or a Jeep Renegade. I picked the Jeep.

Over the wooden crosspiece at the entrance the name "Leighton" had been branded again, in case you'd missed it the first time. Inside the walls, I saw that someone had spent a lot of time, and a lot of money, transforming the broad courtyard from high desert scrubland into English country garden. There was grass, bright brilliant green against the litter of damp petals from the apple and peach trees. There were rose bushes and a bed of tulips, the tulips looking a bit bedraggled after the storm. Carefully tended hedges bordered the winding flagstone walk and, off to my right, a small willow draped its branches over an ornamental pond.

This far out of town, Leighton would be off the municipal water lines. He had to have a well. I wished him luck with it. The level of the aquafer upon which Santa Fe sits is going down every year, and the developers, Leighton among them, keep bulldozing open new subdivisions, throwing together new houses, sinking new wells. One day the air will be shattered by an enormous sibilant rattle as twenty thousand thirsty straws suck at the bottom of an empty glass.

The main house, off to my right, was a fortress of adobe and glass, flanked on either side by wings that extended along the courtyard walls. I walked up the flagstone walk, went up the steps, and pushed the doorbell. From inside I could hear a chime sounding the first four notes of Beethoven's Fifth. I don't want *ding dong*, Sammy, I want *class*.

After a few moments, the door was opened by a young girl, sixteen or seventeen years old. Tousled blond hair, a formless gray sweatshirt, baggy jeans, battered running shoes. One day she might be pretty, maybe even beautiful. Now she was wearing braces and thick-lensed horn-rimmed glasses and she moved inside her body as though it were something she'd ordered from Spiegel's, and she didn't know yet whether she wanted to keep it or send it back.

"Hello," I said. "I'm here to see Mr. and Mrs. Leighton."

Her gray eyes blinked behind the glasses. "You're the private detective?"

"Yep."

"Come on in. Dad's on the phone, but my mother's waiting in the living room."

I followed her through a large foyer and down some broad red tile steps to a huge sunken living room. Three walls were of stippled white plaster, hung with the kind of subdued modern oil paintings that drew attention not to themselves, but to their owner's subdued good taste. The fourth wall was of glass and looked out on the plot of land that was forever England. There was a brick floor beneath me, and *vigas* overhead, long stripped pine logs that ran across the high ceiling. A stone fireplace, broad and round, sat in the center of the room beneath a cylindrical copper chimney with a wide conical mouth. Piñon logs were burning inside, presumably to counteract the chill put out by the air conditioner.

"He's here, Mother," the girl announced.

A woman stood up from a long white sectional sofa, crossed over to me, and held out her hand. Horizontally, so I could kiss it or shake it, whichever I fancied.

"Mr Croft?" she said, as I shook it.

"Yes."

"I'm Felice Leighton. I'm very pleased to meet you." Judging by the trace of accent in her voice, she had attended one of the Eastern colleges that teach women how to wear Harris tweed and talk with their teeth clenched.

Tall and handsome, she wore black pumps, tight pale blue designer jeans, and a tight gray lightweight cashmere sweater opened at the neck to show a strand of pearls. Her body was impressive, with round muscular breasts, a narrow waist, and no excess flesh at all. Her hair was frosted blond, medium length. Her lips were full, her nose straight, and her eyes a deep dark sapphire blue. The color was fake, and had to come from contact lenses, but it did go nicely with the gray of the sweater. Her skin was taut, perhaps a shade too surgically taut over the aristocratic cheekbones, and it had the kind of color that meant weekly visits to the tanning salon. From across the room, she had looked twenty-five. Up close, the figure and face said thirty-five. Only the hands and neck said otherwise.

She held my hand for just a shade longer than necessary, then released it with a smile.

"Please," she said, "sit down." She indicated the sofa. I sat on it, and so did she, a few feet away, folding her left leg beneath her and putting her left arm up on the sofa's back, all of which did some fairly interesting things to the sweater.

"My husband will be with us in a moment. He's on the phone to London."

"To all of it at once?"

She laughed. It was a good laugh, easy and genuine. "Sometimes it honestly seems that way. Would you care for a drink while we wait?"

"No thanks."

"Coffee? Tea?"

"Tea would be fine."

She turned to the young girl, who stood off to the side, no doubt mesmerized by this scintillating adult conversation. "Get that, would you, Miranda? And I'll have a small Scotch and water. And for heaven's sake, darling, stand up straight."

"*Mother,*", the girl said, and rolled her eyes theatrically. Then, without changing her posture that I could see, she turned and marched from the room.

"She's hopeless," Mrs. Leighton told me with a rueful smile.

I nodded sagely. You narrow your eyes and you move your head up and down.

The woman seemed to me, from the way she treated her daughter, to be the sort who liked to control, and to be seen controlling, her environment. Maybe that was why she tended toward the rough trade that Hector had mentioned. Men like Biddle, who would take what they wanted without asking and without much subtlety. Maybe it was a relief, a kind of deliverance, to shrug off all that responsibility.

As though she knew what I were thinking, she looked me over slowly, up and down. It felt a bit like being frisked. "So," she said. "You're with Mrs. Mondragón."

"That's right."

"What a tragedy that was. She was such a beautiful woman."

"She still is."

"Yes, of course. Of course. I only meant that it must be difficult for her. The confinement."

I nodded.

"How long have you worked with her?"

"Almost three years now." I reached into my jacket pocket and slid out my notebook. Reached into my shirt pocket and slid out my pen. "Would you mind, Mrs. Leighton, if I asked you a few questions about the burglary?"

"Why no, not at all." She smiled. "But please," she touched my shoulder lightly with tapered fingers, "it's Felice."

I nodded. "Romero told me that you normally kept the necklace in a safe-deposit box."

"That's right, yes. We have a duplicate, quite a good one, cubic zirconium, and that's the one I kept here. But there was a terrible mix-up, all my own fault, really, and I got the two of them confused."

"When had you last worn the genuine necklace?"

"On Thursday, the day before. Derek and I had gone to the Governor's Ball. And then on Friday, Derek brought the duplicate back to the bank. Thinking that it was the genuine necklace, of course. I realized just before we left that afternoon that I'd made a mistake. And the banks were closed, naturally, so we couldn't get to the box and exchange them. Derek planned to go on Monday. I put the necklace in my dresser, where I normally kept the duplicate."

"So who would've known that the genuine necklace was here?"

"Only Derek and I. And Kevin, our son. Miranda had already left."

"This duplicate," I said. "Would it be good enough to fool a burglar?"

She smiled. "Well, I don't know a great many burglars personally, but I should think so, yes. It wouldn't fool a jeweler, of course. But after all, it fooled me."

"Some cash was taken, too."

"Yes, about two hundred dollars. Ah, here are our drinks. What took so long, Miranda?"

"Elena couldn't find the tea," the girl said. She was carrying a silver tray, which she set down on the coffee table. She stood back and brushed the hair away from her eyes.

"Thank you, darling," said Mrs. Leighton.

The girl nodded, turned, and padded off.

"And a gun was taken," I said. "That was yours?"

She handed me the cup and saucer. "Yes. A pistol my husband had given me."

"Thirty-eight caliber."

"Yes. A Colt, I think. I'd never fired it, and it wasn't loaded. My husband bought it as a joke several years ago."

"A joke?"

She smiled and sipped at her drink. "We were having an argument once, I don't even remember now what about, and I got so angry I told him that if I had a gun I'd shoot him. The next day he gave me the gun."

Very droll. The rich *are* different. "It wasn't loaded when he gave it to you?"

"No." She smiled. "I think Derek felt that would've been carrying the joke a shade too far."

I nodded. "According to Romero, there was no one in the house that night."

She shook her head. "I'd given Elena, our housekeeper, the weekend off. Miranda was staying with Nancy

Garcia, a friend of hers, and Kevin was over at the Palmers' house, across town."

"Has Elena been with you for any length of time?"

"Years and years. Since we moved here. And that was, oh, nineteen-seventy, I think. I'd trust her with my life. And besides, the police talked with her last year. She was home with her mother and brother."

"Did she know the code for the alarm?"

"Of course. But didn't Allan tell you that the alarm hadn't been set?"

I nodded. "Yeah, he did. Why was that?"

"I'm afraid that Kevin forgot to set it before he left. He was the last one to leave that day. He'd had some friends over, and they'd been drinking. You know how boys can be sometimes."

That seemed to call for another sage nod, so I provided it. "It isn't possible that one of them took the necklace?"

She looked at me as though I'd suggested an unnatural act. Probably from her point of view I had. "Certainly not. They're all fine boys. And besides, Kevin never told them the necklace was here."

I nodded and sipped at my tea. Earl Grey. "According to Romero, you were the one who discovered the burglary."

"Yes. I came home on Saturday morning. Derek was staying over in Albuquerque and planned to fly back that evening. I didn't even notice when I came in that the window was smashed. That one." She pointed to a panel in the wall of glass. "I went straight to my room to unpack, and then I saw it. All my things, lingerie, my dresses, scattered around the room. And then I realized, of course, that we'd been robbed. You hear about it—it's even happened to friends of ours—but you never believe it can happen to you. I ran over to the dresser, all the drawers were open, and I saw that the necklace was gone."

I nodded.

"I went to call the police," she said, "and the phone wasn't working. Later, of course, the police told me that the wires had been cut. I had to drive down the road to our neighbor's, the Wheatfields', to call them."

"Was anything else taken," I asked her, "besides the necklace and the cash and the gun?"

"No, nothing. I suppose we were lucky in that respect. But that's not the way I saw it at the time. I was heartbroken. And I had this horrible sense of having been violated."

"The police think that Frank Biddle was involved."

She sipped at her drink. "Yes, so one of them told me. A Sergeant Nolan."

"Would Biddle have known you kept a necklace, genuine or otherwise, in your room?"

She looked at me blankly. "How could he have?"

"What *is* this?" A man's voice, angry, off to my left.

# FOUR

DEREK LEIGHTON stood in the doorway. He was a few years older than his wife and quite a bit taller, a big man midway through the process of going soft. His gray hair had been styled in artful curls that did a good job of concealing how little of it was left. He wore a brown silk Western shirt with mother-of-pearl snaps, and a pair of brand-new blue jeans that, like all brand-new blue jeans, looked vaguely pathetic. Beneath them were a pair of cowboy boots that had cost a large family of lizards their lives. His skin was red, less from the sun, I suspected, than from alcohol. Or possibly apoplexy.

"Derek," said the woman, "this is Mr. Croft."

I set down the cup and saucer and stood up. He came into the room without offering his hand. His face was tight with displeasure. "The police went through all this a long time ago."

"In order to help locate the necklace," I said, "I need to know as much as possible about the burglary."

"Garbage," he said. "Get to this hoodlum Killebrew and beat some sense into him. It's as simple as that."

Mrs. Leighton stood up, smiling. "Mr. Croft is only doing his job, darling. You sit down and relax, and I'll get you a drink. More tea, Mr. Croft?"

"No thanks."

"Please. Sit down. I'll be right back."

I sat, careful not to watch the tilt and sway of nicely rounded buttocks as she walked away. Her husband glowered at me as he sat down in a white padded chair across the coffee table.

"I'm not employing you," he said, "to come here and badger my wife."

"I'm not badgering your wife," I said. "And you're not employing me. No one is. Mrs. Mondragón and I have a speculation contract with Atco."

"I'm paying the bloody finder's fee, assuming you do your job and find that necklace."

Something Allan Romero hadn't mentioned. "That's between you and Atco."

He put his head back as though he'd suddenly smelled something unpleasant. "Are you always this impertinent?"

"Weather permitting."

"This is why," he said, his red face growing redder, "this is exactly why I told Romero to send you over here. I will not have a repetition of what happened last time. People disturbing my wife, my children. Probing into our private lives, asking us questions as though we were the criminals. I know how you two-bit private detectives operate—"

"Three-bit," I said. "Inflation."

"I'm warning you, Croft," he said, leaning forward and pointing a thick index finger at my face. "You do what I tell you and keep your nose out of my family's business."

"Mr. Leighton," I said, "that finger is going to look pretty silly buried in your ear."

He stared at me for a moment and then abruptly stood up. "Get out of my house." He said it through clenched teeth. Maybe he'd gone to one of those Eastern colleges himself.

I nodded. Chalk up another triumph for diplomacy. Just as I stood, Mrs. Leighton returned with a drink in each hand. She looked at her husband, looked at me, looked back at her husband. "What on earth is going on?"

"Croft was just leaving, Felice," he said.

"Thanks for the tea," I told her, and slipped the notebook into my jacket, the pen into the pocket of my shirt.

It might have been my imagination, but her blue eyes seemed to grow brighter. Her left eyebrow rose in an arch and a small smile appeared on her lips.

Happy families are all alike.

I turned to Leighton. "Don't bother showing me out."

I walked across the brick floor, up the steps, through the foyer, and out the front door.


FROM MY HOUSE, I called Rita and told her what'd happened. She suggested I might have been more patient with Leighton and his sensitivities. I said she was probably right. She predicted that Mrs. Leighton, sooner or later, would get in touch with me. I said she was probably wrong; hubby wouldn't let her. I told her that I'd spend the rest of the day trying to pick up some background on the Leightons, and that I'd talk with Hector tomorrow.

I called Peter Ricard, the one man I knew in town who could probably give me reliable information on the Leightons; but he was out. I called the police station, and Sergeant Nolan of the Burglary Investigation Unit was available. After I mentioned a few names—Rita's, Romero's, the Leightons'—he told me that if I made it down there right away, he might be able to spare me a few minutes. It was too gracious an offer to refuse.

His cubicle at the station was identical to Hector's, but Nolan himself looked less like a cop than a bank clerk. He was in his mid-thirties and he was short, not over five foot five. His light brown hair was cut close to the skull and parted on the left with the precision of a razor scar. He wore horn-rimmed glasses, a pale yellow shirt, and a tropical-weight light gray suit whose vest almost hid the beginnings of a small round belly. His tie was banded with red-and-yellow regimental stripes. It hadn't come from the same regiment as Romero's, but I got the feeling, after talking to him for a few minutes, that he and the insurance investigator had probably gotten along splendidly.

He offered me a dry, businesslike hand, and then he offered me a chair. He sat down, pulled a pocket watch from his vest pocket, frowned at it, slid it back, and then patted the pocket twice, as though to reassure himself that the watch hadn't slipped into a time warp and disappeared.

"Normally," he said, pushing his glasses back with the tip of his index finger, "Sunday is off-time for me, but we've got a trial coming up and I had to finalize some reports for the A.G.'s office. I was just leaving when you called."

"I appreciate your giving me the time." It seemed like the thing to say.

He nodded once, in recognition of my appreciation, and said, "I spoke to Allan Romero a few minutes ago, and he's verified your bona fides. As I understand it, you'll be interfacing with Atco on a contingency basis."

"Right," I said. I admire a man who can use *interfacing* with a straight face. I hadn't seen a straighter face than Nolan's in some time.

He picked up a ball-point pen from his desk blotter and began to tap it lightly against the desk. "Sergeant Ramirez assures me that you're more honest than most private investigators, but I do want to caution you about one thing. Any hard data you obtain regarding the perpetrator of the Leighton burglary, or for that matter of any other burglary, is to be input to this office at once."

There would've been more—warnings of the dire consequences to me and my license if I failed to comply. He was taking a break, about to get started, when I interrupted. "Absolutely," I said. "Hector tells me you had Frank Biddle and Stacey Killebrew figured for the theft."

He nodded curtly. "Sergeant Ramirez is correct." With only the faintest emphasis on *Sergeant* to remind me that despite my friendship with Hector, I was still a civilian.

I said, "Biddle was out of town the night the necklace was stolen."

Another curt nod. "Yes. The burglary took place on October sixteenth of last year. And Biddle had left for Amarillo, Texas, on the thirteenth."

"Hector tells me that you think Biddle was involved with Mrs. Leighton."

Still tapping the pen, he nodded again. "I had evidence to corroborate that belief."

"What kind of evidence?"

He shook his head. "Privileged information."

And I wasn't among the privileged. "All right," I said. "Leighton fires Biddle, Biddle gets angry, organizes the theft with Killebrew, then sets himself up an alibi by going to Amarillo. That the way you see it?"

"Yes. The connection between Biddle and Killebrew is established. Neither one of them denied it—they'd known each other since high school in Amarillo. The M.O. of the burglary matches that used in others we know Killebrew committed. And certainly Killebrew is one of the few burglars in town with access to a fence professional enough to dispose of the necklace."

"Good fences make good neighbors."

Nolan smiled faintly. "The majority of thefts here in Santa Fe, both commercial and residential, are committed by drug users, primarily heroin addicts, who steal to support their habit."

"Free Enterprise," I said. "The American Way."

He frowned. And still kept tapping away with the pen—despite the prim exterior, he had a lot of nervous energy tumbling around inside. "The point I wish to make is that Stacey Killebrew is not a part of this system. He is not a drug user who steals to support his habit. He is a professional, full-time burglar who steals only your high-ticket items, primarily artwork and jewelry. Goods that the average Break-and-Enter people could never dispose of because the items are too easy to identify, or because the receivers in this town don't have the cash to pay for them.''

"You make him sound like Raffles."

"Don't let his appearance deceive you. He's sly and he's shrewd and he's extremely competent at what he does."

"He can't be all that competent if he got busted."

Nolan shook his head. "We arrested him only because of a tip from someone who lived near the apartment where the goods were cached. And the burglary counts were ultimately dropped. All we had were the recovered goods, and although they were demonstrably in Killebrew's possession, we had no way of proving his participation in their actual theft."

"So you got him for receiving."

He nodded. "That's correct."

"He only did eighteen months."

Nolan frowned, nodded.

"I remember reading in the newspaper," I said, "about the bust. Weren't the goods valued at over thirty thousand dollars?"

Still frowning, Nolan nodded again. "Thirty-three thousand five hundred."

"Over twenty thousand dollars makes it a second-degree felony. That's eight years' time on a conviction. He plea-bargained?"

"The D.A.'s office is overworked. A trial costs time and money." He spoke quickly, and there was a tightness, an irritation, in his voice. At me, certainly, but also at the system he was defending. It had to be frustrating to make a solid bust and then watch the bad guy get off with only eighteen months in prison. But the frustration was cop-frustration, and rather than share it with a civilian, he was giving me the party line. "They let his lawyer plead guilty to third-degree. Three years. He did half of it."

I said, "The stuff that was recovered was mostly art-work?"

He nodded. "And jewelry. He had burgled at least four galleries here in town, and several homes."

"Was everything recovered?"

"No. We estimate that at least another seventy or eighty thousand is still missing."

"What about Biddle? Did he have a record?"

"Nothing here. And in Amarillo, nothing extensive. Drunk and Disorderly. D.W.I."

"Did Biddle and Killebrew originally come to Santa Fe together?"

"No. Biddle came here about six years ago, Killebrew a year later."

"Did you talk to Biddle after the burglary?"

"Not immediately. We didn't have enough evidence to request extradition. I called him in Amarillo, asked for his cooperation, but it wasn't until a week later that he drove back here." Nolan frowned again, remembering.

"When he did come back," I said, "he denied having anything to do with the burglary?"

A small shrug. "I didn't expect him to confess."

"What was he doing in Amarillo?"

"Looking for work, he said." Another frown. Nolan clearly hadn't been fond of Frank Biddle. "If so, he never found it. He returned to Amarillo after I questioned him, but he stayed only another few weeks before coming back to Santa Fe."

"And you never got the evidence you needed to tie him to the burglary."

"No. Neither him nor Killebrew. But his coming to you as he did, trying to unload the jewelry, is hardly an indication of his innocence."

I nodded. "Getting back to the Leightons. You said something about the M.O. of the burglary."

"Yes. It matched that of the other burglaries. In every case the phone lines had been severed to circumvent a telephone call from the alarm system."

"Did he cut the wires to the siren?"

"You don't merely cut alarm wires," he informed me. "Doing that triggers the system to send an alarm over the phone lines. First you bypass the wires, set up a secondary circuit, and then you cut them."

"Okay," I said. "Did he bypass the alarm wires?"

"At the galleries, yes, but they're all located in town, where the sirens would've been heard. The private homes, including the Leightons', were all out of town and isolated. The phone lines were cut in each case, although only two of the houses had alarm systems."

"Those two had sirens?"

"Yes. The wires were uncut."

"He pulled the plug on the siren when he got inside."

"That's correct."

I nodded. "One thing I don't understand."

"Yes?"

"If Killebrew had the necklace, if he still has it, then why hasn't he tried to get rid of it before now?"

He shrugged. "Waiting for it to cool off, perhaps, and get himself a better price. And possibly he wasn't the one who was trying to get rid of it right now. Possibly Biddle was acting without Killebrew's approval."

I nodded. "You think Killebrew killed Biddle."

"I'm convinced of it," he said.

# FIVE

I CALLED RITA from the public library and told her what I'd learned. Then I called Peter Ricard's house. Still no answer. So I left the library, climbed into the Subaru, and went looking for him. Santa Fa is a small town, and there aren't that many places to hide.

Particularly on a Sunday. Except for the bars in the hotels, which few of the locals frequent anyway, most places shut down from Saturday night to Monday morning. One of those that didn't was Vanessie's, a big piano bar on the west side, and it was here, at seven o'clock that evening, that I found Peter.

He was standing up against the far corner of the large rectangular bar as I walked in, staring down into a brandy snifter as though it were a crystal ball. There were no other customers, and Gordon, the bartender, was using the light above the cash register to do *The New York Times* crossword puzzle in ballpoint. This is a display of arrogance I've always found irritating. Rita does it too.

I walked around the bar and said hello to Peter.

He looked up and nodded glumly. "Joshua. How goes it?" He was wearing a leather windbreaker, jeans, cowboy boots.

"Fine," I told him.

Gordon abandoned the *Times* long enough to take my order, a Jack Daniel's on the rocks for me, another Amaretto for Peter.

"So," I said, "you're looking a little down in the mouth this evening."

Every year, some group here in town puts out a list of Santa Fe's most eligible bachelors. Peter Ricard has made the list every year. Not hard to understand why. He was tall, a little over six feet, with boyish good looks that were becoming more interesting as they began to blur at the edges—Dennis the Menace gone slightly to seed. I knew him because he usually swam at the municipal pool about the same time I did, and occasionally we played racquetball. He was bright, articulate, and he was also one of the richest men in Santa Fe. The third richest or the fourth, depending on whom you talked to. Unless you talked to Peter. He would tell you he was broke.

He nodded. "I violated one of my own cardinal rules last night."

"Which one was that?" I asked. Gordon put the drinks in front of us and I paid for them.

"Never sit down next to an ugly woman when you plan to do some serious drinking. By the time last call rolls around, she's lost forty pounds and gained a face lift."

"Bad night, was it?"

He shook his head in disgust.

I smiled. "I thought you'd already slept with all the available women in Santa Fe."

"Now I'm down to the ones who are *really* available." He tossed back what was left in the first brandy snifter, slid it away from him toward the edge of the bar, moved the full snifter into its place. "We're talking your basic disaster here."

"Look on the bright side," I told him. "Tourist season starts pretty soon."

The thought didn't cheer him. "School teachers from Cincinnati. Secretaries from Dubuque."

"You bring a little excitement into their lives, Peter. Glamour. Romance."

"I've been seriously thinking about entering a monastery."

"The pay's not all that great, I hear."

"Yeah, but the hours are terrific."

I tasted the Jack Daniel's. "I've got a question for you. What do you know about the Leightons?"

He looked at me. "Felice and Derek?"

I nodded.

"You working on something?"

"Yeah."

"For them, or against them?"

"For them, indirectly."

"You'd be better off working against them. They'd probably treat you better."

"Does that mean they're not swell folks?"

"Are we talking professionally or personally?"

"Both."

"It doesn't matter. They're not swell folks in either capacity."

"Why?"

"Where do you want me to start?"

"Professionally."

He shrugged. "Leighton is one of those people who manages to raise mediocrity to new middles. He's the guy who put up the Bel Grande." A new luxury hotel on the outskirts of town, off one of the exits from the main highway. "Everything was substandard. His block, his mortar, even his rebar. The place'll probably topple over in five years. Kill three hundred school teachers from Portland, Maine."

"Peter Ricard found crushed beneath the rubble."

"Not me. I'll be off in the monastery, picking hops. Or hopping picks. Whatever it is they do in monasteries."

Peter was in the same business as Leighton, development and construction. Which was, after all, why I'd wanted to speak to him. But there might have been, I knew, some bias blended with his expertise.

"How'd he get away with it?" I asked. "What about the building codes?"

He shrugged. "Money."

"You know that for a fact?"

"Not anything admissible in court. But a fact, yes. The guy's been involved in more shady land deals than anyone in Santa Fe. And that, believe me, is saying something."

"How's his business doing?"

"A whole lot better than it should."

"No problems, no difficulties?"

"He was in some trouble for a while last year." He sipped at his Amaretto. "A note came due on that project of his over on St. Michael's, those rinky-dink condos, and he was strapped for cash. Overextended, like half the contractors in Santa Fe."

"When was this?"

"Fall sometime. September. October."

"Did he raise the money?"

He nodded. "Probably printed it in his basement."

"How much was involved?"

"Not a lot. Thirty, forty thousand." Peter, who's been known to drive all the way to Albuquerque to save twenty dollars on a pair of slacks, could dismiss thirty or forty thousand with a shrug.

"What about his wife?" I asked.

"What about her?"

"The two of them get along all right?"

"Now we're into the personal stuff."

I nodded.

"Well," he said, "personally, the two of them are a bucket of worms."

"How so?"

"They're into kinky."

"What kind of kinky?"

"Derek likes to watch."

"His wife and other men?"

"Other men, other women, dogs, cats. Otters. Wood-chucks."

"I sense a certain level of exaggeration."

He grinned. "Okay, maybe not animals. But anything human the two of them can drag up there to the house. And just to keep from getting bored, both of them play around on the side. Derek likes little Indian girls. Felice likes truck drivers and props."

"Props."

"Bondage stuff. Handcuffs, paddles. Punish me, you brute."

"Guns?"

"Why not?"

"Are you speaking here from personal experience?"

"Almost."

"Almost?"

He sipped at his Amaretto. "I drove her home one night from some charity thing at the Hilton. Derek was out of town. Probably off laundering money somewhere. We had a drink, Felice and I, and started playing around. She's a good-looking woman, takes care of herself, and I admit I was tempted. But when she told me what kind of games she had in mind, I lost interest."

"What kind of games?"

"Like I said. Handcuffs on the bedpost." He shrugged, smiled. "I've just never felt that I make a very convincing brute."

"Maybe if you took up cigars."

"They hurt my sinuses."

"I think you're right," I said. "Brute is out."

He grinned. "Anyway," he said, "if I were you, I'd do what I could to avoid both of them."

SOMETIMES IT'S NOT so easy to avoid people. After I left Vanessie's, I stopped at the McDonald's on Cerrillos Road and picked up a couple of quarter-pounders at the window. When I reached my house, about twenty minutes later at nine-thirty, I saw that a gray Saab Turbo was parked in the driveway. It was the same one that had been parked at the Leightons', or its twin.

I drove the wagon onto the side of the road, left it there, and carried the McDonald's bag up the moonlit driveway. Nothing like a bag full of hamburgers in your fist to give you that feeling of accomplishment and that air of mystery.

Mrs. Leighton opened the car door and stepped out, wearing the same clothes she'd had on earlier, with the addition of a white fox jacket and a dark scarf at her throat. In the moonlight, the jacket seemed to glow with a light of its own. She wasn't carrying a McDonald's bag, and she looked as if she probably never had.

"I came to apologize," she said. "Your address was in the phone book."

"No need to apologize," I said. "I hope you haven't been waiting long."

She shook her head. "Five minutes. I've been thinking all day about the way Derek behaved this afternoon, and I finally decided to come make amends." She smiled. "He means well, Derek, but sometimes he can be over-protective."

I had circled around her, and now I leaned my hip against the Saab's front fender. Curious, I put my hand out along the hood. Not cold; but not five minutes warm, either. I said, "It happens to the best of us."

"You *are* still going to help me with this, aren't you?"

"I'm going to try to find the necklace, yes."

"Good. Thank you." She smiled. "Is there anything I can do to help?" She said it seriously, with no erotic undertones in her voice.

"Well," I said, "since you're here, you could answer a few more questions."

Nodding to the bag I carried, she smiled again. "I don't want to interrupt your dinner."

"This isn't dinner," I said, lifting the bag. "I just cart this around once in a while to make myself seem poignant."

She smiled. "It succeeds."

I smiled back. "Come on in."

Inside the house, I said, "Let me get a fire started. The heating system here is a little primitive."

The Sunday *New York Times* lay on the sofa where I'd left it, unread. I tore sheets from the business section—I'm not usually planning a merger or updating my portfolio—crumpled them into balls, and tossed them into the *kiva* fireplace. Hands in the pockets of her jacket, Mrs. Leighton moved across the room and stood in front of the bookcase, scanning the titles.

"A private detective who reads books," she said.

"Only the ones with pictures." Squatting, I arranged some piñon logs in a tepee formation above the newspaper, then lit the paper with a kitchen match from the box on the *banco*.

I stood. "Can I fix you a drink?"

She turned from the bookcase. "Please. Scotch?"

I nodded. "No soda. Water all right?"

"Fine."

I went into the kitchen, built a Scotch and water for her, a Jack Daniel's on the rocks for myself. When I returned to the living room, the fire, burning nicely now, had taken some of the chill from the room. Mrs. Leighton had removed the scarf from her neck, the fox jacket from her shoulders, and she was sitting back on the sofa, her long legs crossed. I handed her the drink, she thanked me, and, since the only other available chair was occupied by the jacket and scarf, I sat down on the sofa beside her. It's always been a small sofa, but it seemed even smaller today.

She smiled at me and said, "Well."

"Well," I said.

It was the standard scene. Two strangers alone for the first time, crackle of fire off to the side, click and tinkle of ice cubes in the drinks, the bedroom and its promise only a few short paces away. Except that one of the strangers knew a great deal more about the other's private life than any stranger had a right to.

It wasn't my place to judge the woman. At any given moment, all over the world, people are getting off in every way you could imagine, and quite a few you couldn't, if you were lucky. So long as no one got hurt, so long as everyone had voluntarily bought his own ticket, or hers, then best of luck to them all. But personally I've always found the need for props—handcuffs, paddles, beanies with propellers, whatever—somehow rather sad.

And yet, maybe because what I knew about her was sexually oriented, it was impossible for me not to respond to her as a sexual presence. I was very conscious of the firm tanned flesh beneath her sweater, the faint herbal smell of her perfume, the intelligence and energy alight behind those impossibly blue eyes. She was, as Peter had said, a good-looking woman and, like him, I was tempted.

"My husband," she said, "doesn't know I'm here."

"Ah," I said. Master of the Witty Riposte.

"As I told you, he can be overprotective. He's a good man, and an understanding man, but the burglary last year, the police investigation, it all upset him terribly."

"So I gathered."

She smiled. "Have you ever been married, Joshua?" She tilted her head slightly to the side. "Do you mind if I call you Joshua?"

"No to both."

"Engaged?"

"No."

"Does that mean you're a cynic?" She smiled again. "Or simply a romantic?"

"So far as I can tell, they're both the same thing."

She smiled and nodded approvingly, either at the answer itself or at the fact that I actually had one. Her eyes narrowed slightly, quizzical. "What sort of relationship do you have with Mrs. Mondragón?"

"We work together."

She nodded. "Allan Romero said something interesting."

"That surprises me."

She laughed. It was still a good laugh. "He's not really a very interesting man, is he? But he does know Mrs. Mondragón, apparently. And he knows you, at least *of* you. He tells me that there're all sorts of rumors about the two of you."

"When did you speak to Romero?"

"This afternoon. After you left." Another smile, another tilt of her head. "Does it bother you that I was curious?"

"No. Why should it bother me?"

"It shouldn't. But aren't *you* curious about the rumors?"

"There are more rumors in Santa Fe than there are green chiles. I can't keep up with them all. But Mrs. Leighton—Felice—none of this is getting us any closer to finding that necklace."

A smile. "You really don't like talking about her, do you? You did the same thing when you were over at the house."

"We're business associates. We work together."

"Allan said that when you found the man who shot her, you nearly beat him to death with your bare hands. Is that true?"

"No. Suppose I ask you a question, Felice."

She smiled, then sighed in mock resignation. She waved her drink gently. "All right. Ask ahead."

"When did you stop sleeping with Frank Biddle?"

It was a cheap shot, but she took it well. She stared at me for just a moment, and then she laughed. "I love the way you phrase it. The syntax presumes the guilt. *Mr. Jones, when did you stop molesting little boys?* What can I say? That I *didn't* stop?"

"Did you?"

"Well," she smiled, "after all, the man is dead. That's about as final a stop as you can get." She sipped at her drink. "But what makes you think there was a beginning?"

"The police think there was."

"Do they now." Still amused. "That boring little man, Nolan?"

"Among others. They think that you and Biddle were having an affair, that your husband found out and fired him."

She laughed again. "Then they're even more ridiculous than I thought."

"You never slept with him?"

"Slept with him? We're being rather circumspect, aren't we? Are you asking me if we fucked?" She smiled as she said the word. I think I was supposed to be shocked.

"Yeah," I said. "In my circumspect way."

"Twice, as a matter of fact." She tilted her head. "Does that surprise you?"

"No. You get old enough and nothing surprises you."

She smiled. "You're not that old yet, Joshua. But in any case, he was not a particularly inspiring lover. And two times hardly constitutes an affair. And they had nothing whatever to do with my husband's firing the man. My husband and I have an arrangement. We *sleep* with whomever we please."

I nodded. "An interesting marriage."

"As a matter of fact, it is. Some people may not approve, but for Derek and me, it works out very well. Neither one of us is a hypocrite. We both accept each other for what we are."

Whatever that might be. "Why did your husband fire Biddle?"

She moved her shoulders lightly, in a shrug. "He said it had something to do with the accounts."

"Did Biddle know the number code for the alarm system?"

"No."

"Who did?"

"Only us. Derek and I and the children. And Elena, the housekeeper."

"Did Biddle know about the necklace? The real one or the duplicate?"

"I don't see how he could've."

"What about the cash and the gun? Did he know they were in the dresser?"

"He knew I kept cash there. Sometimes he'd need to buy things for the garden, and he had to have cash to get them."

"And the gun?"

She nodded. "He knew about the gun."

"He knew where it was?"

"Yes," she said. "I showed it to him once."

"Why?"

She smiled. "Are you asking out of prurient interest?"

"Were they prurient circumstances?"

"Yes," she said, still smiling. "They were. We played with it for a while, the two of us."

I nodded.

The blue eyes watched me over the rim of her glass as she sipped at her drink. "Would you like to know how?"

"Not really."

She shook her head, smiling. "Don't you ever have fantasies, Joshua?"

"Not about Frank Biddle."

"Oh, Frank had a certain feral charm. Initially, at any rate. And a certain amount of stamina. Unfortunately, he totally lacked imagination." A smile. "And that, nothing can make up for."

"How'd he get along with your children?"

She shrugged lightly, dismissively. "I don't think Miranda even knew he was alive. Kevin liked him. He and Frank did quite a lot of male things together. Camping, hunting, horseback riding. At that sort of activity, Frank was actually very talented.

"I'd like to talk to your son."

She frowned. "I thought we were discussing fantasies." She smiled again. "And somehow Kevin doesn't strike me as your type."

"You were the one talking about fantasies. I was the one talking about getting your necklace back. Could you ask him to come to my office tomorrow?"

"I suppose so. If you think it's absolutely necessary."

"I do." I stood up. "And now, Felice, I'm sorry, but it's been a long day."

She glanced at the watch on her wrist, a small gold Rolex. She smiled. "It's not even eleven."

"Beauty sleep."

"You don't need it," she said. She set her glass down on the end table and stood up, turning to face me. "I know something that'll be even better for you."

I'm not sure how I would've handled the situation. It's not very often that I have to fend off attacks from attractive women, and the few times it has happened, I haven't succeeded very well. I feel fairly preposterous acting the coy maiden.

But the question suddenly became academic. As Felice Leighton swayed toward me, the bullet smashed through my window and shards of glass went ripping through the room.

# SIX

TAKING A SIP of his bourbon and water, Hector Ramirez nodded to the window. "I kind of like the cardboard there. You should smash out the glass in all the windows and put cardboard up everywhere. And the duct tape adds a nice touch. Elegant."

The cardboard had come from a box I'd found down in the basement; the uniformed police had let me tape it to the window after they finished taking their measurements and digging the slug out of my wall from just beneath a framed black-and-white photograph of Canyon de Chelly. I would've been annoyed if the picture had been shattered. It'd been a gift from the photographer friend who took it.

I was annoyed anyway. The two uniforms and the plainclothes detective, Parker, had taken almost two hours to finish their preliminary investigation. It was two in the morning now, I still hadn't had a chance to eat my quarter-pounders, and the adrenaline that had pumped through me earlier had washed away, leaving me limp and slack. I sat slumped down on the sofa, Raggedy Andy in his dotage, my drink in my lap, my feet on the coffee table.

"I think what I'll do," I said, "is smash all the windows and put up steel plate."

"It's too bad you didn't get a good look at the guy."

"I had a few other things on my mind, Hector."

Mrs. Leighton for one, and my gun for another. I had reached for the woman and dragged her down with me as I went to the floor, and she was lying beneath me, her breath coming rapidly, her arms clutching at my neck. My

gun was in the bedroom closet, thirty feet away. There's
never a gun around when you need one.

"Are you all right?" I'd asked her.

"Yes," she said. "Yes, I think so." We were both
speaking in whispers. I could feel her heart beating against
my chest. Or maybe it was my heart.

"You stay here," I told her. "Don't move."

Her arms tightened around my neck.

"You'll be all right," I said. "Just don't move."

"That was a bullet," she said. There was fear in her
voice, her throat muscles tight, but she was dealing with it.
The control that had served her all her life was serving her
now. I felt a flicker of admiration for the woman, reluctant but real.

"Yes it was," I said.

She swallowed. "What if he comes in while you're
gone?"

Good question.

"If he were going to come in," I said, "he would've
come in already." Not really unassailable logic, but she
seemed to buy it. The tension began to leave her arms. I
said, "I'll be back as soon as I can."

She let out her breath in something like a sigh, and
nodded. Her arms slid away from my neck.

I got up into a crouch, keeping below the level of the
window, and smiled down at her to show her that everything was just swell. My strength is as the strength of ten
because my heart is pure.

She smiled back weakly, and licked her upper lip.

Awkwardly, I scurried across the living room into the
hallway. Straightening up, I ran down the hall to my bedroom door, swung through it into the darkness, remembered the window, and realized that the shooter could have
circled the house. I went into a crouch again to cross over
to the closet. Opened the door, found the shoebox in the

dark, opened that, slipped out the revolver, flipped open the cylinder, checked by feel to make sure it was loaded, flipped it back. Duckwalked over to the window. Waited for my breath to return. It didn't.

I leaned forward and tugged a pillow off the bed. Waved it once in front of the window. *Yoo hoo.*

Nothing happened. Either he wasn't out there or he didn't have a grudge against pillows.

Standing up, stomach to the wall, I snaked out my left arm and pushed back the latch at the top of the window. Brought the heel of my left palm against the frame, pushed. The angle was wrong but after a moment I felt the window give. I slid it up as far as it would go. It made no noise.

No shots, no sound from outside.

The idea was to get out there and take a look around. I could go slowly and try for quiet, or I could go quickly. Quickly seemed better. The rocky ground below the window would play hell with my Woolrich chamois shirt, and possibly with some bones and ligaments, but so would a bullet or two.

I dove, tucking my chin against my breastbone. I hit with my shoulder, lost some more breath, rolled in a sloppy somersault, scrambled to my feet, and scuttled into the trees.

Panting, the pistol raised to my shoulder, I waited.

Nothing.

I waited some more, panted some more, with the same result.

After a while, moving through the trees, keeping close to the ground, I checked the front. No one there, either. Whoever he was, he was gone.

I looked back at the house. The picture window was untouched, but the smaller window that adjoined it to the right was shattered. Beyond them both was the brightly lit living room. Standing there, outlined by the frames, the two of us had been an easy shot.

I glanced around, searching for tracks. Found none. And there was no point searching for a spent shell casing by moonlight.

I called out toward the broken window, "Felice? It's okay." I headed for the front door.

Felice opened it, stood there in the rectangle of light looking down at me. Her hair was mildly disheveled, as though she'd run her fingers through it, but otherwise she looked as cool and self-possessed as she had when she first stepped from the Saab. She let out a deep breath. "Well," she said, crossing her arms beneath her breasts, "you certainly know how to show a girl a good time." Her smile was a bit shaky, but it was a smile.

"You all right?"

She nodded. A tough lady. She said, "What happens now?"

"Now," I said, "we call the cops."

And so we had. And the cops at the station had called Hector, who was off duty. He had showed up half an hour after the others arrived. Parker had asked the questions and the uniforms had taken the measurements and searched the yard and driveway with flashlights. No tracks. No spent casing. The missing casing wasn't much of a surprise, though, because the slug they dug out of the wall had come from .38 revolver. Everyone was gone now but Hector.

I asked him, "How long will it take for Ballistics to compare the slug with the ones that killed Biddle?"

Hector shrugged. "A week, if I'm lucky."

I nodded. It was only on television that a ballistics report came in overnight. The State Crime Lab, like crime labs everywhere, has a backlog to contend with, and comparing any two slugs requires taking literally hundreds of photographs of each.

Hector stroked his bandit's mustache. "There is one thing," he said, "that disturbs me some."

"What's that?"

"The driveway's only about twenty feet away. You and Mrs. Leighton were standing up, and the lights were on."

"And he missed." I took a sip of bourbon and nodded. "Yeah, the same thought had occurred to me. But maybe he's just a bad shot."

"He didn't just miss. He missed by a good six feet."

I drank some more bourbon. "A warning of some kind, you're saying."

He nodded. "Yeah, but what kind?"

"Beats me. My book club payments are all up to date."

"Jealous husband?"

"Leighton? No. According to her, they've got an open arrangement."

"Does he know that?"

True, I had only her word for their arrangement. But there was another objection. "We weren't doing anything, Hector. We were just sitting here, talking about the theft of the necklace."

Hector smiled. "Maybe he suspected you had lust in your heart."

As indeed I had. And the bullet had come through the window just as Felice leaned toward me. But I shook my head. "I don't buy it, Hector. It's possible, but it doesn't feel right."

"Maybe next time, the bullet'll hit you, and you'll feel better about it."

"Thanks."

"I'd feel a lot better about all this myself, Josh, if you and Rita would forget that finder's fee."

"We've already signed a contract with Atco."

"A speculation contract. Doesn't mean a thing."

"It means ten thousand dollars if we find the necklace."

"Ten thousand should buy you a real nice funeral. What do mourners go for these days?"

"Last I heard, you get a discount on groups of six."

"Should be quite a soirée."

"I think I'll pass on it, myself." I sipped at the bourbon. "You find out anything more about Biddle?"

"Like who killed him, you mean? Nope. We're still leaning toward Killebrew, but his alibi's tight. We'll talk to him tomorrow, find out where he was tonight."

"Probably out playing poker again."

"Probably."

I asked him, "Did Biddle have a girlfriend?"

Hector frowned. "Why should I give you that?"

"Because you're a prince?"

He snorted. "Try again."

"Because you want to find Biddle's killer and I want to find the necklace. Maybe the two things aren't connected and maybe they are. But it looks to me like a little cooperation could benefit both of us."

He drank some bourbon. "Silver-tongued bastard."

I nodded. "That's what Mom always said."

"Chavez," he said. "Carla Chavez. Biddle lived with her. On Fremont Street. Two thirty-one."

"Did she give you anything?"

"A pain in the neck."

"But nothing helpful."

"No. She says she doesn't know anything about Biddle. They'd been living together for two years and she doesn't know anything about the guy."

"You have anything on her?"

"She was working the night he got killed. Plenty of witnesses. And she's clean. No record. Her brother's got one. Benito. Works for Norman Montoya, up in Las Mujeres. But we don't have any connection between Biddle and the brother."

"Montoya's a fence."

"No one's ever been able to prove it."

"He's also coke, I hear."

"No one's ever proved that either."

"Was Biddle selling coke?"

"We don't think so."

"But it's possible."

"Shit, anything is possible. As far as I know, Biddle got iced by creatures from Venus. Listen, Josh, talk to Chavez if you want, but stay away from Stacey Killebrew. I don't want to be prying you up from the sidewalk."

"A tender sentiment, Hector, and I appreciate it."

"You're good, Josh, but I don't think you're that good. Killebrew would as soon pound your face in as look at you."

"I'll try to bear that in mind."


IN THE MORNING, I drove downtown to the police station, signed the first statement I'd made, about Biddle's visit to the office, and then dictated another, about the shooting incident last night. Hector pointed out that I was making more statements lately than a politician.

Afterward, I drove out to Allwood's on Cerillos Road and picked up a new pane of glass for the window. Fitting it in occupied most of the morning, and I didn't get back to work till after twelve.

Fremont Street lies to the west of St. Francis Drive, in what local Anglos, with a certain smug complacency, once referred to as the *barrio*. Until fairly recently the area was entirely Hispanic; but now, with land prices inflated everywhere else in town, those same Anglos are beginning to move in. Two-story adobe haciendas with clerestory win-

dows and solar heat collectors are sprouting up next door
to tiny, carefully tended frame cottages. Jaguars and
BMW's prowl down the narrow streets, coolly ignoring the
Chevy lowriders and the Ford pickups that slumber along
the sides.

Carla Chavez's house was neither a hacienda nor a cot-
tage. Even in its better days, three or four decades ago, it
would have barely qualified as a hovel. A small, square,
featureless building, it sat on a small, square lot surrounded by a rusting chain-link fence. Two small, square
windows, one on either side of the front door, stared
blankly out at the street. The brown paint that was supposed to make the walls resemble adobe had flaked off in
large irregular patches, revealing the gray cinderblock beneath. There were more cinderblocks to the left, these
holding up a red '58 Chevy, missing all four tires and
blotched with primer. To the right of the house an ancient
refrigerator lay on its back, its door yawning open. The
yard was brown dirt, still sodden from the meltwater, and
bare, as though not even weeds would grow here.

The latch on the gate was ajar, and looked as if it had
been for years. I pushed through the gate and walked up
through the mud to the front door. There was no doorbell. I knocked. Ever resourceful.

After a moment, the door opened.

She surprised me. Probably I had expected someone
whose disrepair would match that of the house and
grounds, someone slovenly and unkempt, a slattern. She
was in her mid-twenties, and she was short, maybe five
foot three. Her black hair, thick and shiny, fell to her
shoulders. She wore light metallic blue eye shadow, jet
black mascara, lipstick the color of arterial blood. It was
more make-up, especially in broad daylight, than anyone
needed, and she needed none at all. Her lush young body,
flared-hipped and firm-breasted, was encased in spray-on

jeans and a red Danskin top so tight that one deep breath would've given her thread poisoning. In a few years, unless she took care of herself, that opulence of body would fill out, thicken, and she'd become a fleshy parody of herself. But right now, young and sensual and ripe, she was stunning.

The dark brown eyes moved up and down, taking me in. The striking face was vacant, an empty sullen mask. "Yeah?"

"Carla Chavez?"

"Yeah?"

"Joshua Croft. I'd like to talk to you about Frank Biddle."

"I already talk to the cops." A lot of Hispanics in town speak English with a lilt, as though it were Spanish. Usually it gave color and music to the language. In Carla Chavez's case, however, it sounded simply petulant.

"I know," I said. "But I saw Frank the day he died. I thought we might be able to help each other."

"Yeah? How?"

"I don't know yet. Suppose we talk."

She pursed her lips together. At last she said, "You're not a cop."

"No. Private investigator."

She nodded. "Like 'Rockford Files.'"

"Yeah," I said. "Exactly."

She nodded again. "Okay, come in. But not for long. I gotta go to work soon."

I wiped my feet on the mat and followed her in, shutting the door behind me. The living room was tiny and most of the furniture was cheap—a burgundy recliner chair, its naugahyde arms spotted with cigarette burns; a sway-backed second-hand sofa, cream colored; an end table and a matching coffee table, each of whose oak veneer, paper thin, was beginning to peel back at the edges.

A black portable stereo cassette player sat on the end table; a beanbag ashtray lay on the coffee table beside a package of Marlboros and a red Bic lighter. The only thing there that cost more than fifty dollars was the television, a big color console that was set against the wall opposite the couch.

Lying atop the television was a battered leather Bible, and hanging on the wall above it was a large wooden crucifix with a nickel-plated Jesus. I suspected that Frank Biddle hadn't had anything to do with either the Bible or the cross.

I suspected that he hadn't had anything to do with the house at all. He had lived here, stayed here, but the place was more hers than his. It was a young woman's replica of her family home, and she clearly spent time and energy keeping it up. No dust lay anywhere, and although the threadbare brown wall-to-wall carpeting showed trails of wear, it was spotless.

On the television screen, a man swathed in bandages, lying in a hospital bed, was telling a woman dressed in an evening gown that she'd be better off without him. For no real reason that I could see, she was disagreeing.

Carla Chavez nodded to the TV. " 'Days of our Lives.' You ever watch it?"

I shook my head. "I'm usually working."

"That's Mickie, the guy in the bed. He got hit by a truck. He just got married again to Maggie, that's Maggie there, but he hasn't told her yet that he's the father of Marcella's baby."

I think she was explaining all this just so she could postpone turning the thing off and missing something wonderful. I said nothing. She looked back at me and then, with obvious reluctance, reached out and pushed the button. The picture folded in upon itself and the screen went black. She turned to me again. "You wanna drink?"

"No thanks. Just talk. May I sit down?"

"Yeah, sure, go ahead."

I sat in the recliner; she sat on the sofa. She leaned forward, picked up the pack of cigarettes from the coffee table, slid one out, and lit it with the Bic. She sat back and inhaled the smoke up from her mouth into her nose, two thin streamers, then blew it out in a pale blue billowing cone. Very sophisticated. I wondered then if she were a good deal younger than she looked. "So," she said, "what you wanna talk about?"

"I'm working for the company that insured a diamond necklace that was stolen last year."

"Yeah," she said, "I know all about the necklace from the cops. They were buggin' us about it last year." With her thumb and fourth finger, she plucked a flake of invisible and—filtered cigarettes being what they are—probably nonexistent tobacco from her lower lip. "Frank din't steal no necklace, man. We were in Amarillo, Texas, a thousand miles away."

"Did the police tell you that Frank came to my office last Friday and offered to sell it back to the insurance company?"

"How could he sell it, man? I tole you, he din't have it."

"Did they tell you that he came to see me?"

"Yeah, sure, they tole me. But Frank din't have no necklace."

"You didn't wonder why Frank would offer to sell something he didn't have?"

She laughed. "No, man. Frank was always cooking up some scam. Frank was good at scams."

There was something in her voice, but I couldn't tell whether it was bitterness or admiration. Maybe she couldn't either.

I asked her, "What kind of scam do you think Frank had in mind?"

"How do I know, man?" She sucked in the cigarette and put her head back to exhale, staring at me, eyes narrowed, over the plume of smoke. "You said you were gonna help me. So how you gonna help me?"

"There's a reward," I said, "a finder's fee being offered for the necklace. If you can provide information, any kind of information, that helps me locate the thing, I'll see to it that you get some of the money."

"Yeah?" Dubious. "How much, man? Five bucks?"

"That depends on the information."

"Yeah, well, I don't have no information. And Frank din't have no necklace."

"Do you know Stacey Killebrew?"

"Yeah, I know him. He's a pig." She leaned forward to stab the cigarette out in the ashtray.

"He was a friend of Frank's," I said.

"No, man, not for a long time."

"Since when?"

"Since we got back from Amarillo."

"And that was when, November?"

"Yeah."

"Why'd you leave Amarillo?"

"Thing weren't workin' out." Her eyes narrowed. "What difference does it make?"

"Just curious."

"Yeah, well, curiosity, man." She nodded. "You know what it did to the cat."

"In a private detective, it's considered a plus."

She leaned forward and slipped another cigarette from the pack. Holding the lighter poised before it, she said, "How much they payin' you, that insurance company?"

"Nothing unless I find the necklace."

She lit the cigarette, sat back. "Rockford gets a hundred bucks a day."

"Rockford retired. Why weren't Frank and Killebrew getting along?"

"How do I know? Frank din't talk business with me."

"What kind of business was Frank involved in since he came back from Amarillo?"

"This and that. Odd jobs. Cars. He fixed cars for people. He was good at cars." She narrowed her eyes. "Shouldn't you be payin' me some money for all this?"

"For all what? So far you haven't told me anything."

"I got bills to pay, man, it's not gonna be easy now I'm on my own."

"Where do you work?"

"At the Donut House. My tips are okay. The truck drivers like me, but the tips, they don't cover everything."

"Maybe I can help. Tell me about Frank and Killebrew."

She shrugged. "Nothin' to tell. They used to hang out, go hunting and stuff. Then Frank got pissed at him."

"Why?"

"How do I know? Stacey, he called here one time, just after we got back, and Frank tole him if he ever come around again he'd break in his head."

"Killebrew's a pretty big guy for Frank to be talking to him like that."

"And he's crazy, man. Mean. Evil-mean. I seen him beat up on people, nearly kill 'em, just 'cause he don't like the way they look. But Frank wasn't afraid of nothin', man. Someone lean on him, he get a baseball bat and come back and break their knees. He was short, you know? But strong. And he wasn't afraid of nothin'."

As good an epitaph as any, probably. "Did Frank have a gun?"

"A rifle. Like I say, sometimes he went out hunting deer."

"No pistol."

"Uh-uh."

"Did Frank have any close friends beside Killebrew?"

"No. Not anyone close, you know? Acquaintances, like, he had a lot of acquaintances. Everybody liked Frank a lot."

"Did your brother Benito like him a lot?"

She frowned. "Why you asking?"

I shrugged. "Curiosity."

"Me and Benito, we don't get along too good. Benito only saw Frank one time, maybe two."

"Did Frank do coke, Carla?"

She nodded. "I knew that was why you were askin'. No, never. *Never.* I don't have no drugs in my house. I tole him, that's the one thing I don't put up with."

"Frank never dealt coke?"

"I tole you, no. I don't allow it."

"Okay. What about these acquaintances of his. Do you know any of them? Know their names?"

"No, man. How'm I gonna know? They were guys. You know. Guys who hung out at the bars. Guys Frank knew."

"Which bars?"

She shrugged. "He liked the Lone Star. Everybody knew him there."

"The country-western place north of town?"

"Yeah."

"What about other women? Was he seeing any?"

She frowned. "What's he need other women for? He had *me.* He take care of me; I take care of him."

Involuntarily, I glanced around the tiny room, took in the shabby second-hand furniture. I kept to myself my opinion of Frank's abilities as a provider.

But it must have shown on my face, because suddenly her mouth turned down in a frown and she said, "This was only temporary. We were only staying here until Frank made his score, and then we were off. We were history, man.''

"Off to where?"

"Mexico. We were going to buy a ranch down there and settle down for good. Frank was good at that, at ranching. He knew all about it, the animals, everything.''

"What was his score going to be, Carla?"

She shook her head, her lips pursed. "He never tole me.''

"When did he start talking about it?"

"Always," she said. She looked away, remembering. Her voice softer, she said, "Ever since I knew him. He was always talkin' about it.''

"How long was that, Carla?"

In the same soft faraway voice, still not looking at me, she said, "Two years. We been together—" she corrected herself, "—we *were* together for two years, almost. Two years in June. We met in June.''

This wasn't helping me. I had probably learned all I could from the girl.

It wasn't helping her, either. I saw that her mascara was making dark slick trails down her cheeks. Sitting there, immobile, silently crying, she suddenly looked somehow smaller, and even younger, like a child badly made up for a costume party.

I asked one more question. "Carla," I said, "do you have any idea who killed him?"

Silently she lowered her head, silently shook it.

I stood up. "All right, Carla, thank you. If you think of anything else, give me a call.'' I put my card, and a twenty dollar bill, on the coffee table. And then, as I had at the Leightons', I saw myself out.

# SEVEN

"WHY ON EARTH didn't you call me?"

"Rita," I said into the phone, "I didn't—"

"Someone shoots at you, smashes your window out, and it never occurs to you to let me know?"

"It occurred to me, but I didn't see that there was a whole lot you could do about it. There wasn't a whole lot *I* could do about it."

"So I have to wait until I read about it in the newspaper."

"I'm calling you now," I pointed out.

"Thanks, Joshua. Thank you very much. Now do you think you could see your way to explaining what happened?"

"I can *tell* you what happened, but I'm not so sure that I can explain it."

"Joshua, don't play word games with me."

"Ah, Rita, those are the only kind you'll let me play."

"Stop smirking."

"How do you know I'm smirking?"

"You have a very loud smirk. Where are you, at the office?"

"Yeah. I'm waiting for the Leightons' son to show up."

"All right. In the meantime, tell me what happened."

I told her. About the conversation with Mrs. Leighton, parts of which I edited slightly, about the smashing of the window and the discussion last night with Hector. Told her I'd fixed the window and talked with Carla Chavez, Biddle's girlfriend.

"So you and Mrs. Leighton were just sitting there, innocently, and someone took a shot at you."

"Actually, we weren't sitting at the time. We were standing."

"Innocently."

"Absolutely." I told her what Hector had suggested, that perhaps the shot had been a warning of some kind.

"Maybe," she said, "but even if that's true, you and Hector are both making an assumption."

"Which assumption?"

"That the warning was meant for you."

I frowned. "You think it was meant for Mrs. Leighton?"

"I don't think anything yet. I don't know enough."

"That doesn't make any sense, Rita. It was a thirty-eight slug that came through the window, so it's probably safe to assume that whoever fired it was the same person who killed Biddle. What would he have been warning Mrs. Leighton about?"

"What would he've been warning you about?"

"Beats me, Rita. You're the brains of this operation. I'm just the muscle."

"Sometimes I can almost believe that. By the way, are you carrying your gun?"

"No."

"I think you should, Joshua."

"It spoils the drape of my jacket."

"Get a new jacket. What did Carla Chavez have to say?"

I related the conversation.

Rita said, "Do you believe her, about the drugs?"

"I believe that *she* believes Biddle wasn't involved in drugs. But she also believes that Biddle wasn't involved with other women. And we know from Felice Leighton that he was involved, at least temporarily, with her."

"Felice, is it?"

"Aha," I said. "Do I detect a note of jealousy?"

She laughed. "No. Sorry. But I have a hard time picturing you with someone like her. You'll have to buy yourself a pair of handcuffs."

"Hector has some nice ones, he tells me. Maybe he'll let me borrow them."

"If you're planning on a long-term affair, it might be better to invest in a pair of your own."

"We'll see how it goes. Maybe she carries some with her, just in case."

"Before you begin this courtship, do you plan to do anything else to find the necklace?"

"I talked to Peter Ricard yesterday, and he tells me that Leighton was in a bind for money last fall, around the time the necklace was stolen. He needed thirty or forty thousand to make payment on a note, and somehow he managed to come up with it. I thought one of us could give Aaron a call, at the bank, and see if he can find out where Leighton got the money."

"If it's insurance money, the claim might've been fraudulent."

"Yeah."

"I know Allan Romero. Atco wouldn't have paid out the money if there were any question of fraud."

"I'd still like to know if it was the insurance money that saved his ass."

"All right. I'll call Aaron. What else did you have in mind?"

"Like I said, I'm talking to Kevin Leighton this afternoon. Tonight I'll drive out to the Lone Star and talk to the bartender there. I know him. Maybe he can tell me something about the people Biddle hung around with."

"I wonder why Biddle and Killebrew had a falling out."

"Well, sooner or later I'm going to have to talk to Killebrew. I'll ask him that very thing."

"From everything I've heard about Killebrew, he sounds a dangerous man."

"You forget, it seems, that you're talking to a guy who can bend steel in his bare hands."

"Steel doesn't try to bend you back. I know you're terribly strong, Joshua, and terribly competent, but I suggest you be careful with this one."

"Right, Rita. I'll talk to him on the telephone. Long distance."

"And wear the gun when you do."

"Right."

AT FOUR O'CLOCK, half an hour late, Kevin Leighton sauntered through the door, hands in his pockets, and walked across the room with a wrangler strut that immediately reminded me, as perhaps it reminded him, of Frank Biddle. "You Croft?" he asked, his head canted slightly back.

He was medium tall, five foot eight or nine, slender. He was wearing a gray plaid flannel shirt, faded jeans, and that bland insolent mask with which some teenagers confront a potentially hostile adult world. His hair was fine and wavy, so blond it was nearly white, and he was good-looking in an almost delicate way. A well-defined and sensitive mouth, a narrow pointed nose, and pale blue eyes with a wariness to them that didn't quite match the arrogance of expression.

Nodding, I stood up behind the desk and held out my hand. "Kevin Leighton?"

Reluctantly he slipped his hand from his pocket and took mine, shook it.

"Have a seat," I told him.

He sat down in the client's chair in a manner so like Biddle's it was uncanny. Legs stretched out and crossed at the ankles of his cowboy boots, fingers interlaced atop his chest.

"Did your mother tell you," I asked him, "what I wanted to see you about?"

He nodded. "Yeah, right," he said, his voice flat. "The necklace that got ripped off."

I nodded. "You think Frank Biddle stole it?"

"Nah," he said. His face twisted with scorn. It's an emotion that comes easily to someone who hasn't lived for very long. "Frank wasn't even in town."

"The police think that Frank planned the thing with a man named Killebrew. You know him?"

He shrugged. "Seen him around once or twice."

"With Frank?"

"Yeah," he said. He raised his eyebrows. "That doesn't prove anything."

"I'm not trying to prove anything, Kevin. I'm just trying to find the necklace."

He nodded, mouth compressed, looking wearily up to the ceiling to demonstrate how fascinating he found all this.

I said, "You were the last person to leave the house the night the necklace was stolen."

"Yeah." He shrugged again. "What're you, gonna arrest me?"

"I understand that you forgot to turn on the alarm."

He snorted slightly. "That's what they tell me."

"And what's that mean?"

He winced with impatience. "I was drunk, man. Ripped. I had some friends over and we partied. I don't remember what I did. They say I didn't turn it on; I didn't turn it on."

"Were you doing coke that night?"

He looked at me, puzzled, as though he'd never, never ever, heard of the stuff. "Doing what?"

"Kevin, if you were in kindergarten instead of high school, I might buy the innocence number."

"Hey, man, we partied. We had drinks, seven and sevens, some screwdrivers. That was it."

"Why am I suddenly having a hard time believing that?"

"Don't know, man, and I don't care. None of this was my idea, my coming here."

"I thought you might want to help me find your mother's necklace."

"Right, yeah," he said, and studied the ceiling some more.

I asked him, "Did you see anything that night, when you left? An unfamiliar car parked near the house?"

Another wince. "I did all this with the cops last year. Ask *them*."

"They're not here. You are."

He sighed a long elaborate sigh. "Right," he nodded. "Okay." In a monotone, staring at the ceiling again, he chanted, "No I didn't see any cars, no I didn't see any strangers around the house, no I don't have any idea who stole the stupid necklace, and no, I don't give a shit." He looked down at me. "Can I go now?"

"Kevin," I said, "I know you're not going to believe this, but you are really beginning to piss me off."

"Well, that's just too bad, isn't it?"

I stood up and came around the desk.

"You touch me," he said, sitting up straight, fingers clutching at the arm of the chair as he tucked his feet beneath it, "and my father'll sue you for everything you've got."

"Uh-huh." I sat down on the edge of the desk, put my hands against its top. "Kevin, do you have any idea what a thirty-eight caliber slug can do to the human body?"

He sneered. It wasn't a completely successful sneer, but then I outweighed him by about fifty pounds. "What're you, gonna shoot me now?"

"I'm talking about your friend Frank. Your dead friend Frank. Someone pumped four slugs into him. Let me tell you a little something about that, Kevin. A thirty-eight slug travels at around a thousand feet per second. I don't know how good you are at math, probably not very, but that works out to a little more than seven hundred miles an hour. I want you to think about that, Kevin, think about this little piece of lead, doesn't weigh more than a quarter of an ounce, but it's traveling faster than a seven forty-seven. Now what it does when it smashes into you, it shatters bone into splinters and dust and it ruptures blood vessels; the shock just explodes them, and it piles up flesh ahead of it, muscle and ligaments and fat, and rams it all out through a hole in your back the size of a coffee cup."

His face had gone pale. He cleared his throat, discovered his bravado along with his voice. "So what's the point?"

"In Frank's case, two of the slugs stayed inside him. One of them smashed a couple of ribs and turned his heart into Alpo."

He leaned forward, hands on the arm of the chair. "Why are you *telling* me this?"

"Because we're talking about a human being here, Kevin, maybe not much of one, but a human being that someone put four bullets in, and your mother tells me, goddammit, that you *liked* him."

His face clenched with fury. "I did *like* him!"

"Then forget this James Dean shit and *talk* to me. Whoever shot him is still out there, Kevin. He's still got the gun and he's probably still got the necklace."

His anger and his hurt were still carrying him. "I don't *know* anything about the necklace."

"Then tell me about Frank. Did he ever get coke for you?"

"What difference does it make now?" His voice was beginning to fray.

I leaned toward him. "So he did."

"All right, *shit*, yes. So *what*?" But this last bright flare of defiance, the words spat at me, consumed whatever was left. Suddenly he lowered his head, cupping his hand around his forehead so I couldn't see his eyes. His shoulders moved slowly up, slowly down, in a long, deep, ragged sigh.

I said, more softly, "I'm not the cops, Kevin. You want to do coke, that's your business. And your problem. But I need to know about Frank. I need to get a handle on him. How often was he dealing for you?"

"He wasn't *dealing*." He looked up at me, and his face was flushed, his mouth awry. A sob was trembling just behind his voice. "He did it as a *favor*."

I was feeling extremely pleased with myself just then. Within the space of only three or four hours today I had managed to reduce two people to grief, both of them barely out of childhood. J. Croft Inc., Freelance Funsters. Spreading mirth and merriment wherever we go. Ask about our group rates.

"All right," I said. "Tell me about the first time."

The first time, he told me—slowly, haltingly, with me nudging him gently along—had been on a horseback camping trip in the Kit Carson National Wilderness, north of town. He and Biddle had put in a good day, having traveled perhaps ten miles or so into the forest before set-

ting up camp. Biddle had cooked the food, Kevin had
helped clean up afterward. And then as the two of them sat
against their bedrolls, the campfire flickering at their
boots, a scene straight out of *The Trail of the Lonesome
Pines*, Biddle had produced a pint of V.O. and a gram vial
of coke.

"Was this the first time you'd done coke?"

"No. Practically everybody at school does it."

The teachers? I wondered. The principal? "All right,"
I said, "so then what?"

So then Biddle and Kevin had sipped at the pint and
snorted from the vial and Biddle had regaled the boy with
tales of Life on the Range amid the dogies and the tum-
bleweed. From the warmth in Kevin's eyes as he related all
this, it was clear he was fond of Biddle. Years ago the
fondness would've been called a crush; today, most likely,
it'd be called unresolved Oedipal conflict, or, worse, la-
tent homosexual propensities. To me, having met the boy's
parents, it simply seemed that he needed someone to look
up to, and that Biddle had filled the bill. And Biddle, for
his part, would've enjoyed an audience for his cowboy
theatricality.

"Did he ever get coke for you after that?" I asked.

"Three or four times." He looked at me, the face open,
the blue eyes pleading. "But really, like I said, only as a
favor. He never made any money off it. He always charged
me what it cost him."

"How much was that?"

"A hundred and twenty a gram."

The standard price, last I'd heard. "You only bought
grams?"

"Once a bunch of us got together and bought an eightball."

An eighth of an ounce, a little under three grams. "For
how much?"

"Two seventy-five."

Again, as far as I knew, the standard price. Maybe Biddle *was* charging what he'd paid. Which didn't make him any more of a peach in my book. But on the other hand, despite Kevin's hero worship, I found it difficult not to picture the man picking up every bit of spare change he could locate.

Something occurred to me. "Kevin, you weren't selling the stuff? At school?"

"No, no. It was just for us, for me and my friends. We never sold any."

Maybe so, maybe not. I tended to believe him, but I've been wrong before. Something that becomes easier to remember, unfortunately, the older you get.

"Did any of your friends buy from Frank?"

"No. I was the only one. Frank made me promise not to tell where I was getting it."

"And you never did?"

"*No.*" Surprised and indignant. After all, he'd given his word. Code of the West.

"Were you buying from him before or after he stopped working at your house?"

"Before, mostly. It was hard to get in touch with him after. I think he got me some one more time, before he went to Amarillo."

"And after he got back from Texas?"

He shook his head. "I only saw him once or twice. He was too busy, he said."

"When was the last time you saw him?"

"Last week."

"Where?"

"At the house."

"At your house?" My turn to be surprised; Felice Leighton had told me she hadn't seen him. "Why'd he come?"

"I don't know. To see me, probably. But I never got a chance to talk to him. My sister opened the door first, and then my father was there, and he told Frank to get off the property or he'd call the police."

"Was your mother there?"

He shook his head. "She was out." He looked at me with what appeared to be genuine curiosity. "Why do you want to know so much about Frank?"

I told him that Frank had come to my office to sell some stolen jewelry. "The more I know about Frank, the more likely I am to learn something about the necklace."

"Yeah," he said. "But you don't know for sure that the jewelry he was talking about was my mother's necklace."

Everybody's a detective. "No," I said, "I don't. Kevin, why do you think your father disliked Frank so much?"

"I don't know. He used to like him a lot, and then suddenly, last year, he fired him."

"You and Frank never talked about it?"

He shook his head. "I asked him, and Frank said it was like a personality conflict. I said—" he paused, uncertain.

"You said what?"

"Well, I called my father a bastard, and Frank got real mad and told me never to badmouth my old man. He said it was okay to badmouth your old man to his face, but never to other people."

It was a piece of homespun morality I wouldn't have expected from Biddle. I asked the boy, "Kevin, did you know any other close friends Frank may've had?"

He shrugged. "Only the big guy. Killebrew. I didn't really like him. He was pretty scary."

"What about women? I got the impression that Frank liked the women."

Kevin grinned. "And they liked him."

"Did he mention any in particular?"

"He never used names. He said a gentleman never used names. He told some pretty funny stories, though."

"No names at all?"

"Well, there was Carla, the girl he lived with. And once—" another hesitation.

"What?"

"Well, once I saw him with Silvia Griego. They were in her car and Frank had his hand, you know, on the back of her neck."

"And who is Silvia Griego?"

"She's a friend of my mom's. She owns an art gallery on Canyon Road."

"Is there anything else you can tell me, Kevin, that might help?"

He shook his head. "But I don't think Frank took that necklace."

"Someone did," I said.

IT WAS ALMOST SIX when Kevin Leighton left my office. I called Hector and caught him just as he was leaving his own.

"So how's it going, Philo?" he asked me.

"Interesting," I told him. "I've got something I think you can use."

"And what's that?"

"Biddle was dealing coke. Small-timing it, anyway."

"Uh-huh. And naturally you're not going to give me your source."

"Sorry, Hector."

He sighed. "You think the information's solid?"

"I think so. The source bought from him. Grams and eightballs."

"Where was Biddle getting it?"

"I don't know. But Benito Chavez is a possibility."

"He lives in Las Mujeres. I'll have the Sheriff's Department up there talk to him. Not that it'll do much good."

"You sound dispirited, Hector."

"Is that the same as shitty?"

"Nothing new on Biddle?"

"Nothing."

"I'm going up to the Lone Star for a drink. Why not join me."

"Why the Lone Star?"

"Biddle used to hang out there. I know Phil, the bartender. Maybe he can tell me something about Biddle's friends and relations."

"Stacey Killebrew hangs out there these days."

"Good. It's about time I talked to Stacey."

"Josh, stay away from Killebrew."

"Everyone keeps telling *me* that, Hector."

"Listen to them. Killebrew's a fruitcake."

"According to *Psychology Today*, all your basic fruitcake needs is a little kindness and sympathy."

"You can't believe everything you read...."

"Yeah, I read that somewhere. So you coming?"

"Not tonight. Errands to run."

"All right. Talk to you later."

"Leave Killebrew alone, Josh."

"Sure, Hector."

"It's your funeral."

# EIGHT

SOMETHING JABBED once at my right shoulder, quick and hard and insistent, and when I turned on the bar stool I found myself staring into the center of a T-shirted chest that seemed about six feet wide. I looked up, and kept looking up, and finally my stare found the dark brown eyes of Stacey Killebrew. They were set deeply back, above the high Slavic cheekbones and below the sandy eyebrows that matched the sandy mustache and the sandy thinning hair, and they were as friendly and inviting as a pair of gun muzzles.

"You wanna talk to me?" he said in a flat West Texas drawl.

I'd seen Killebrew one or twice a few years ago, before he became a guest of the state, and he'd always been a big man who kept himself fit. But a year and a half of pumping iron in the slammer had turned him into a fine figure of a man indeed. The sleeves of the T-shirt were rolled back to his thick shoulders, displaying biceps that were a tad thicker than my thighs, with pectorals as rounded as grapefruit. His skin was so taut, stretched tight over the swollen muscles and the cable-wire ligaments, that it looked as if it could repel bullets. I wouldn't have a chance to find out, not today, anyway. I still wasn't carrying the revolver.

I said, "Yeah, I would, as a matter of fact. Sit down and I'll buy you a drink."

"You won't buy me shit," he said. His thin-lipped mouth moved hardly at all as he spoke—something else, perhaps, he'd picked up in prison. "You wanna talk," he said, "we go outside." He hooked his thumbs over an ornate silver and turquoise belt buckle.

Phil, the bartender, had moved down to this end of the bar again and now he leaned toward the two of us and said, "No trouble, Stacey." He kept his hands below the bartop.

With no change of expression, Killebrew turned to him and said, "Tell you what, Phil. You pull out that billy and I'll cram it so far up your ass I'll pop your eyeballs out."

Phil had been a Green Beret in Vietnam and the bartender here for ten years. He was prepared to take this thing as far as Killebrew wanted to go with it. His hands still below the bar, he said, "I'm telling you, Stacey. It doesn't happen here."

I stood up. Sitting on the stool I'd been in a bad position anyway. "No problem, Phil," I said. "Mr. Killebrew and I are going to have a little chat."

"Right," Killebrew said. He had eased smoothly away, a step or two, when I stood. Giving himself room. He jerked his head toward the entrance. "Out."

"I don't think so," I told him. Standing, I was eye to eye with him and as ready as I would ever be. Feet braced, knees loose, body away from the bar but left elbow resting casually on its top, ready to come up in a block. I would've felt considerably better about it if I hadn't known that he was ready too.

I said, "Right here is fine with me. If you've got the time, I'd like to ask you a few questions about Frank Biddle."

Right here was also fine with Killebrew. He said, "I hear you been badmouthin' me behind my back."

"You hear wrong." I was wondering if there was anywhere on that body I could hit him without hurting myself. Not the stomach; beneath the tight T-shirt it looked like washboard.

For the first time, he smiled. His teeth were large and mulish, discolored yellow, and the smile didn't do much for him. It didn't do much for me, either. He said, "You callin' me a liar?"

"I'm saying you've been misinformed."

"So," he said, still smiling, "now you're callin' my friend Albert a liar." He nodded his head to the left, and I recognized the ferrety little man who'd been sitting at the bar when I arrived. He was standing now, off behind Killebrew, smirking, arms crossed, practically hugging himself in anticipation.

I shrugged. "Why? You planning on defending his honor?" As musclebound as Killebrew was, he wouldn't be able to move with any speed. Or so I told myself.

The smile grew wider and his eyes took on a sleepy, almost blissful expression.

And then he moved. I had been wrong about his speed.

I HAD REACHED the Lone Star a little after seven. I knew that the band didn't start until eight-thirty. I'd heard it play once before and I didn't really want to repeat the experience.

The bar was nearly full, but there were a couple of empty stools next to the waitresses' service area. I took the one nearest it and looked around.

As big as a barn—it had been one, twenty years ago— the room was dominated by the long wide wooden dance floor, empty now. The bandstand, also empty, sat at the far end, opposite the bar. Running along the sides of the building was a raised wooden platform that held small round tables and straight-backed wooden chairs. Most of these were unoccupied, but scattered in the dimness were four or five couples, each pair huddled over drinks, sharing privacy the way couples tend to do in a nearly empty lounge.

No couples huddled at the bar. Three construction workers sipped Coors; a pair of heavy-set Indians did the same; three young Hispanics in white shirts drank highballs; a couple of old men with lined red faces who could have been farmers sat behind shots of what could have been bourbon. My nearest neighbor, two stools down, was a small skinny guy about forty years old with a narrow ferret's face, wearing denim pants and jacket and a green Caterpillar Tractor cap. Leaning forward, bootheels notched against the stool strut, he had both hands wrapped around his glass of draft beer as though he were afraid someone might try to snatch it away.

And, later on tonight, when things got lively, someone might. The Lone Star was the place you went when you wanted to hear honky-tonk and kick a little ass. The management had kept the place simple and unadorned—"thoroughly unpretentious," as Rita liked to put it, smiling—because anything elaborate in the way of furnishings was liable to get stomped on or, during especially festive occasions, shot at.

"Been a while, Josh," someone said, and I turned back to the bar to see Phil standing behind it. He was Irish, in his forties, balding and red-bearded, barrel-chested and slowly, over the years, becoming barrel-bellied. With his beefy freckled forearms, his white shirt and apron, he would've looked more at home at P.J. Clarke's in New York, or maybe McSorley's, than he did here, in a cowboy bar in a cowboy state.

He held out his hand. "How's it going?"

We shook, and I said that everything was dandy. He asked if I was still drinking Jack Daniel's and I told him I was. He poured it for me and I asked him if he'd heard about Frank Biddle.

Phil's face didn't change—he'd been a bartender too long for that—but he scratched for a moment at his beard. "Yeah," he said. "I heard he got wasted."

"Four thirty-eight slugs."

Phil nodded. "Slow you down some."

"He used to hang out here," I said.

He shrugged. "Once in a while. Wasn't what you'd call a regular."

"When he did hang out here, who did he hang out with?"

He shrugged again. "No one in particular. Why?" Phil owed me a favor, and he wanted to know whether he was paying it back.

"I'm trying to get a line on him."

"Business?"

I nodded.

He shook his head. "He was a loner, mostly. Everybody knew him to say hello to, and he was friendly enough, but mostly he kept to himself. Sometimes he brought in the girl he lived with."

"Carla Chavez."

"Yeah. Sexy little thing."

"Did he ever bring in any other women?"

Phil smiled. "I don't think Carla woulda gone for that. Probably put a knife between his ribs if she heard he was doing someone else."

"Would Carla have to know?"

He shrugged. "A lot of the women come in here, they know Carla. They'd tell her if Frankie showed up with someone else."

"But he could've had something on the side and never brought her in here."

"Wouldn't surprise me. Frankie was the type. You could tell from the way he looked at them."

"How do you mean?"

Bartenders are like interns; they like explaining their observations. "Some guys," said Phil, "married guys, they look at women like little kids at a candy store, you know? Wanting something they know they can't have, and a little sneaky just for wanting it. But Frankie looked at them like he coulda had them anytime he wanted, only now wasn't the time. Not here, where it might get back to Carla."

"So he never moved in on any of them."

He shook his head. "Not here."

"Was he selling coke, Phil?"

Phil's face once again took on its bartender blankness. "Not here, he wasn't."

"But somewhere else?"

He held up his hands, palms out, and raised his eyebrows: I don't know, don't ask me. "I know for a fact he wasn't moving anything through here."

"How do you know?"

And then, from down the bar, someone called out Phil's name. He turned. "Yeah?"

It was one of the construction workers, short, squat, his long blond hair kept in place with a headband. "Phil," he called, "what time you get off tonight?"

"Two," Phil called back.

"Any chance of getting another beer before then?"

Laughter down the bar. Phil grinned, turned to me. "Back in a minute."

I sipped at my Jack Daniel's. The ferret-faced man to my right sipped at his draft. When Phil had covered the rest of the bar, he returned. Leaning toward me, hands clasped, forearms against the bar, he said, "Look, even if he *was* dealing—dealing somewhere else, I mean—he wasn't dealing in quantity. A gram here and there, maybe an eightball or two. Small change. Frankie was a small-change guy."

I nodded. "You ever see Frank with Carla's brother?"

He frowned, shook his head. "You're really stuck on the coke thing."

"And it looks like you're really stuck on protecting ol' Frankie's reputation."

"I liked him. He never gave me any hassle, never bitched and moaned about how crummy life was. He was cocky, maybe, he never took shit off anybody, but he never went looking for it either." He shrugged. "I liked him. He was all right."

Another epitaph. "Phil," I said, "for all I know, he was a prince. I'm just asking if you ever saw him with Benito Chavez."

"All right, yeah. So once, twice maybe, they were here together. But I'm telling you that no coke deals went down in this bar."

"You talked to Biddle about it. You told him no dealing here."

He shrugged again, his face empty.

Code of the West.

"Okay, Phil," I said, "Fine. If you believed him, that's good enough for me. What about Frank and Stacey Killebrew?"

"They used to hang around together, last year, before Frankie took off for Texas. But something happened, and after Frankie came back they weren't talking to each other. It was like Frankie got pissed at him for something."

"You don't know what."

"No."

"What do you know about Killebrew?"

"Enough not to want to know anything at all."

"He hangs out here."

Phil glanced quickly around the bar, then nodded. "Now and then." He leaned closer. "Listen, Josh, I don't

think you want to have anything to do with Stacey Killebrew."

"Everybody keeps telling me that."

"No offense, babe, but he's out of your league. The guy
is crazy. He *likes* to hurt people."

"Do you know what he does for a living?"

"Officially, he owns a piece of a garage over on St.
Francis."

"And unofficially?"

"Who knows?" He shrugged. "Like I say, I hear
things."

"What things?"

Another shrug. New Yorkers shrug almost as much as
Frenchmen. "That he's working something not totally
kosher. I don't know what it is, but it must bring in a fair
amount of cash, because he throws the stuff around like it
was monopoly money. Last week he gave the band a hundred bucks for playing what he wanted to hear."

"What was that?"

"Silence."

I smiled. "He's got better taste than I would've
thought."

Phil smiled back. "You've heard the band too, huh?"

"Who does Killebrew hang out with when he comes
here?"

"Guy named Lucero, usually. John Lucero. An Indian.
He's supposed to be an artist, but I never saw him paint
anything so you couldn't prove it by me."

"Is Lucero here now?"

He shook his head. "Doesn't come in till later." He
looked at his watch. "Around eight. Another twenty
minutes, half an hour."

I asked him for a description of Lucero, and he gave it:
in his thirties, tall, slender, wispy black mustache, long

black hair usually worn in a braid. It was a description that would've fit half the Indians in Santa Fe.

And then I asked him if he thought Killebrew could've killed Biddle.

"I dunno," he said. He shrugged again. "It's possible. Killebrew could shotgun his mother and then go out for pizza."

"Okay, Phil," I said. "Thanks. If you hear anything about Biddle, let me know."

"Will do."

He went off to attend to the rest of the bar, and I sat there, sipping my Jack Daniel's and wondering what had caused the rift between Biddle and Killebrew. Had it something to do with the burglary at the Leightons'?

Rita would've said that I didn't have enough information to form suppositions, but I sat there forming them anyway. Suppose that Sergeant Nolan was right, and Killebrew and Biddle had planned the robbery together. Suppose that Biddle had taken off to Amarillo to give himself an alibi. Suppose that when he returned, Killebrew refused to split the take with him.

But what take? The necklace hadn't been fenced, not if it was still around last week. There had been no take to split.

Out of the corner of my eye, barely noticing it, I saw the ferret-faced man to my right swing himself off the stool and walk away.

A few moments later, I felt the tap on my shoulder.

A LONG TIME AGO in a magazine—*Esquire*, I think it was—I saw a life-sized photograph of Mohammed Ali's fist. My own fist is hardly tiny, but when I held it up against the picture, it looked like a child's. The fist that came rushing at me that night in the Lone Star, delivered in a fast, effortless right jab up from Killebrew's belt, looked as big as Ali's.

Reflexes took over and snapped my head to the side, but even so, the fist smashed along the side of my skull, scraping away at my left ear.

I spun around, going with the momentum of the punch and swinging away from the bar. As I turned to face him again, Killebrew moved in with a roundhouse left. I caught it on my right shoulder and drove my own left, all my weight behind it, into his middle, just below the rib cage.

I doubt that it hurt him, but it must've surprised him because he backed away, fists coming up.

His smile didn't change at all.

The left side of my face, my cheek, my ear, had gone numb. Adrenaline had over-ridden the pain circuits and sharpened all the others. My vision was working with abnormal clarity; everything in the room had an outline sharp enough to slice fingertips. I was aware of the smells of cigarette smoke and beer, of the sounds of the crowd around us, the men jostling each other for position and hooting us on.

Someone shouted, *"Fair fight, leave 'em alone!"* and I knew without looking that it was Killebrew's ferret-faced friend.

Both big fists making small tight circles in the air, left fist above and slightly forward of the right, Killebrew danced toward me.

He was very good. His grin never wavered and his eyes never left mine, never signalled his intent. He feinted a left jab, his heavy torso weaving, then shot a straight right at my heart. I backpedalled away, but he came with me, moving more lightly and swiftly than I thought possible. Another feint, this time with the right, and then a wide left. I stopped it with my right forearm, felt the arm lose all sensation, and moved inside and jabbed twice at his face as hard and as fast as I could. It was less painful than hitting a cinderblock, but not much.

When I moved quickly away, I saw that I'd drawn blood. A red trickle of it, bright as paint, ran from his nose down over his lips.

Killebrew wiped at his chin, glanced down at the shiny scarlet smear on his palm, then showed me his yellow teeth in another grin. He said, "You're dead, boy."

There was something unreal, theatrical, about the whole scene. Bar brawls don't work this way, not in real life. In real life, people slam at each other with beer mugs, plates, anything available—ketchup bottles are good, because they're heavy and because when they do break, the guy you've hit thinks he's bleeding to death.

In real life people don't put up their dukes and dance around the room the way movie cowboys do, the way Killebrew and I were doing. I didn't know, at the time, what either one of us was trying to prove. Since then, of course, Rita has explained it all to me, several times.

I still couldn't quite believe, even as I saw it, how quickly the man could move. He sailed into me now, fists pumping like pistons in a Maserati, pounding at my upper body, my head, my chest, my belly. Most of this I blocked or slipped away from, but my arms had begun to feel as though they were made out of sandbags, and I couldn't send him anything back. And, heavy shoulders hunched, teeth bared in his mulish grin, he kept coming at me.

Finally he hit me with a gut shot, a good one, a left, and, paralyzed with the shock of it, my guard went down. I can remember thinking, *Shit, this is it,* and it was, because his huge right fist came roaring in like a bullet train and crashed square against my cheek. And then the room did an extraordinarily clever trick and flipped over on its axis, dumping me flat on my back.

Lying there, staring at the ceiling, I knew that I had to get up, knew that if I didn't, Killebrew would finish me off with his boots, kick me or stomp me into a pudding.

But my body, unaccountably, didn't seem to share my brain's anxiety. It liked staring at the ceiling. As ceilings went, it felt, this one was awfully nice.

# NINE

CANYON ROAD may be the oldest road still travelled in the United States. Years before the Mayflower reached Plymouth Rock—or the drafting board—it was a pathway for Indians trekking up over the Sangre de Cristo mountains to the pueblo at Pecos. Later, outside the township called Villa Real de la Santa Fe de San Francisco, Spanish settlers and their descendants built homes here. Some of these still stand, but they've become art galleries and boutiques and eateries that supply food—*quiche, ceviche, pasta al pesto*—that would've made the *hidalgos* scratch their heads in wonderment, and at prices that would've made them roll, giggling, across the quaint hardwood floors.

The building I wanted had been a large home, fronted with a territorial wooden portal. The rectangular bronze plaque to the side of the door was engraved in black anodized script: "The Griego Gallery." The main door, of some heavy dark wood, was open, but the screen door was shut. I opened it and stepped inside. There must have been a buzzer under the floor mat; somewhere, far off, a discreet set of chimes announced that an intruder had arrived.

The walls were white, and so were the broad Greek flokati rugs, two of them, atop the dark polished hardwood floor. Pottery and other objets d'art nested throughout the room on white boxlike display stands, and nestled in spotlit alcoves inset along the walls. To my right an older couple stood peering into one of the alcoves. She wore a lime green pants suit and he wore khaki slacks, a suede sport coat, and a cowboy hat. Up from Dallas or Houston, most likely, to find themselves some art; it was only Texans who attached a certain amount of importance to wearing their hats indoors.

A woman came around the corner to my left, smiling pleasantly. Perhaps twenty-two years old, short, nicely proportioned, she wore a black silk blouse, a black mini-skirt, and black pumps. She had very good legs and she walked as though someone had informed her of this, frequently. Her blond hair was curled in tight ringlets close to her scalp and her features were even and regular, with the kind of blue-eyed outdoorsy good looks that you see, maybe a shade too often, in Pepsi commercials.

"Can I help you?" she asked me, and her smile didn't waver even as her glance took in, quickly, the flamboyant bruise gleaming below my left eye.

"I'm looking for Silvia Griego," I said, smiling back as pleasantly as I was able to do with a cheek that felt the size of a cantaloupe.

"Silvia's on the phone right now. May I give her your name?"

I took a business card out of my blazer pocket, one of the cards that had only my name embossed on its front, and handed it to her.

She looked at it, then looked up at me, still smiling amiably. "And what's this in reference to?"

"It's a personal matter."

Briefly, her glance skated up and down my height and her smile took on a knowing quality. Mine probably took on a befuddled quality. What did she know that I didn't?

Probably, like everybody else, quite a lot.

She nodded. "I'll tell her," she said and moved off, back the way she'd come. I ambled after her into the next room.

She crossed the room, opened a door at its far side, and disappeared within. I looked around me. To my right, more pottery, bowls and pitchers, all of them heavy, black, and glossy. Most likely from the Santa Clara pueblo whose Indian artisans were famous for their black ware. I picked up one of the bowls from its stand and turned it over. No price tag; this wasn't Safeway, after all. Then I noticed the small, tastefully printed card, tented, standing atop the stand. It described the object, in case there was the least shadow of a doubt, as a bowl, and then gave the name of the Santa Clara artist who produced it, and then its price. I set the thing down with a lot more caution than I'd used to pick it up.

Opposite the pottery were the kachinas, handcarved wooden dolls, painted and feathered. There were four of them, each perched on one of the display stands, each lit separately by a small spotlight. I strolled over to the nearest one.

It was two feet tall, an animal figure of considerable power, a wolf or a bear. Below a sort of skullcap made of feathers was a head of white fur and a white wooden snout filled with needle-sharp teeth. Its eyes were blood red, with round black pupils. Its body was that of a man, smoothly sanded, painted white. More white fur ran down its spine, and tufts adorned the back of its hands and its white leather boots.

A good deal of care had been taken with the details. The leggings and armbands were of leather, painted black and dotted with white. Its loincloth was white cotton, embroidered with a geometric design of green and red. Each tiny, carefully shaped finger was tipped with a claw carved from thin translucent shell.

I took a look at the card taped to the stand. The price was $3,500. Took a look at the artist's name.

John Lucero.

"That's *Hon*," said a voice behind me.

I turned. "It's who?"

She smiled as she came up to me. She had wide hand-some lips and bright white teeth with an attractive over-bite. There was a small cleft in her chin and another one, barely visible, at the tip of her nose. Her eyes were brown, laugh lines crinkling at their corners. In her late thirties, or early forties, she wore a beige cashmere sweater, a black skirt, and black flat-soled shoes. Her hair was her most impressive feature. Deep brown, laced heavily with silver, it was long and thick and it outlined her shoulders like an aura. To make it look so artlessly dramatic, she probably spent the cash equivalent of a Santa Clara bowl every month or two.

She said, "*Hon*. The Bear kachina. The Hopis believe he can cure serious diseases."

"How is he at bruises?"

She looked at my left cheek. "Did you walk into a door?"

"Three or four of them."

She laughed softly and held out her hand. "Silvia Griego."

I took it. "Joshua Croft. Are all the kachinas as expen-sive as this one?"

If she resented the question, she didn't show it. She smiled, and in a reasonable, well-modulated voice that probably sold a lot of kachinas, she said, "That's actually one of the least expensive. I couldn't let you have that Buffalo over there, for example, for less than forty-five hundred." She nodded to the figure on the stand farthest away. No bigger than this one, it sported an elaborate headdress of feathers.

"Lot of money for a doll," I said.

No doubt she'd heard the same sentiment expressed be-fore, and more diplomatically, but once again she merely smiled. "They take time," she said, "and they take care. The artist, John Lucero, is one of the few today who works from a single piece of cottonwood root. Assuming you can locate a piece, which is getting more and more difficult to do, the wood has to be dried for a period of time before it can be worked. And John makes the paintings himself from native materials. Iron oxides, copper carbonates, vegetable dyes. The others use acrylics.''

"Acrylics are bad," I said.

"Acrylics are perfectly fine," she said, "if you like them, and many people do. It's a matter of taste. But personally, I happen to prefer a somewhat softer tone." End of lesson. Her smile became speculative. "But I don't think you came here to discuss kachinas."

"No," I said. "I came here to discuss Frank Biddle."

I've discovered that one of the advantages, or disadvantages, or simply one of the side-effects of growing older, is that whenever I meet people now, I can somehow see in each of their faces the face of the child they once were. Long ago, before things started happening. It's not a trick I do intentionally; it simply happens, more or less easily.

And Silvia Griego, just then, made it easy. All at once, her grown-up face collapsed. One moment she was a handsome, friendly, self-assured career woman; the next she was a stricken young girl, mouth open, eyes tight with fear, shoulders slightly hunched against an expected blow.

Surprised, a little alarmed, and maybe a little guilty, I watched as she pulled herself together. With a visible effort she straightened her back, brought her adult face back into focus. Without looking at me, she said, "In my office," and she turned and strode off toward the door at the far end of the room. I followed her.

She pulled open the door, stepped inside, and said something to someone in there. I waited, and after a moment the Pepsi-Cola girl sauntered into the doorway. She gave me another knowing smile as she passed by, heading back toward the front of the gallery.

Silvia Griego turned to me, mouth set, eyebrows lowered, eyes staring somewhere in the middle of my chest. "Come in."

The office was airy and spacious, with cream-colored walls and white shag wall-to-wall carpeting. To my immediate right, an L-shaped desk held a computer workstation and a bulky printer. On the opposite wall was a painting of a landscape that I recognized as Diablo Canyon, down by the Rio Grande. Beneath the painting sat a couple of comfortable-looking white chairs; and high above it on the wall, braced with metal struts, were two television screens, each showing a view of the gallery. When I'd been in there, I hadn't noticed any cameras. I wasn't supposed to, of course.

Beyond the desk, an open door led out onto a small enclosed courtyard of Russian olive and flagstones. Although there was no one visible out there, Silvia Griego crossed the room and shut the door. Her eyes still avoiding mine, she came back around the desk and sat down behind it in the padded leather swivel chair. She put her arms along the arms of the chair, took a deep breath, and looked up at me.

"What do you want?" she said, her voice flat. She was back in control now, or she'd convinced herself she was.

"Mind if I sit down?" I asked her.

Pursing her lips as though she minded very much, she nodded to the pair of white chairs. I took one, sat back, crossed my legs. Casually, taking my time. I had an advantage over the woman, even if I didn't know yet what it was, and I couldn't afford to lose it before I did.

I said, "Frank and I had a little business deal going."

She crossed her arms beneath her breasts. A defensive gesture, shielding herself against me. "What sort of business deal?"

"Frank had something I wanted."

Even as wary and guarded as she was, she was able to look me over clinically, head to toe and back again, and say, "I'm not surprised."

I ignored that. "I figure you and Stacey Killebrew know where I can find it."

"Then why not ask Stacey Killebrew?"

I smiled, shook my head. "Wrong question. The right question would've been, 'Who's Stacey Killebrew?'"

She frowned. "Just what is it you want from me?" Anger was beginning to build up behind the wariness. At me, possibly at herself for the slip.

"You know Killebrew," I said.

"I know of him."

"Never met him?"

"Not that I can recall."

When people make equivocal statements and stare at you defiantly, they're lying.

I said, "Was Lucero in on this?"

Her eyelids fluttered briefly and her voice, when it came, had lost its anger and become uncertain. "John? In on what?"

"The necklace."

She frowned again, looking genuinely puzzled. "Necklace?"

"Felice Leighton's diamond necklace."

"Felice?" She sat back, put her arms along the arms of the chair. "What *are* you talking about?"

"I'm looking for the necklace," I said.

She shook her head. "I don't know anything about any necklace."

"Why'd you fall apart out there when I mentioned Frank Biddle?"

"All right," she said, crossing her arms again. "Just who are you?"

"I'm a private investigator," I told her. "I'm working for the company that insured the necklace."

She looked at me for a moment. "Do you have any identification?"

I reached into my jacket, took out my billfold, opened it, leaned across the desk, and showed her the ticket. Still sitting back, she studied it, nodded.

She said, "The diamond necklace Derek gave her a few years ago?"

Sitting back down, I nodded.

"When was it stolen?"

"Last year. October."

She shook her head. "She never told me."

"Biddle never mentioned it?"

A surprised look. "You don't think *Frank* stole it?"

"The day before he died, Frank was talking about offering it back to the insurance company."

"Frank wasn't a thief." A simple statement.

"How long were you involved with him?"

"I don't really see that that's any of your business."

"Maybe not. Maybe you'd rather talk to the cops."

She smiled, and I knew then that whatever my advantage had been, I had lost it. "I've nothing to hide from the police. Or from anyone else. But now, if you'll excuse me, I have an opening tomorrow and I'm really quite busy." She stood up.

I stood as well. "Thanks for your help," I said.

She nodded, and the smile became ironic. "Anytime."

WHEN I GOT BACK to the office at one o'clock, the telephone on the desk was making noises. It's not one of your

more expensive models, and it sounds like a large re-
tarded bird in considerable distress. I snatched up the receiver and plopped myself down into the chair.

"Mondragón Agency."

"Joshua?" The smoky aristocratic voice of Mrs.
Leighton.

"Felice. How are you?"

"Rather confused at the moment."

"How so?"

"I just had a call from a friend of mine, Silvia Griego.
She tells me that she had a visitor this morning who wanted
to know about a necklace of mine. She described him, and
I'm quoting now, as 'an attractive thug,' and said that he
gave his name as Joshua Croft."

"It's a common name, I understand, among attractive
thugs."

"Joshua, why are you asking Silvia about the necklace? She's one of my oldest friends, and she never even
knew the thing was stolen."

"One of your oldest friends, and you never told her
about the burglary?"

"I didn't tell anyone about it. Derek asked me not to. All
of us, me and the children. You have to understand his
sense of pride. More than anything else, I think, he was
embarrassed about the theft. He saw it as a personal thing,
as though it happened through some mistake of his."

"What about the newspaper? It wasn't listed in that
update they run of all the local burglaries?"

"No. Derek's got a friend down there, one of the edi-
tors, and he called him and asked him not to mention anything about the necklace."

The Incorruptible Press strikes again.

"I don't understand," she said, "why you're bothering
Silvia."

"Silvia knows some people who knew Biddle. I was just following up some leads." I saw no need to tell her of Biddle's involvement with Griego. "And how are you doing these days?"

"Much better than when I left your house the other night."

"You seemed fairly composed at the time."

"Bravura acting. Oscar material. I was a shambles. Couldn't sleep a wink all night. I kept hearing that window of yours crashing apart. You were very brave, you know, rushing outside like that."

"Careful," I said. "You'll turn my head."

"And Kevin's quite taken with you as well."

"Yeah?"

"He's decided he wants to be a private investigator himself."

"That should tickle your husband."

A throaty chuckle. "Derek's out of town for a few days. Actually, that's my ulterior motive for calling. I'm getting cabin fever, sitting around all day. I was wondering if we could get together, you and I. We could have lunch—I was thinking the Toad Garden, my treat—and we could discuss your progress." The Toad Garden, despite its name, dished up the most expensive lunches in Santa Fe.

"It wouldn't take a whole lunch to discuss my progress," I told her. "One appetizer would just about do it."

"You don't feel you're any closer to finding the necklace?"

"It's still too early yet. And thanks for the invitation, Felice, but I'll be busy all day today. No time for lunch. Maybe later in the week."

"Oh drat," she said with mock petulance. "I was looking forward to it."

"When's your husband coming back?"

"Tomorrow. Why?"

"Sooner or later I'm going to have to talk to him again."

"He's not really an ogre, you know. Most of the time, he can be quite reasonable. I'm sure that the two of you, given a second chance, would get along very well."

"Let's hope so. Could you ask him to call me?"

"I shall. And give me a jingle tonight if you get tired of sitting alone while bullets come whizzing through your window."

"I'll do that. Bye now."

"Bye." She put several more syllables, and several more shades of meaning, into the word than I remembered it having.

I hung up and noticed that the green indicator on the answering machine was lit, telling me that urgent messages, maybe even Clues, awaited me on the tape. Just as I was reaching for the rewind switch, the phone squawked again.

"Mondragón Agency."

"I am not going to get angry." Rita's voice, cold and flat, precisely enunciating every syllable.

"Good for you."

"You have every right in the world to make a total and utter fool of yourself."

"Says so right in the Constitution."

"If you want to get your brains, such as they are, splattered all over some barroom floor, it's really none of my business."

"I'm glad you're being reasonable about this. And I truly admire the way you turn a phrase."

"I spoke to Hector this morning."

"And he finked on me."

"He told me what happened last night."

"Like I said."

"Hector was less than straightforward, but I gather, reading between the lines, that if he hadn't shown up there last night, you'd probably be dead today."

"A bit of an exaggeration, Rita."

But not by much. Killebrew had drawn back his leg for the kick, and, lying there groggy and immobile, all I could do was watch it happen and know that when it did, my head would snap like a football off a tee, spinning up toward the goal post.

And then, behind him, someone had called out, *"Freeze!"*

The crowd parted and Hector was standing there. He wasn't holding his gun, but his sports coat was open and if he wanted to, all he had to do was reach inside and slip it from the holster. Most of the people, like Killebrew, who have an interest in these things know that the Santa Fe Police Department favors the Smith and Wesson 586, and they know that the magnum .357 load it carries will do some fairly serious damage to bodily organs.

A fair fight, everyone had said as they gathered around, most of them grumbly and querulous, disappointed that Killebrew hadn't scored the extra two points. After hauling myself to my feet, I had refused to press charges against Killebrew, who still hadn't lost his wide yellow grin. Hector had walked me out to my car, explaining that he had had second thoughts about my going to the bar alone. I had thanked him for those. A bit incoherently, but profusely.

Rita said, "I thought you were going to avoid Killebrew."

"I thought so too. Killebrew had his own ideas on the subject."

"You shouldn't have gone there," she said.

"You're right, dear."

"Someday you'll go off somewhere and Hector won't be around."

"Yes, dear."

There was a silence on the line, and then she said, "Joshua." Her tone turned the word into a warning.

"Yes, dear?"

*"Stop it."*

I laughed.

"You think it's *funny?*"

"Moderately, yeah. Rita, I'm all right. I appreciate your concern, and I'm grateful for it, but I'm sound in mind and body, and I feel tip-top, absolutely hunky-dory. I've already filed away the thing last night as a learning experience."

"I'm not so sure about the sound-in-mind part."

"Thanks."

"Do you still have all your teeth?"

"Sure. I'm keeping them in a cigar box in the desk drawer."

"Joshua." Another warning.

"I'm okay. Really. A tiny bruise, nothing else. A little Max Factor and no one will ever know. By the way, I spoke to Silvia Griego today."

"You're changing the subject."

"Someone has to."

She sighed. "All right. What did Griego have to say?"

I related the conversation and my feelings about it.

Rita said, "So what you're saying is that she knows something about Biddle, something that frightens her, but it's something that may have nothing to do with the stolen necklace."

"Yeah, that was the hit I got. I don't think she knew about the necklace. Felice Leighton never told her, and it looks to me that Biddle never did either."

"You've been in touch with Felice again?"

"We had," I said, "a brief but enlightening chat. She didn't know, apparently, that Biddle was seeing Griego."

"Are you sure?"

"Fairly. From the way she talked, it was the last thing that would've entered her mind. She seemed much more interested in inviting me to the Toad Garden for lunch."

"Trying to ply you with Perigord truffles and Dom Perignon eighty-three."

"I refuse to surrender myself for anything less than the sixty-four."

"A man of principle. So what are your plans for the rest of the day? Working, or sporting with the fair Felice and her magic manacles?"

"I take it back."

"What?"

"What I said before, about your turning a phrase. Magic manacles?"

"What are your plans?"

"I don't really have any. But I suppose you do."

"Why not talk to Silvia Griego again? So far, she's the only one who seems to know anything."

"Yeah, but not about the necklace."

"So find out what she *does* know and use it as leverage to learn more about Biddle."

"And how, exactly, do I do that?"

"Exercise that notorious charm of yours. The one that's working so well on Felice Leighton."

"Griego's busy at the gallery, setting up for an opening tomorrow. I won't be able to talk to her until tonight. What do you suggest I do until then?"

"Call Felice, why don't you, and tell her that Woolworth's just got in a new shipment of heavy-duty nylon rope."

WHAT I DID DO that afternoon, after I checked the messages on the machine—three from Rita, one from Felice Leighton—was drive over to Tomasita's on Guadalupe and treat myself to a beef burrito with green chile and a Corona beer. Then I drove back to Carla Chavez's house and asked her where I could locate her brother, Benito. She was reluctant at first, but after I explained that it might help me locate whoever had killed Biddle, she gave me his address in Las Mujeres, and the name of the local bar where he often hung out. I gave her another twenty dollar bill.

I found Silvia Griego's address in the phone book, and that night, at eight-thirty, I drove over there.

She lived in another adobe compound, this one on Cerro Gordo, a long dirt road that winds through an area that the realtors like to call Santa Fe's Fashionable East Side.

In the asphalt driveway there was a BMW, bright shiny red beneath a floodlight attached to the side of the house.

I know I parked the Subaru beside the BMW; I can remember that part. And I can remember leaving the car, walking up through the piñon and juniper to the gate, unlatching it, and stepping onto the brick walkway that ran diagonally across the courtyard.

After that, what must have happened is that I walked up to the front door and found it ajar, or at least unlocked. I must've pushed it open, and probably I stood there for a moment, wondering what to do and looking fairly stupid. Probably I called out Silvia Griego's name. Maybe I heard something in reply. Whether I did or not, I must've gone into the house, and inside there, in the hallway, is where it happened.

It's called retrograde amnesia, and I'm told that it's fairly common with a sudden, concussive blow to the skull.

# TEN

THE FIRST THING I realized when I opened my eyes was that I was lying on a brick floor. The second thing I realized was that, any moment now, I was going to be sick. Extremely, elaborately sick. Small parachutes of pain were opening at the top of my head and fluttering down through my brain, and every time they landed at the base of my skull, my stomach gave another lurch.

I pulled myself up onto my hands and knees and looked around. A mistake; the parachutes became packing crates. I didn't know where I was—whose house, what city, what universe—and I didn't care. I stood up, head pounding, legs wobbling, and set out to find a toilet. My progress through the unfamiliar house was not lacking in dignity. I don't think I clawed at the walls for support or bumped into the furniture more than eight or nine times.

At last, down a hallway from the living room, I found a bathroom, knelt down, and got rid of dinner. I flushed the toilet. Then I stayed there for a time, forehead resting on arms and crossed atop the bowl.

After a long while, I sat back and began to take stock.

No bones seemed to be broken, but I had a welt on the back of my skull the size of a corncob. I stood up, still a bit woozy, and lumbered to the mirror. I looked remarkably chipper for someone who'd just spent a lifetime leaning over a toilet. Both pupils were the same size, and neither seemed particularly constricted. Good. Concussion, yes, but no hematomas spreading around inside there like clusters of dark gray tubers.

Not yet, anyway.

I turned on the cold water, splashed some on my face, sucked some up from cupped hands to wash away the taste of bile. Dried my face and hands with a small pink towel hanging to my right. I glanced around the bathroom and noticed, for the first time, that the toilet was pink, the same shade as the towel. So were the sink and the bathtub and the bathmat atop the blue tiled floor. The translucent plastic shower curtain was printed with a bright blue floral pattern, and it was pulled shut.

But not all the way, because a flat-soled woman's shoe was jutting out from one end, and there was a foot in it.

I jerked back the curtain.

Someone had hurt her badly. Her face had been battered, her cashmere sweater torn, a white rounded rim of shoulder poking through the rent. Silver-brown hair lay in a wild tangle across the pale pink porcelain, and to the left, just behind her temple, it was limp and wet with thickening blood. I felt for a pulse at her throat and found none. Already her flesh was losing its warmth and taking on that sad unmistakable final slackness.

I turned from her and left the room. Maybe I blacked out again for a few moments, or maybe sometime since then I've blocked those moments out, but the next thing I remember I was in the kitchen ripping open cupboards, looking for a bottle. You're not supposed to drink after a head injury, but you're not supposed to find attractive women beaten to death either.

I found some Stolichnaya in the freezer, tore off the cap, drank straight from the bottle, felt the ice-cold liquid turn miraculously warm as it hit my stomach. I got myself a glass, filled it halfway, and sat down with it, head hanging, at the round kitchen table.

I couldn't think about her, not just then. Just then, it seemed to me, I had to make a decision. I could get out of there, I could call the cops, or I could take a look around.

Tomorrow. At Tara.

I looked at my watch. Nine o'clock. Eight-thirty arrival. Figure a few minutes finding my way through the house. Ten or fifteen minutes in the bathroom before I discovered her. A few more minutes in the kitchen. That left me unconscious for only ten minutes, maximum.

Whoever had clubbed me was long gone. If any of the neighbors had seen anything, they'd remember it just as well in an hour as they would now.

That was a rationalization, and not a very good one. Any cop will tell you that the sooner he talks to a witness, the more likely he is to get information. He'll also tell you that he doesn't much appreciate your messing around with a crime scene.

But I was reacting—to the woman's death, to the blow I'd received—and I was disguising it to myself as making a decision.

And what I decided to do was take a look around.

I STARTED in the kitchen. Because I was already there and because some women use the kitchen as an impromptu office, grabbing whatever's handy to jot down phone numbers, addresses, reminders.

Under the sink, I found a pair of yellow dishwashing gloves and tugged them on. A tight fit, but workable. The last crime solved with fingerprints in the States probably took place back in 1933. But the police, traditionalists all, still dusted religiously for latents, and I didn't want them to find mine.

Nothing had been scrawled on the cover of the phone book or on any of the pages inside. A small white memo pad lay on the counter below the wall phone, but it was blank. I held it obliquely up to the light, looking for impressions in the paper, just like they do in the movies, and it was still blank.

After a few minutes I began to get the feeling that the woman had seldom set foot in here. The place possessed every conceivable household marvel, each of them spotlessly clean. There was a food processor, a blender, a coffeemaker, a toaster oven, a microwave with a digital timer display and enough dials and switches to pilot a space shuttle. In the refrigerator door was an ice-cube dispenser, so you could freshen up your gimlet without chilling your pinkies.

But inside, in the lower section, the only food was a jar of Scottish marmalade and, in the vegetable bin, a few limp stalks of celery. No eggs, no bread, no milk. The freezer above was full, but with neat stacks of expensive TV dinners. No leftovers.

One cupboard contained dinnerware, plates and crystal glasses; the other held a box of Triscuits, a can of coffee, a box of coffee filters, another jar of marmalade, this one unopened, and two cans of chicken bouillon.

Silverware in one drawer, utensils in the other. Everything looked new and untouched.

In the dishrack, a single coffee cup, a single fork.

Even the garbage was immaculate. A plastic trash basket with a carefully installed white plastic bag. Inside, a used coffee filter and an opened TV dinner carton. Inside that, a disposable plastic plate, scraped clean.

The room could've been a stage set. Silvia Griego had apparently not been a homebody. When she got hungry, she either ate out somewhere or she tossed one of the frozen dinners into the microwave and nuked it.

All the electrical outlets were being used, hooked up to the different appliances. I turned them all on, one by one, and they all worked. She hadn't installed one of those cute little plastic safes that masquerade as outlets.

I tried the living room next. Wall-to-wall carpeting, an antique sofa, two Queen Anne chairs, two large colorful kachinas on the mantel over the square brick fireplace. An oak coffee table supporting a single copy of *Artspace* magazine. A largish oak bar, the bottles inside all very expensive and all precisely aligned. Behind the doors of a wide oak cabinet, a Bang & Olufsen stereo system and a slim collection of record albums, Mr. Sinatra heavily represented. Paintings on the wall, one of which looked like, and probably was, a genuine Remington. The frames, of course, oak; a good-sized grove had been leveled to furnish this room. Two tall—oak—bookshelves, one packed with books on Southwest history and art, the other with paperback novels, mostly romances. Later, if I still had the time, and I still hadn't found anything, I'd take the books out and riffle through them.

I peeked behind the paintings, tested the outlets, checked the furniture. Beneath one of the sofa cushions, I found a dime. Progress.

I skipped the bathroom, blanking my mind as best I could to what lay in there. Skipped the room opposite, the guest bedroom, it looked like, and even more unused and sterile than the rest of the house. Moved on to the last door. The master bedroom.

Lace curtains. A queen-sized bed. A slight depression in the pale yellow down comforter and in the pale yellow pillow bunched up against the antique wooden headboard. Perhaps she'd lain down for a nap. Or perhaps she'd watched some television—a large stereo TV sat opposite on the broad oak dresser. A remote-control unit lay on the nightstand beside a half-filled glass. I picked up the glass, sniffed it. Scotch, single malt. The ice had melted, but even through the rubber gloves it was still cool. I set it back down.

I did the dresser first, working it like a burglar, opening the drawers from the bottom and, for the time being, leaving them open. On the left side, sweaters and blouses, and rising up to me as I poked and prodded, the scent of Chanel. Rebuking me for trespassing. Above, in the next drawers, lingerie, panties, bras, hose, scarves. Everything simple, unadorned, functional. No peek-a-boo nighties, no whalebone corsets.

I found two cameras in the bottom drawer, right side. A Nikon and a Polaroid, both containing partial rolls of film. There were a couple of photo albums, and I leafed quickly through them. Silvia Griego, from young girl-hood to womanhood. Only one other familiar face: Felice Leighton, making much the same trip.

Nothing interesting in the remaining drawers. I pushed them all shut and went into the adjoining bathroom.

It was the one place, apparently, where she'd let her sense of neatness slip. The mirror, a long one atop the makeup counter, needed cleaning. On the counter, a fine dusting of talcum powder lay over the moisturizers, creams, lipsticks, eyeliners, perfumes, and colognes. The cap was missing from the toothpaste and the tube had been squeezed from the sides, not carefully rolled up from the bottom the way parents, and other maniacs, are forever insisting it should be. One toothbrush, not too vigorously cleaned after use and tossed to the side of the sink. A woman's razor on the rim of the pink porcelain tub, its blade flecked with dark stubby hairs.

In the medicine cabinet, aspirin, Alka Seltzer, Maalox, Pepto-Bismol, a plastic diaphragm holder with its dia-phragm in place, a tube of Ortho-Novum spermicide, a bottle of Valium that had been refilled a week before and was now half-empty.

I went back into the bedroom and into the closet. Smell of Chanel stronger here. Handbags and purses arrayed along the top shelf. Checked through them all. Nothing.

Dresses and coats, three of them fur, hanging from the rack. Shoes in neat formation on the wooden floor. Nothing slipped away in any pockets, nothing tucked away in any shoes.

I came back out and sat down on the bed. I knew that I'd missed something, seen something important and let it slip away.

Mentally I replayed the search. From the kitchen through the living room to here.

I got up, stepped over to the dresser, and pulled open the drawer. I took out the albums and leafed through them again. None of the prints were Polaroids.

And yet there was the camera. It didn't look like a new model. Some of the current roll had already been shot.

So where were the prints?

Maybe she'd tossed them.

All of them?

As I sat there mulling this over, it occurred to me that there were other items missing from the house. Insurance forms, mortgage papers, tax records, bills and receipts, all the dry dreary paperwork that serves to establish our existence in the eyes of our Lord, the Banker.

Maybe they were in her office, along with the Polaroids. Maybe they were in a safe-deposit box.

But I was here, not at her office, not at her bank.

Work on the assumption that they were here, too.

I looked at my watch. An hour had passed. Give it another thirty minutes.

It took me twenty to discover that two of the floorboards in the closet, below the row of shoes, were loose. I lifted them up, reached down into the hollow, and my fingers found the metal strongbox.

What have we here, Silvia?

I wrestled it up, carted it over to the bed, sat down with it on my lap. It was locked. One of those heavy steel padlocks with a four digit combination on the bottom. The numbers read 4832, and that provided me a certain amount of optimism.

What you're supposed to do, when you lock one of these things, is spin all the number wheels back to zero. But people are lazy. What they often do is spin just one of the wheels, and because they read from left to right, they usually spin the first wheel on the left. This is a snippet of information that professional burglars find most useful.

Professional burglars and me. I spun the left wheel up one digit, to five, then jerked at the lock. It didn't budge. I spun it up to six and jerked again, with the same results. I worked my way up to nine, then back down to three. On two, the padlock snapped open.

IT WAS ONE O'CLOCK in the morning when Rita opened the front door and rolled back her chair to let me in. She said, "You said it was tiny."

I shut the door behind me. "What was tiny?"

"Your bruise."

I reached up and touched it. "It was," I said. "It grew. Got anything to drink?"

She frowned quickly, involuntarily, probably thinking what I already knew, that I'd had enough. "There's Jack Daniel's and ice on the coffee table," she said.

"Ah," I said. "The Total Woman."

I'd been trying for light and sophisticated, William Powell to Myrna Loy. But I saw Rita blink at me from the wheelchair, shrink slightly away; and I heard in my voice, almost as an echo, the snarl. "Oh, Jesus," I said. I took a deep breath, let it out. "Jesus, Rita, I'm sorry."

Lips compressed, not looking at me, she shook her head. "Come on into the living room."

I followed her down the hallway, into the room, and across the floor. As she turned the chair around, I sat down on the sofa. There was an ice bucket beside the bottle of Jack Daniel's and the bottle of Glenlivet, and I flipped open the lid, grabbed some ice, and plonked it into the glasses. I poured her a Scotch, poured myself a bourbon. I didn't spill a drop; she was watching me.

She was wearing a loose-fitting black robe of some silk-like material that buttoned up to her throat, and she looked like she'd been quietly reading a book all evening, rather than sleeping soundly, as she actually had been. Until I'd called her, half an hour ago.

I handed her the drink, sat back, and took a hit of mine. It tasted the way it'd been tasting all evening, ever since I got back to my house from Silvia Griego's. It tasted bitter.

"I'm sorry," I said.

She shook her head again, but this time her eyes met mine. We were going to pretend that I'd never said it. She sipped at the Scotch. "So," she said. "Griego is dead."

I nodded. It had been the only thing I'd told her over the phone, before I asked if I could come over.

She said, "And you're feeling guilty."

"Yeah." I drank some more bourbon. "I scared her this afternoon. She called somebody. He went to her house and he killed her."

"You don't know for a fact that she called someone. And even if she did, it wasn't you who killed her."

"It was me who scared her. If I hadn't, she'd still be alive."

She sipped at her Scotch, looking at me for a moment. At last she said, "Joshua, I understand how you feel, and I'm sorry for you. You know I am. But if you're determined to take all this guilt upon yourself, there's nothing I can say. You do know, I hope, that you have no moral responsibility for what happened."

"He beat her to death, Rita. Then he dumped her like a sack of potatoes."

"Start from the beginning," she said. "When did you get to the house?"

I knew what she was doing. Refusing me the absolution that a part of me wanted, because absolution would only validate my guilt. Trying to take the power from the woman's death by turning it into a dry, dispassionate recital of facts. I was resentful, and I was irritated, and I was grateful. William Faulkner, I think, once said that a good indication of intelligence was the ability to hold at least two conflicting ideas simultaneously. It's also a good indication of drunkenness.

But I told her all of it, everything up to the point where I worked the padlock open.

"And what was inside?" Rita asked.

"Tax records, bank statements." I reached into my back pocket, took out my notebook, flipped it open. I spent a moment or two focusing on the columns and rows of numbers I'd scribbled in Griego's bedroom. "She was doing pretty well for herself. Paid off the mortgage on the house three years ago, fifteen years before she had to. Paid off the mortgage on the gallery two years ago. Stocks, mostly preferred, worth about fifty thousand. Fifteen thousand in seven-percent municipals. Another sixty-five thousand in an IRA. Two thousand in interest-bearing checking—that's her personal account, the records for the business must be at the gallery." My mouth was dry from all the talking. I took another drink.

Rita sipped at her Scotch. "It's a lot of money for a gallery owner. Even a successful gallery owner."

I shook my head. "There's more. There's a numbered account at the Credit Suisse in Berne with four hundred and twenty thousand in it. So far as I can tell, it's undeclared income."

"Did you learn where's it coming from?"

I nodded, fairly pleased with myself. "Germany. Munich. Something called Liebman and Sons, Art Dealers. She's been doing business with them for the past five years, and they've been depositing drafts directly to the Berne account. The receipts and the bank statements involving the Liebman deals were the only business records she had at the house."

"She kept them off the gallery books."

I nodded. "What it looks like."

"What were the deposits like?"

"Interesting." I read them off to her from the notebook. They had begun over five years ago and, for the first year, the deposits had been relatively small, ranging from two thousand to just under five thousand dollars. They had been made approximately every four months, giving her a total of slightly over twelve thousand for the first year. And then, four years ago, in April, there had been a deposit of twenty-five thousand dollars. After that, none of the deposits were less than thirty thousand, and they'd been made, as before, every three or four months. Except for a period of about a year and a half, during which only two deposits had been made. In the past year, there were three more deposits, averaging about fifty-five thousand each.

Rita nodded. "What was her total worth?"

I rubbed at my forehead with fingers and thumb. "Not sure," I said. "She's got a safe-deposit box at the Bank of Santa Fe, and I wouldn't be surprised if she's got some cash stashed away there. Maybe some jewelry, too—there wasn't much at the house. But from the records in the box, counting the real estate, she was worth a little under a million dollars. Nine hundred thousand and change." I tossed the notebook to the coffee table and sat back.

"You're right. She was doing very well for herself."

"The records weren't the only thing in the box."

"What else?"

"For one thing, some coke. Not much, a couple grams."

"You put the box back?"

"Yeah."

"And you called the police?"

"Not yet." Too busy brooding and boozing. "I'll do it now."

She shook her head. "It's too late. And they can make voice prints from the recording. Did anyone see your car?"

I had to think about that for a moment. After nearly half a bottle of Jack, my mind was finally beginning to sludge up. Thank God for Jack. "Don't think so," I said at last. "There was no one driving around. And the driveway's got a bend in it, trees all over."

She nodded, looking off for a moment, thinking, then turned back to me. "I'll call Pedro and have him phone it in." Pedro was one of her cousins, usually out of work; Rita sometimes used him for small-time jobs.

She rolled the chair over to the end table and picked up the phone. "The address?"

I told her. As she talked to Pedro in Spanish too rapid for me to follow, I sat and stared at my bourbon.

She hung up and rolled the chair back to the coffee table. She glanced at my drink. "You shouldn't be doing that, Joshua. Not after a head injury."

"Right," I said, and swallowed what was left in the glass. I picked up the bottle, unscrewed the cap, and poured myself some more.

Rita sighed. "When you were at Griego's gallery, did you give your name to anyone else?"

I had to think about that for a while, too, before I remembered the Pepsi-Cola girl and the card I'd given her. I told Rita.

She nodded. "So Hector or one of his people will probably be in touch with you. You'll have to act surprised about Griego's death. We don't want him charging you with obstruction."

"Obstruction's not the only thing he could charge me with. I did a little evidence tampering too."

"What evidence?"

"These." I slipped the Polaroid prints out of my inside jacket pocket and flipped them onto the table. "They were in the box."

Rita leaned forward.

You can buy photographs like that almost everywhere now. If your local newsstand doesn't carry them, you can get them shipped to you, in a plain brown wrapper so your neighbors never know. Probably everyone has seen people doing those particular acrobatic things to one another.

The only surprise, for me, had been who these particular people were. Felice Leighton. Derek Leighton. Silvia Griego. And a few others.

"The cute little naked guy in the cowboy hat," I said. "With the vibrator. That's Frank Biddle."

# ELEVEN

NORTH OF SANTA FE, the High Road to Taos lopes
through badlands where ragged sandstone ridges rising up
from the bare arid countryside look like the spines of
mammoth fossilized lizards. Now and then it dips down
into small neat adobe villages huddled among lush cot-
tonwoods, but always it climbs again, heading up through
the sandy high desert to the distant mountains.

Directly overhead that morning, the sky was a clear en-
ameled blue, only a few sedate white clouds loafing across
it. But far off, beyond the raw red gullies and the empty
red buttes, where the mountains surrounded me like the
rim of a bowl, thick gray tumbles of storm clouds were
lowering. The thickest and grayest of these were directly
ahead, just above the nose of the Subaru, up there in the
shrouded peaks where Las Mujeres lay.

Quite a few of the Anglos in Santa Fe don't like travel-
ling in the northern New Mexico mountains. Living here
are descendants of the original Spanish settlers, many of
whose families saw their private land stolen by the United
States government, their grazing land appropriated by the
Park Service. Some of them, not surprisingly, still bear a
grudge.

And up here, too, live *Los Hermanos Penitentes*, the
Penitant Brothers. They've inspired a lot of talk, some of
it distrustful, and some of it horrified, with a ribbon of
boogie-man excitement running through it. I've been told,
by more than one Anglo, and with complete conviction,
that up until recently the *Penitentes* were offering human
sacrifices.

It's not very likely. Humans, up here, are too precious to waste.

Whatever the truth might be, for hundreds of years in these isolated villages they were the sole source of religious comfort for the sick and the dying. And apparently the only people they've ever actually hurt, collectively or individually, have been themselves. Which is a good deal more than most of us can say.

It's a hard country. Where the green stops, not far from the banks of the narrow rivers and the tiny streams, the desert begins, unrelenting and unforgiving. A sudden shift in the weather, a brush fire, a flash flood, a pack of wild dogs savaging the livestock, almost any fluke of nature can mean disaster. The emphasis on atonement, on making peace with an all-powerful God, isn't difficult to understand.

I was doing a certain amount of atoning myself that morning. The piercing headache that had greeted me when I woke up on Rita's sofa had softened itself to a dull gray shadow, somehow slightly larger than my skull. But my stomach was still queasy, my mouth still lined with material torn from the inside of an old sleeping bag.

We had talked for a while last night before I collapsed. I had wondered whether the Polaroid prints might've had something to do with Griego's death.

"Blackmail, you mean?" Rita had asked.

"Sure," I said. "Why not?" It wasn't the world's most persuasive argument; but I was a long way, just then, from being Perry Mason.

The photographs, maybe fifty of them, were spread out on the coffee table. Leaning forward, Rita pushed through them with her fingertips. "They all knew about the camera. Some of them are posing for it. So the photographs weren't shot secretly. And they were all shot in the same room. Her bedroom?"

I nodded.

"But you can tell from the light behind the curtains," she said, "that they weren't all shot at the same time."

"No," I said. I took another hit of bourbon. "Three separate occasions, I figure."

She pointed to one photograph. "That's Peter Ricard."

I nodded. "Sure is. And that's Felice Leighton with him."

She looked up. "Didn't Peter tell you he'd never been involved with her?"

"Uh-huh. But he looks pretty involved right there, doesn't he?"

She stared at the photograph. "I wonder why he lied."

"People always lie," I said. "It's easier than telling the truth."

She looked up at me, frowned. "Maybe you should have some coffee."

I waved my glass, somehow managing not to spill any liquor. "Never touch the stuff."

Another frown, a glance down at the pictures, a glance back up at me. "Did the house look like it'd been searched?"

I squinted at her. "Searched?"

"By someone else. Before you got there."

"No. Don't think so. Why?"

"Which is it?" she said. "No, or you don't think so."

I considered it for a moment. "No. I would've noticed."

"If someone killed her because she was blackmailing him with these, wouldn't he have searched for them before he left?"

I lifted my eyebrows, dropped my mouth open. "You astound me, Holmes."

She looked off, frowning at the thoughts she saw. "Except that he was still there when you arrived." Looked back at me. "Maybe he didn't have time."

"Ah," I said, and nodded sagely.

"Stop it," she said, more amusement than irritation in her voice. Or so I told myself.

I said, "I thought we were trying to find that stupid necklace. I'm pretty sure Silvia Griego didn't know anything about it. Maybe she was blackmailing somebody; maybe she wasn't. But I don't think it had anything to do with us."

"She was involved in something with Biddle. Something that frightened her."

I pointed my glass at the photographs. "Those, maybe."

"Maybe. But it looks like Biddle wasn't there every time."

"Maybe he was the one taking the pictures. Someone had to."

"Unless the camera had a timer."

"Oh," I said. It had. "Yeah."

"How many of those people do you recognize?"

I sighed. Concentration was becoming more and more of an effort. "Let's see. The Leightons. Biddle. Peter. Silvia Griego. That little curly-headed blonde is the Pepsi-Cola girl from Griego's gallery. The redhead with her, I don't know who she is."

She nodded. "If we accept the possibility of blackmail, any one of them could've had a motive for killing Griego."

"Can't see Peter beating anyone to death. Not over photographs like that, anyway. He probably wanted a couple copies for himself, blow-ups, to hang in the den. And I can't see Felice, either."

She nodded. Once again, as usual, I couldn't tell whether she was agreeing with me or placating me.

"So what should we do with these?" I said, nodding to the photographs.

"We'll hold onto them for a while. We can always mail them in to the police later. But right now, we're going to bed. Both of us."

"Aha," I said, and stood up, grinning merrily, and weaving only slightly. "Proud to be of service, ma'am."

Rita smiled. "Down, boy. I'm sleeping in my room, and you're out here on the sofa. Joshua, sit down."

I sat. Sitting was a lot better. I said, "But what if you need something during the night?"

"Then I'll get up and get it."

"What if *I* need something during the night."

"Then you can get up and go home and get it. And stop leering. Take your boots off and lie down."

I grumbled for a bit more, then sat back, wrestled off my boots, stood them up beneath the coffee table, and swung my legs onto the sofa. Lying down was even better—I must've passed out right away.

When I woke up, it was seven in the morning and someone had thrown a blanket over me. I flipped it off, scooped up the photographs and staggered out to the Subaru. After a hot breakfast at my house, and a hotter shower, I still felt as if I'd been kicked down a stairway. I didn't really want to contend with Hector that day, so I decided to vacate town for a while. But before I slipped on my windbreaker, I strapped on the shoulder holster and tucked the .38 inside. I'd been banged around enough already this week.

I had the High Road pretty much to myself. It was too early in the year for tourists to be making the drive up to Taos, and with the rain coming, none of the locals would be out.

The road climbed higher, clouds gathering overhead and casting black shadows that lumbered up and down the hills. I left the tiny village of Cordova behind, and then the village of Truchas, and then I was in the mountains, green ponderosa pines thick around me, gray clouds thick overhead.

The village of Las Mujeres perches on the side of a deep pine-covered valley, and from it, on a clear day, you can see all the way to Albuquerque, over ninety miles to the south and maybe a hundred years in the future. But this wasn't a clear day. Just above me, not fifty yards away, the clouds were trailing between the dark tree trunks like the tentacles of some enormous smoky beast.

On the outskirts of town was a small cemetery, the forest looming around it, the flower wreaths on the graves looking drab and somber in the gray. After that came the houses, the first of them fairly new, of cinderblock or framing. Very soon these gave way to squat brown adobe structures, some with thickets of bushes growing atop their flat roofs, all with woodpiles of piñon logs. For most of the year up here you needed a fire in the hearth.

I drove through town to the general store, as Carla Chavez had directed me, and turned right into a dirt alleyway.

Her brother's house was like the houses that flanked it: a small square adobe building. But unlike those, whose tiny front yards were littered with rusting auto parts and deceased kitchen appliances, the yard here was neat and well-tended, with a narrow rectangular garden running along the wooden fence. And here the future had arrived; a satellite dish was tilted back, ready to receive signals from the stormy sky.

I parked the station wagon in front, got out, went through the gate and up to the door. Knocked on it. Nothing. Knocked on it again.

A window swung open in the house to my left and a heavy-set woman, gray hair pulled back in a bun, poked her head out.

"Benito Chavez?" I said.

Without a word, expressionless, she pulled her head back in and shut the window.

"Have a nice day," I said.

LA CANTINA was on the other side of town, set far enough away from it that the sounds of revelry wouldn't vex the villagers, but close enough for the villagers doing the revelling to totter home when the night had ended. Lying just off the road, it was a ramshackle rectangular wooden building with a rambling wooden porch and a neon Budweiser sign in one of its two dusty windows. In the gravel parking lot in front were two Chevy Impala lowriders, one candy apple red, the other midnight black.

I parked the Subaru, got out, and stood for a moment admiring the cars.

What you do is you find yourself a '63 or '64 automobile in good condition—Impalas and Monte Carlos are popular—then you go down to Albuquerque and you locate a junked Citröen. You strip away its hydraulic suspension system, including the interior switches, and you slap everything onto the Chevy's frame. You add three or four batteries to the electrical system. You customize the interior with a steering wheel six inches in diameter, and wall-to-wall carpeting, or wall-to-wall fur. You slide a stereo cassette player into the dashboard and install speakers, as many as you can afford, anywhere they'll fit. You customize the exterior with flared fenders and an ornate grille and bumpers. You buy a thousand dollars worth of spoke wheels and a couple hundred dollars worth of white-wall tires. You paint the body with three or four coats of irridescent paint. You sandblast and seal the underbody, and, if you're really a purist, you chrome it, along with anything else that'll take a coat of chrome. For the finishing touches, you might drape a pair of foam rubber dice over the rearview mirror, or stick a marijuana leaf decal to the rear window. The whole deal will run you, not including the original cost of the car itself, at least ten thousand dollars.

Then, on Saturday nights, you drive the thing slowly, at three inches off the ground, down around the Plaza at Santa Fe. If you spot a cop—the legal minimum height for a license plate is twelve inches—you flip a switch and your hydro, powered by the extra batteries, quickly pump-hops the car back up to legality. If you spot a couple of cruising chicks, you do the same. It's a kind of mating dance.

Together, the two cars in the parking lot at La Cantina represented something over thirty-five thousand dollars. That was a lot of money for this neighborhood. It was a lot for mine, come to that.

La Cantina itself represented a good deal less. It needed a coat of paint, although that particular shade of sickly gray would probably be difficult to come by. The planking on the porch, worn down to bare wood, was curling up at the edges and it creaked beneath my feet like rotten ice on a frozen lake. I pulled open the screen door and stepped inside.

Maybe the three men standing at the bar, and the bartender standing behind it, had been silent even before I arrived. They were certainly silent now, watchful and appraising.

I crossed the floor, my footsteps sounding louder than they should. Wooden chairs and tables were haphazardly arranged around the room. To my right was a small pool table. To my left, a pair of video arcade games, one of them pinging inanely away to itself. Overhead, a ceiling fan whispered as it slowly turned.

The three were in their twenties, and before each sat a bottle of Coors. The two men nearest me were so alike they could've been bookends. Both were about my height and slim, both wearing jeans and T-shirts and wispy mustaches. The one farthest away was taller, thicker in the body, more muscular, and above his jeans he wore only a buttoned leather vest. No mustache. High, almost Indian cheekbones. A red headband holding down the thick black hair. On the large bicep of his left arm was a tattoo of an eagle.

The bartender, maybe forty years old, was short and fat and wore a shirt that hadn't been white for some time. His apron had probably never been white. Like the others, he kept his face empty as I approached. Like them, he was waiting.

I felt as if I'd walked into a Gary Cooper movie. Felt as if I should've tipped my Stetson and drawled, "Howdy." I wasn't wearing a Stetson, so I smiled instead and asked the bartender what kind of beer he carried.

Lip protruding slightly, he shook his head. *"No habla inglés."*

The line provoked huge guffaws in the two slim men. The third, with the headband, only smiled faintly and kept watching me.

*"Bueno,"* I said, still smiling at the bartender. *"Una cerveza. Corona, por favor."*

He nodded, his face still empty, and turned and bent down to open the wooden cooler behind him, beneath the cash register. He took out a bottle of Corona, pushed the door shut, turned back, snapped the cap off with a churchkey dangling from his belt, then slammed the beer down onto the bartop. It foamed up immediately, gushing out the spout, down the sides of the bottle, and bubbling along the counter. He produced a glass and set it down, with elaborate precision, exactly in the center of the puddle.

I nodded appreciatively, as though this was exactly the way I preferred to receive my beer.

*"Cinco dólares,"* he said.

I smiled again, nodded, reached into my pocket, pulled out a five, and handed it to him. Ignoring the cash register, he slipped the bill into his pocket.

"Five dollars," I said in cheerful Spanish. "This is an excellent beer, but the price seems a little excessive."

He shrugged. "The beer is cheap." He waved a hand, indicating the room. "You are paying for the atmosphere."

More mirth from the two bookends. Despite what was probably a family resemblance, they weren't really identical. The one nearest me was better looking, with a sensitive mouth and sharp, intelligent eyes. The second one had a nose that had been broken at least once, a wide mouth that he kept mostly open, and narrow deep-set eyes that seemed faintly glazed. Grass, or beer, or maybe just stupidity.

Smiling at them fondly, watching Headband out of the corner of my eye, I raised the dripping glass. *"Salud."*

"Sure, bro," said the bookend nearest me, in English. He elbowed his friend, and the two of them held up their Coors bottles. *"Salud,"* they grinned. Headband merely nodded at me, still smiling faintly.

We drank. As I set my glass back down in the puddle, the nearest bookend smiled at me. "So you speak Spanish, huh, bro?"

"A little."

He nodded, eyes narrowed, lips pursed, thoughtful. "Too bad you speak it so shitty, huh."

The second bookend laughed.

"It certainly is," I said. "It's a good thing you speak English so well." I drank some beer. "You know," I said earnestly, "maybe you can help me. I'm trying to find someone."

Bookend Number One looked at me. "And who's that, bro?"

"Guy named Chavez. Benito Chavez."

He squinted, looked off at the ceiling, considered for a moment, then shook his head. "Never heard'a him."

At the mention of the name, Bookend Number Two had dropped open his mouth and glanced at his near-double. Now, turning away, his shoulders were tight to stop them from shaking and he was trying to hide an excited grin behind a long pull of beer. From such subtle clues I deduced that Bookend Number One was most probably Benito Chavez.

Headband was still smiling. Waiting to see how I handled the two *cholos* before he stepped in.

I said, "No, I didn't think so. You look too smart to be involved with a guy like Chavez."

He frowned. "How's that, bro?"

I shrugged. "From what I've heard, Chavez is a real loser. He was dealing coke to a guy named Biddle down in Santa Fe, and Biddle got blown away. Word is, Chavez is involved."

He nodded thoughtfully and said, "And this Chavez dude, you're lookin' for him."

I nodded. "I need some information." I took a drink of beer. A few drops from the bottom of the glass plopped onto my windbreaker.

"Hey, careful, bro," he said. Grinning, he brushed at my chest with the back of his fingers. Forcefully.

I smiled at him. "Thanks."

"Hey, no problem." He punched at my shoulder, pretending at playfulness but going for the nerve endings along the curve of the joint. I smiled some more.

He turned his back to the bar and leaned up against it, hooking the heel of his boot over the rail, holding the beer bottle loosely. He nodded to my cheek. "Some bruise you got there, bro."

I nodded. "Fell off a horse."

"Uh-huh," he said. "So what kind of information you lookin' for?"

"Information about Biddle."

"That dude that got blown away."

"Right."

"I can tell you one thing about him, bro."

"What's that?"

He grinned and pronounced the words like a redneck cowboy: "He's *daid*."

This inspired more hilarity in Bookend Number Two.

I was getting a little tired of playing straight man. And if Bookend here was Chavez, he wasn't going to tell me anything worthwhile with his two compadres hanging around. "Well," I said, and reached into my windbreaker pocket. Headband didn't react at all, but the other two stiffened for a moment, then relaxed as I brought out one of my calling cards. I set it on the bar. "If you run into Chavez, give him my card. Tell him there may be some money in it for him." I moved to leave. Bookend Number One put the hand holding his beer against my chest.

"You can't leave now, bro. You didn't finish your beer."

"That's all right. I'll come back later."

"No later, bro." He smiled at me and dropped his hand, nodding to the glass. "Finish the beer."

I smiled back. "You're right. Why waste good beer." I picked up the glass, drained it. I nodded at the three of them. "See you later." And then I moved again to leave. Again his hand came up.

He called out over my shoulder to the bartender, "José, another Corona."

I shook my head. "No thanks."

"Hey, bro, *relax*. Take it *easy*. We'll have a few beers, we'll talk, we'll smoke some good grass, we'll pass some time. Later maybe we'll go out and find ourselves some women. What you say?" Leaning forward, grinning, he poked me in the chest. "You like the Spanish women, bro?"

"Maybe some other time."

Behind me, the bartender picked up the empty beer bottle and put a full one in its place.

Bookend Number One was facing me now, his foot off the rail, his left hand holding the beer bottle, his right resting along the bar. Setting himself up to pull off a trick that'd been old before he was born.

"What's the matter, bro?" he said. "Spanish women not good enough for you?"

"Spanish women are swell."

"Maybe you like boys better, huh, bro?" His eyes were narrowed and I could smell the stale beer on his breath.

"Not especially," I said.

"Maybe you just a fuckin' faggot, huh, bro? You like doin' little boys, that what it is?"

And it was then, after he'd got himself worked up for it, that he tried.

The trick is simple. As you talk, you suddenly drop your beer bottle, or your glass, whatever you're holding. The person you're talking to is distracted, his eyes instinctively following the bottle, and that's when you sucker punch him.

He dropped the bottle and I hit him with a very good left along the cheek.

As he went spinning off, face awry, his friend came bulling in, head lowered, fists up. I smashed down on his instep with the heel of my boot. He screeched and doubled over. I pounded my fist against the back of his neck, grabbed at his shoulder and hurled him off to the right, out of the way.

Because Headband was dancing toward me now, his hand snaking out of his pocket. The knife was a Balisong, the Filipino fighting knife that can whip open as quickly as a switchblade if it's handled properly.

He handled it properly, but by then I had the .38 out, pointing it at his nose. I pulled back the hammer and it made a satisfying click.

"Nice knife," I said. "You wouldn't want to get brains all over it."

# TWELVE

HEADBAND LOOKED for a moment at the gun. Then he smiled, straightened up, and tossed the knife casually to the floor. From the way he shrugged, he might've been making a comment on the weather. *"Otra vez,"* he said. Another time.

I nodded. *"Otra vez."*

Bookend Number Two was out for the count, slumped in a fetal ball on the floor, but Number One was pulling himself to his feet, and from the anger in his face I knew he was going to try a rush at me.

I said to Headband, "Tell him to lie down. Face to the ground."

*"Calma te,"* Headband told him. Bookend hesitated, and Headband snapped, *"Acostado de suelo."* Bookend lay down.

I heard the floorboards creak behind me, on the other side of the bar. Still watching Headband, I called out in Spanish over my shoulder, "Do not even think about it, José. I will shoot your friend and then I will shoot you. Does your insurance cover such situations?"

Silence.

I said, "Come out here, José."

After a moment, he shuffled around the bar, his hands wringing at his apron. "It is not a good thing," he said in Spanish, and nodded nervously to the gun, "to bring that in here."

"It is not a good thing," I said, "to charge five dollars for a glass of beer. Lie down."

He looked down with distaste. After all, he knew better than anyone what had been on that floor over the years.

"Lie down," I said again. Muttering to himself, grimacing, he got down onto the floor. I turned to Headband. "You, too."

Headband shrugged again, and then slowly, eyes never leaving mine, lowered himself to the floor. I crossed over to Bookend Number One and told him, "Hands out. Straight above your head, palms along the deck."

*"Maricon,"* he said.

Gently, silently, I released the hammer on the pistol. I didn't particularly care for the guy; but the revolver, cocked, has a very light trigger pull, and I didn't want to turn him into a mess that José would have to clean up. I bent over and put the snout of the barrel against the back of his neck. "Hands out."

He slid his hands out.

Holding the gun to his neck, keeping an eye on Headband, I squatted down and reached into his back pocket, slipped out his wallet. I flipped it open. The driver's license was behind the plastic window. The photograph was a good likeness.

I stood up and tossed the wallet to the floor. "Well, Benito," I said, "I don't suppose there's anything you want to tell me about Frank Biddle."

He hissed a few colorful unpleasantries about my mother.

"I didn't think so," I said. *"Otra vez,* maybe."

I turned to Headband. "I think it'd be a good idea if the three of you stayed where you are for a while. Don't get up. Don't go outside. You understand?"

He nodded.

"Good. *Adios.*"

I backed across the room and out of it, punching the screen door open with my elbow. The door swung shut and

I turned and sprinted off the porch, down the steps, and across the parking lot, the gravel clicking and clittering beneath me. At the lowriders, I raised the .38 and fired at all four front tires. Three hits, a miss, another hit. Splendid shooting. But the tires were blown and the front ends were sagging.

I ripped open the door to the Subaru and jumped in, tossing the gun to the passenger side. Found the keys, jammed them in the ignition, started the car, slammed it into reverse, backed out, slammed it into forward, hit the gas, took off with a rattle of pebbles.

My hands were shaking. Adrenaline buzz. No wonder I'd missed.

The shaking didn't stop until I was far below the town, until I was past the village of Truchas. It stopped right about the time I spotted the two new lowriders behind me.

FOR A FEW MINUTES after I noticed them, they maintained their speed, keeping the distance between us to about a hundred yards. They could've been kids or a pair of young couples, out for an afternoon spin. On the other hand, the three men back at the bar could've used a telephone or a C.B. radio to call in reinforcements.

Below Truchas the road goes downhill almost all the way to Santa Fe, coiling and uncoiling, turning and winding through the high desert. It's a good road with a firm solid surface, except when the winds dump drifts of sand across the tarmac, or when a storm slicks it up with rain. There was no sand today, but the storm that'd been threatening all morning looked ready to deliver. Far ahead of me, to the south and just about the location of Santa Fe, I could see where the black rolling cloud cover ended; shafts of bright yellow light hit the mountains aslant and made them gleam with green and gold. I was wondering if I'd make it there without getting drenched when I glanced into the rear-view mirror and saw that the lowriders were moving up.

I was going a little over sixty on the straights, in direct violation of the national speed limit. Coming at me that quickly, the two cars had to be violating it by at least thirty miles an hour.

If these two were after me, there was no way I could outrun them. The little Subaru engine, game as it might be, was no match for even a small-block Chevy eight.

When they both got within thirty yards of me, the rear lowrider dropped back, and at that point I was pretty sure they weren't just a couple of kids out for a ride. And it was just then that the rain started, fat round drops splatting against the windshield.

One eye on the mirror, I flipped the wipers on. Magically, this made the rain fall harder.

It was a nifty situation. Chased by two big Chevies, either of which could run rings around the Subaru, at exactly the time when the rain was starting to lift the embedded oils up off the road surface, turning it into a skating rink.

The rain was drumming against the windshield and, despite the frantic thrashing of the wipers, smearing away the landscape. But ahead of me, barely, I could make out a sharp leftward curve coming up in about half a mile. I kept my speed steady at sixty as the lowrider behind me moved into the other lane and began sailing up alongside. There were two men in the front seat.

The driver was cocky. He'd seen car chases at the drive-in, and thought I was dead meat. He and his passenger were both grinning as he swung the massive bulk of the Chevy toward the Subaru. I braked and let him shoot past me.

He was almost at the curve, where the road dropped off on both sides, when I flipped the Subaru into four-wheel drive and floored the gas pedal. The little wagon surged forward. I was braced, fingers tight around the wheel, elbows locked, when it smacked into the left side of the Chevy's rear fender.

Suddenly propelled faster than his wheels were moving, the driver lost his rolling traction, and then, only a moment later, he lost the road. He went over the side and down the slope.

I didn't have time to congratulate myself. Going into the curve too quickly, I could feel the tires sliding away beneath me. I let up on the gas, countersteered, ignored the brakes, and felt the tires bite into the road again. I steered back onto track, and let out my breath. Okay.

Now if the second lowrider stayed to help the first get his machine back onto the road, I was safe for a while.

No. He had slowed down, maybe, but not stopped. He was right behind me, and coming up fast. If he had any imagination, he could do the same thing to me that I'd just done to his friend.

Either he didn't have any imagination, or he was trying to prove something that didn't require it. He began moving up on my left. I glanced in the side mirror, saw the silhouette of his head behind the swishing windshield wipers.

When he was nearly level with me, I tapped the brake, dropped back a few feet, then jerked the steering wheel to the left, held it firm, and hit the gas. The Subaru's bumper smashed into the Chevy's right front fender, crumpling it and jamming it up against the tire. With his front wheels suddenly locked in place, he went into a skid.

Accelerating past, I watched in the rearview mirror as he tried to ride it out. There wasn't much he could do—his steering wheel was useless. He stayed on the road for fifty or sixty yards, and then the road made a gentle curve, sweeping off to the right, and, like his friends, he was gone.

I think I may have grinned. I had handled the three men back at the bar—rather well, I thought—and now the little Subaru and I had bested a couple of big lowriders. And without killing anybody, I was fairly sure. Getting the two cars back up onto the road might take a bit of grunting, but it seemed unlikely that anyone inside had been badly hurt; the slope down from the roadway wasn't steep enough. Maybe a broken arm or two, a bloody nose. So what. Dumb bastards had asked for it, right?

Not a bad day's work.

Hubris. I rounded a bend in the road and saw another two lowriders parked across it, blocking both lanes.

I eased up on the gas.

They had arranged it well. The road dipped down here toward a small bridge crossing an arroyo. They were on my side of the bridge and I couldn't go around them without winding up in the arroyo, which was filling up now with the rush of run-off water. And I couldn't ram them head on. When you're driving a Subaru, you don't ram any stationary object that weighs over ten pounds.

Not much choice. They were sixty yards away and I was down to forty-five miles an hour. I used my left hand to turn the wheel slightly to the left, used my right to jerk up the emergency brake. The front wheels seized and the rear end of the car began a quick swoop out from under me. Before the wagon swung a half circle, I slapped down the emergency brake-stick, grabbed the wheel with both hands, floored the gas peddle.

No dice. A bootlegger's turn needs more traction than the slippery road could give me. Suddenly I was in an uncontrolled spin, thrown back against the seat.

I don't know how many times the Subaru whirled around itself while the world whipped by. I was too busy holding onto the steering wheel to count.

The carousel finally stopped with a sudden sickening jolt that slammed my teeth together and hurled me to the right, against the safety belt, and then a jolt to the left as the car rocked on its suspension. I was off the road, in the sandy soil, and the engine had stalled. I smelled gasoline fumes, piercing and sweet. I looked out the rain-streaked window and saw the lowriders twenty yards away to my left. Three or four men were standing behind the cars in the rain, but none seemed to be doing anything. They were probably all too stunned by the display of precision driving they'd just witnessed.

I shook my head, trying to clear it. Didn't really succeed. I shifted into neutral, switched the ignition off, then on again. The engine caught. I turned the wheel to the right, uphill, toward the road, shifted into first, and hit the gas. The wagon lurched forward about a foot, then stopped abruptly and shuddered, its wheels racing. I shifted into reverse, floored the peddle. A lot of noise, no movement. The front wheels were in muck and the rear wheels were off the ground, suspended above a ditch.

I looked back at the lowriders. One of the men had come around from the left and begun walking toward me.

I unsnapped my seat belt, reached for the gun. Couldn't find it. I groped around, discovered it stuck between the seat and the passenger door. I opened that door and pushed myself out into the rain, remembering that I had only two shots left.

Soaking wet all at once, crouching behind the car, I pulled back the hammer of the pistol and poked my head up over the hood to take a look.

The man had stopped maybe thirty feet away. He was wearing a black plastic raincoat and a black cowboy hat with a flat crown. He had his hands up.

"We mean you no harm, Mr. Croft," he called out to me.

I had the pistol's sights centered on his belly. "Don't move," I told him.

How the hell did he know my name?

I remembered. The card I'd left back at La Cantina.

He called out, "Mr. Montoya would like to talk with you."

"Keep your hands up and tell your friends to come around the front of the cars and lean against them. They probably know the position."

He nodded. "Very good." Hands still in the air, he turned and shouted back toward the lowriders. Three men, all wearing black raincoats, emerged from behind the cars and walked around to the front, turned and leaned against them, hands outstretched. In the rain, I couldn't see their hands very well, and any one of the men could've been holding a snub-nose. But at that distance a snub-nose, mine included, didn't represent much of a threat.

I stood up, covering him. "Okay. Get over here. This side of the car."

"We mean you no harm," he said again, coming toward me. Medium height, slender build, mestizo face, about thirty years old.

"Yeah?" I said, backing up as he came around the Subaru. "Two of you just tried to run me off the road. Okay, stop. Turn around. Feet spread, hands against the car."

"They are idiots," he said, shrugging. "They were supposed to follow you here. Nothing more." He had no real accent, none of the New Mexican lilt, but he spoke the kind of formal English you hear in people who have been very well educated in another language.

"Lean against the car," I said.

He did as I said, rainwater spilling from the brim of his hat and splashing against the window of the wagon. I frisked him. Very carefully. He was clean. I stood back.

"Okay," I said. "Stay against the car. What's the story?"

He twisted his head over his shoulder to look at me. "Mr. Montoya wishes to speak with you."

"I've got a telephone."

"He prefers to speak face to face. He says it will be to your advantage. He gives you his word you will not be harmed in any way."

"Great."

"Mr Croft, we have deer rifles in the car, with scopes. If we wanted to kill you, we could have."

If they did have rifles, he was right.

He shook his head, more rainwater sloshing from his hat, and looked down at the ground. "This is unnecessary, Mr. Croft. I apologize for the stupidity of the two fools who followed you. Mr. Montoya only wishes to speak with you about your investigating business. He does not wish to harm you. He says it will take only a half an hour of your time." He looked up at me and smiled. "I am getting very wet, Mr. Croft," he said.

He, at least, had a raincoat. I was wet to the skin, clothes clinging to me everywhere, hair slicked against my forehead, ice-cold rain pouring down my face, down my neck, and into the windbreaker.

"All right," I said. "Tell one of your friends to get over here. Unarmed."

He put up his head, called out, "Carlos! Come here!"

Carlos came at a run. He was shorter than the first man, and a lot younger. He wasn't wearing a hat, and he kept his face in a squint, blinking his eyes against the rain. I put him up against the car and frisked him. Clean.

"Okay, Carlos," I said. "Here's the way it's going down. You get in the car and drive it back onto the road. Your friend here will push." I turned to the first man. "What's your name?"

"George," he said, twisting his head around again. He smiled wryly. "Very pleased to meet you."

"George," I said, "I'm going to stand behind you while all this is going on. I guess you can figure out what happens if Carlos here takes off with my car."

He glanced at the gun. He smiled again. "I believe so, yes."

I turned to the other. "Carlos, when the car is back on the road, you put it in neutral, set the emergency brake, and get out and go back to your friends. And then you all drive away. Back toward Santa Fe. When you get there, go to a movie, do some shopping. Whatever you want. But don't come back this way until tonight. If I spot you, you'll never see George again. You understand?"

Blinking, Carlos nodded.

"George," I said. "How does that plan sound to you?"

George nodded, more rain spilling from his hatbrim. "Excellent. Do you think we could put it into action soon?"

"Go," I said.

With George pushing, it took Carlos only a few minutes to haul the Subaru out of the ditch. George stood back, slapping his hands together, as it rolled onto the road. Carlos stopped it, got out, and, without looking at either of us, walked back to the lowriders. He and the other two got inside. The cars backed up onto the shoulders, turned around, and headed south. I waited until they were out of sight.

The whole thing, from the time I spotted the roadblock till the time they drove away, hadn't taken more than twenty minutes, and not a single other car had come along the road.

"Okay, George," I said. "You drive."

He turned to me, smiling. "Where to?"

"To see Mr. Montoya."

# THIRTEEN

As WE DROVE OFF, the windshield wipers swishing rhythmically, George turned to me and said, "You almost made it."

"Made what?" Holding the pistol in my lap, I leaned forward and switched on the heater.

"The turn. Back there, when you saw us on the road. You did it well. If the road had been less slippery, you would have succeeded."

"Yeah," I said, using my palm to brush wet hair back over my scalp. "But if's don't count for much."

He looked at me, smiled. "Truly," he said, and nodded. Water fell from his hat and spattered onto his raincoat.

The car was crowded with the smell of damp clothing. I cracked the window open a bit and unzipped my windbreaker, tugged the limp clammy shirt away from my chest. There have probably been times in my life when I was more uncomfortable, but I couldn't remember them and I didn't see any point in trying.

Two miles up the road the driver of the second lowrider was standing on the shoulder in the rain. He was wearing only jeans and a black T-shirt, his arms hugging his chest, his hands buried in his armpits, his long black hair plastered down his face. He looked even more miserable than I felt. He saw who was driving and began waving frantically at the Subaru.

George grinned and saluted him, index finger flicking the brim of his hat, then drove on without stopping.

"Where is the other car?" he asked me.

"Another mile or two up ahead."

"Also off the road?"

"Yeah."

"You knocked them both off the road with *this*?" Eyes wide in mock wonder, he opened his hands against the Subaru's steering wheel.

"I keep an atomic cannon in the glove compartment."

He smiled.

At the spot where the first lowrider had sailed off the road, a Ford Bronco was parked at the edge of the slope and a man in a yellow slicker was lowering a winch cable down over the side. Presumably the driver of the lowrider had used a C.B. to call for help.

I said, "You people have good communications."

George nodded. "Mr. Montoya believes in them."

I sat back and tried to remember everything I'd heard about Norman Montoya.

Over the years, there'd been a lot of stories, none of them substantiated, and a lot of charges, none of them proved. A descendant of one of the original Land Grant families, he was supposed to be a big-time drug dealer, running Mexican smack and Bolivian coke up through El Paso, then west to L.A. He was supposed to be a fence, the biggest around. He was also supposed to be the political honcho for the area. Although he'd never run for county office himself, he approved or selected, according to the stories, everyone who did. Those who ran without his approval usually disappeared suddenly, and ended up, according to the stories, feeding the rainbow trout at the bottom of Abique Lake.

So far as I knew, he'd never been tried for anything, or even been arrested. From time to time the state police or some branch of the federals brought him in for questioning, but invariably they let him go. A few years ago, a state attorney general swore, publicly, that before his term was up he'd see Norman Montoya rotting in the federal penitentiary. He resigned for undisclosed personal reasons three months later, with two years of his term unexpired.

Montoya was Big Time. I wasn't, and I couldn't imagine what he wanted with me.

We drove through Truchas, and then up into the mountains, the windshield wipers fighting a steady losing battle against the rain. We drove through most of Las Mujeres, turning off just past the general store onto a dirt road that wound up through the dark ponderosa pines. Signs nailed to the trees at about fifty-yard intervals kept reminding us that this was private property and that trespassers would be prosecuted.

After a mile or so the trees fell away and the road leveled out to cross a few acres of green pasture. Then it climbed again, up the flank of a large grassy hill, and I could see the house at the top.

It was a big place, very imposing against the storm-blackened sky, a modified A-frame with cedar and redwood wings rambling from the main structure. As the Subaru swept around the curve leading to the driveway, I saw that from the rear of the house, on a clear day, you'd have a view all the way down the valley, and beyond it to the Sandias and faraway Albuquerque.

George parked the car and we got out, heads ducked against the pelting rain. Holding the gun at my side, I followed him up the broad slatted wooden stairway to the front door. He thumbed the doorbell.

It opened immediately, as though someone had been standing behind it.

Someone had. Headband, the man from La Cantina.

He wasn't carrying the knife, and if he were tickled to see me, or disappointed, or miffed, he didn't show it. His face remained neutral as he stepped back to let us in. Ignoring me, he turned to George and said, in English, "He's downstairs, in the spa."

George nodded and turned to me. "Come."

I shook my head. "First," I said, "I make a telephone call."

George smiled. "Of course. This way."

I wiped my feet on the doormat. Then smiled at myself—two of his people had tried to kill me, and here I was being careful not to track mud into Montoya's house. Screw it. He could afford the cleaning bill. I followed George from the entrance hall into the living room.

It was an enormous room, maybe forty feet square with a high ceiling and white wall-to-wall carpeting. But what I noticed first wasn't the room itself, nor its furniture, which was all handsome enough, white leather sectionals and chairs, walnut coffee tables and bookcases crammed with books. What I noticed was the valley spread out beneath me, beyond the wall of glass that took up the entire opposite side of the room. Gray clouds were moving down between the black stands of pine, slowly whirling and swirling, and then as they neared the silver ribbon of river at the valley bottom, slowly unraveling and fraying, wisping away like wood smoke. The view stretched on for miles, until both sides of the dark valley became lost in rolling white mist.

"Formidable, no?" said George.

"Not bad," I admitted.

Smiling, he handed me a cordless phone.

I kept the gun in my right hand, punching in Rita's number with my middle finger. She answered on the third ring.

"Hi," I said. "I'm at the home of Norman Montoya in Las Mujeres. I'm here voluntarily, more or less, and right now everything is just ducky." I looked at my watch. Eleven o'clock. "But if I don't call you back in thirty minutes, then you should give some serious thought to springing into action."

Rita said, "Give me the phone number there."

There was no number on the phone. I turned to George, asked him. He told me and I gave it to Rita.

"Hang up," she said. "I'll call right back. I want a record of an outgoing call from here to there."

"Right," I said, and hung up.

All of New Mexico shares one area code, and to call anywhere in the state from Santa Fe, you merely dial one before the number. Naturally, the phone company's computers keep track of all these calls, so they know exactly how exorbitant to make your bill. With a record of a call to this number, if anything did happen to me, Rita could at least verify that she'd been in contact with the Montoya house.

It gave me some leverage. Not much, but maybe enough to keep me from providing protein to the rainbow trout.

George smiled at me. "Mrs. Mondragón?"

"Yeah."

He nodded. "I understand she is a most impressive woman."

"Most impressive," I said.

The phone rang. I spoke into it, "Hello."

"All right," Rita said. "Half an hour from now, or I call Hector."

"Right," I said. "And look, let's get together, the two of us, and have lunch sometime. I'm in the book."

She hung up.

I handed the phone back to George. "It was unnecessary," he said, "but you are wise to take precautions. Now, please, follow me."

I looked back at Headband. He had sat down in a leather chair in the entranceway, and he was reading a magazine as though there was nobody else around.

"Right," I said to George.

WE WENT THROUGH the living room, down a wooden stairway, and along a narrow hallway carpeted in white, both of us leaving a trail of dampness, like a pair of snails. Faintly, I could smell chlorine. We passed two doors, both closed, and when we came to the third, also closed, George stopped and turned to me. He nodded to the gun. "I'm sorry, but I must take that."

I frowned.

"It is a rule," he said. "Mr. Montoya does not permit them in his presence. You are quite safe, I assure you." He smiled. "And besides, if we wanted to keep you here, or to harm you, the gun would not help you."

I nodded and handed it to him. He held it loosely at his side.

"One thing more," he said.

"What's that?"

"You must strip."

"Strip," I said.

He shrugged, smiling. "Your clothing. All of it. Another of the rules. And it will allow us to dry it for you."

"Strip," I said.

"Strip," George nodded. He had the grace not to point the gun at me, but both of us knew he could have.

I stripped, letting my soggy clothes fall to the carpeting, and then stood there feeling very naked and trying to look extremely casual about it. I think that Man invented clothing so that no one would know how tiny his penis can get in a good breeze.

George nodded, opened the door, stood back. "May I bring you something to drink?"

"A beer," I told him. Casually. "A Corona."

He nodded, and waved a hand to indicate I should enter. I did, and he closed the door behind me.

The chlorine smell was stronger and the air was hot and moist, as thick as soup. Opposite me was another wall of glass. The glass must've been treated somehow; despite the humidity it hadn't fogged over, and through it I could see the same spectacular view of cloud-wrapped valley that I'd seen upstairs.

On a sunnny day, the room would be blinding. The floor was tiled with white, and so were the walls. On the wall to my right were three chrome showerheads, chrome nozzles and knobs running down the tiles beneath them. In front of the window was a raised white fiberglass platform. Set into it was a hot tub about ten feet across, and sitting inside that, nodding pleasantly to me, pale thin vapor rising all around him like mist off a lake, was a man who had to be Norman Montoya.

"Mr. Croft," he said. He had a raspy voice that sounded like three packs of Marlboros a day. "Good afternoon. Please be so good as to use one of the showers to rinse off and then come join me."

Well, why not. A hot tub was as good a place as any to conduct business. Henry the Eighth and LBJ, I'm told, conducted it on the toilet.

I soaped up and rinsed myself off, then padded over, climbed up the rubber-coated steps, crossed the platform, and stepped down into the water. It was nearly scalding.

Montoya stood to greet me, steam curling from his shoulders, and I was surprised at how short he was, no more than five foot three or four. His hair was white, cut close to the scalp but not so close you couldn't see the waves in it. His eyes were dark and shiny and shrewd. Beneath a small, almost Indian nose was a thin, white, carefully trimmed mustache. His skin was tanned and his face was creased, lines crinkling out from his dark eyes and hollowing his cheeks. But he was in good shape, his body compact and wiry, the muscles taut. From what I knew about him, he must've been close to sixty years old. He could've passed for late forties.

I shook his damp hot hand and he smiled at me. "Please, sit down. Shall I turn on the jets? They're very good for muscular aches and pains, and I understand that you've had quite a strenuous morning."

I sat down on the wide bench that circled the tub at knee level. The hot water rose halfway up my chest. "The jets'd be fine," I said.

He nodded and sat down opposite me, the water lapping at his shoulders. He reached out a thin arm and tapped at a button on the platform. There was a whooshing sound and the water suddenly foamed up creamy white. I could feel pin-point bubbles whizzing along my back, rushing along my legs. It was like sitting in frothy warm champagne.

He smiled at me, benevolently. "Did George ask you if you wanted anything to drink."

"He did, yes. He's good, George."

The old man nodded, pleased. "My nephew. A graduate of the University of Mexico. And of Stanford, in California. He's Phi Beta Kappa, you know."

"And he drives a lowrider?"

He smiled. "He prefers his BMW—he appreciates German technology, you see—but he knows that frequently it pays to be underestimated." He lifted his arm from the water waved it toward the window. "Do you like the view?"

"Very nice."

Gazing out over the valley, he said, "It's strange, isn't it, how people become proprietary about the view from inside their homes. As though they owned everything they see. *My* lawn, *my* tree, *my* mountain, *my* sky." He turned to me, smiling. "In my case, it would mean I owned most of northern New Mexico."

I smiled back at him. "In your case, I hear it's not far from the truth."

"Now, now, Mr. Croft." He waggled a dripping finger at me. "Never try to flatter a vain old man. Vanity is bottomless, you know. You could spend the rest of your life, fruitlessly, attempting to fill it." He sat back in the tub, water bubbling beneath his chin, and eyed me through the steam. "Tell me," he said. "Are you a religious man?"

"No," I said. "Not really."

He nodded. "Do you believe in an afterlife?"

"Do I have faith in one?"

He smiled. "An important distinction, isn't it? Let me rephrase the question. Are your actions grounded on the assumption that one exists?"

I shook my head. "No."

He nodded again. "Good. I dislike dealing with people who expect to be playing harps on a cloudbank somewhere. I find them untrustworthy. I, myself, am a Buddhist. Do you happen to know anything about Zen, Mr. Croft?"

I shrugged. "I know you're supposed to sit a lot."

Another approving nod. "*Zazen.* I sit in lotus for half an hour every morning, and another half hour every night. Merely sit, keeping my mind empty as possible and staring at an empty wall."

I nodded, but I was beginning to wonder where all this was leading.

He smiled. "I'll be getting to the point in only a few moments, Mr. Croft. Please be patient and bear with my ramblings for a while longer."

I shrugged, smiled. "It's your nickel," I said.

"Thank you. Ah, here's George with your drink."

George came in, carrying a round silver tray that held a bottle of Corona, an empty glass, and another cordless

telephone. He set the tray on the platform, close enough
for me to reach it, and nodded to the old man.

Montoya said, "And what of Luis?"

George jerked his head toward me. "He ran Luis off the
road too." He grinned. "With a Subaru."

"Very enterprising. Perhaps he can explain the tech-
nique to us before he leaves. Is someone seeing to Luis?"

George nodded. "Vincent is picking him up. He's already gotten Raoul's car back on the road."

"Very good. Thank you, George."

George nodded again, grinned at me, turned and left.

"I apologize," said Montoya, "for the two cretins who
tried to run you down. They were exceeding their instructions. I wished them only to follow you until you met with
George. They will be reprimanded, and of course we will
pay for any damage inflicted on your vehicle. Please, Mr.
Croft, drink your beer."

The ice-cold bottle was sweaty with condensation. I
filled the glass, sat back, and tasted it. Good.

The old man spoke. "As I said, Mr. Croft, I sit in *zazen* two times every day. Now a curious thing happens
when you stare at a blank, empty wall. Your vision flick-
ers and fades for a while, and sometimes goes into a complete white-out. Sometimes a faint hollow in the surface of
the wall, barely perceptible under normal circumstances,
will fill up with waves of gray, or green, or red. And
sometimes images will float across the wall, some of them
so finely detailed they could have been drawn by a master.
A dog or a horse, a Balinese dancer, a field of grinning
skulls."

I took another sip of beer and nodded. I wondered how
often he saw fields of grinning skulls.

"We call this *makyo*, illusion, and we learn to ignore it.
The point I wish to make, Mr. Croft, is that I believe
something much like this has happened to you in your

search for the necklace belonging to Mr. and Mrs. Leighton."

I thought I kept my surprise fairly well hidden—I hadn't mentioned the Leightons or the necklace at La Cantina— but the old man smiled again and said, "Oh yes, I know all about it. Mr. Frank Biddle's visit to your office last Friday, your contract with the Atco Insurance Company, your discussions with Ramirez and Nolan at the police department. At the risk of sounding self-satisfied, I must tell you that I am very well-informed."

"Sounds like it."

He nodded. "My existence depends upon it. And although this particular existence is only one of many and, like all of them, illusory, I confess to having become attached to it." Another smile. "As Diogenes once said, 'Old habits are hard to break.'"

"He was a caution, Diogenes."

He smiled again. "As I said, Mr. Croft, I believe you have become a victim of *makyo*. From somewhere you've heard that Mr. Frank Biddle was involved in small-time cocaine dealing. You have persuaded yourself that this fact is somehow connected to his death. This has led you to one of my people, Benito Chavez, and would have led you, ultimately, to me. I invited you here, Mr. Croft, to assure you that Mr. Biddle's dealing in cocaine and his death are in no way related."

"What *was* related to his death?"

"I have no idea. But I know that cocaine was not."

I drank some beer. "Assuming that's true, why would you bother to tell me?"

"We are all seekers after truth, are we not, Mr. Croft? And is it not our responsibility, if we see that one of our fellow seekers is following the path of error, to correct him?"

"Sure it is," I said. "Especially if we get something out of it ourselves."

He smiled. "Very well, Mr. Croft. What I get out of this is Mr. Stacey Killebrew."

"Get him how?"

"Get him back in the prison, where—and here I'm sure your friend Ramirez will agree with me—he most certainly belongs."

"Why would you want Killebrew back in prison?"

"He sets a bad example."

I laughed. "You mean he doesn't fence his stuff with you."

Montoya raised his eyebrows. "Receiving stolen property is a criminal offence, Mr. Croft. Suffice it to say that the man offends me. He is violent. He is cruel. He has a fondness for very young girls. There are certain individuals whose karma is so dark, so black, that they seem to personify evil. Killebrew is such a one."

"Maybe next time," I said, "he'll come back as a mollusk."

"I think not," he said. "A mollusk would be a decided improvement."

"Did Killebrew kill Biddle?"

"Once again, I have no idea. But I think it likely that he killed Mrs. Silvia Griego."

So Griego's death must've made the news. "Why would he kill Griego?"

"Should I tell you everything, Mr. Croft?" He shook his head, clicking his tongue against his teeth. "It would seem unsporting to deprive you of the discovery."

"That's okay," I said. "Deprive me."

He nodded once. "A single small hint, then. Mr. Killebrew, Mr. Biddle, the artist John Lucero, and the late Mrs. Griego, they were all…" and he smiled slyly, as though he were about to impart one of the Great Secrets of the Orient, "... they were all birds of a feather."

"Uh-huh. And what does that mean, exactly?"

"Think of it as a *koan*, Mr. Croft. A puzzle to be solved on the way to Enlightenment. You're an intelligent man. I'm sure you'll come upon an answer."

I glanced at my watch. Eleven-thirty. I asked him, "Could I use your phone?"

A gracious nod. "Of course."

This time Rita answered on the first ring.

"Everything's still hunky-dory," I told her.

"All right," she said. "Call again in another half hour."

"I will."

I put the phone back on the silver tray and turned back to Montoya.

He said, "I met Mrs. Mondragón once, you know."

I shook my head. "I didn't know."

"With her late husband. Some years ago, at a political gathering in Santa Fe. This was shortly after the late Mr. Mondragón had opened the detective agency. You were not, I believe, associated with it at that time."

"No," I said.

"I'd known him and his family for years. A fine old New Mexico family. I believe they were all very pleased that William was finally doing something with his life, even something as *outré* as opening a detective agency." He smiled. "Later, of course, after he was killed, they all blamed Mrs. Mondragón, said that the agency had been her idea."

"I know," I said.

He nodded. "Of course. You were the one who found him, were you not? Found the man who killed William and wounded Mrs. Mondragón."

"Yeah."

He smiled. "How does it feel to be a part of the local mythology?"

"You'd know the answer to that a whole lot better than I would."

He smiled, shook his head. "Flattery again. You're incorrigible, Mr. Croft."

"Listen," I said, "would you mind if I asked you a couple of questions?"

"Not at all," he said, nodding graciously. "That is, after all, your job."

"Did Killebrew steal the Leightons' necklace?"

He shrugged lightly. "He seems the likely suspect, wouldn't you say?"

Not really an answer, but probably the best I'd get from him. "No one's fenced the thing?"

He shook his head. "If it had turned up anywhere, I would know."

"One thing I don't understand. If you want Killebrew back in jail, why not go to the police with what you've got?"

He shook his head, his lips pursed in distaste. "On general principle I avoid the police whenever possible. And explaining to them my sources of information in this instance would set in motion a chain of circumstances I prefer to avoid."

I nodded. "Okay. One thing more. A personal question."

"Certainly."

"How does a Buddhist get into your line of work?"

He smiled. "According to the statements I submit annually to the Internal Revenue Service, investing in real estate is my line of work."

I shrugged. "So how does a Buddhist get into real estate?"

"Karma, Mr. Croft. The failures and successes of previous lives have led me to this one, with its particular rewards and burdens. And because I'm well aware of my imperfections, I know that this one will not be my last. I cannot devote myself, unfortunately, to the meditative life as completely as I would like. I have too many commitments and responsibilities to an extended circle of family and business associates. Can you understand that?"

"Sure," I said. "I saw *The Godfather.*"

He smiled. "You're an amusing man, Mr. Croft." He put his head back against the edge of the tub. "Perhaps we can do business together at some time in the future."

"I suppose that means we're finished with our discussion."

"Sad but true, alas. I'm an old man and I need my rest. But I'm sure you're anxious to return to Santa Fe and put to useful work the information I've provided you."

"Right," I said. "The information. Birds of a feather."

Smiling, he nodded. "Precisely. Your clothes will be hanging in the hallway."

"Thanks."

"Not at all. Please feel free to contact me whenever you think it necessary. It's been a great pleasure talking with you." He nodded to me, smiled again, and closed his eyes.

I clambered up out of the tub, grabbed a towel off the rack on the wall, and dried myself. Wrapped the towel around my waist and padded down off the platform and across the room.

When I looked back, through the mist rising off the water, his eyes were still closed.

# FOURTEEN

THERE AREN'T MANY THINGS to do in Santa Fe until summertime, when the opera season begins, and I'm one of the philistines who believes that there aren't many things to do then, either. But one of the things you *can* do, year-round, is attend openings. New restaurants, new supermarkets, new shopping malls, new shows at the local galleries—all of them kick off with an opening. Openings provide an excuse for the locals to dress up in their Navajo silver and get out of the house to see who's seeing whom, and be seen by whoever's seeing whom. There are one or two individuals in town, it's been said, who'd be willing to attend the opening of an envelope.

I had thought that the opening at the Griego Gallery would've been called off. But when I telephoned the gallery after I got back into town from Las Mujeres, I learned that I was wrong. Despite Silvia Griego's death, The Show Must Go On.

There was a message from Hector on the machine at the office, asking me to call him. I did, and he asked me if I'd known that Griego was dead. I said I had. He asked about my visit to her gallery yesterday, and I told him I'd spoken with her because of a reputed connection between her and Biddle. He said that was very interesting, and asked if Griego had admitted the connection. I said she had, more or less, but that I didn't think she'd known anything about the stolen necklace. He said he liked the way I used the word *reputed* and suggested I come down to his office tomorrow to use it again in the statement he wanted me to make. I said I would.

I called Rita, gave her the rundown on what'd happened up at Las Mujeres, skipping lightly over the scene at La Cantina and the chase on the highway, emphasizing my talk with Montoya. I mentioned the old man's cryptic remark about "birds of a feather," but it didn't mean any more to her than it had to me. After I hung up, I drove over to the municipal pool and swam my mile. Then I went home.

For my outing that evening I selected a pair of clean Levis, Luchese lizardskin boots, a pale blue silk shirt, and my Adolfo blue blazer. Understated elegance. The sort of thing Hoot Gibson might wear to the Four Seasons.

When I arrived, fashionably late at seven o'clock, the gallery's parking lot was packed with cars, and so were both sides of Canyon Road for a hundred feet in each direction. Apparently the death of the owner could really punch up a gallery's business. I wondered if this would start a trend.

I drove on until I found a space, parked the Subaru, and walked back. Dusk was becoming evening. The air was cooling off, but it carried the sweet purple smell of lilacs and, with it, the promise of summer.

The people milling around on the gallery's portico, illuminated by the soft glow of kerosene hurricane lamps, seemed prepared to take the promise for the reality. Most of them were dressed ten or fifteen degrees warmer than the weather. Nearly every male there was outfitted, as I was, in Middle-Class Cowboy, although there were a few three-piece suits circulating among the denims. A lot of the Hispanic women were wearing Hispanic-flavored outfits, long skirts set off with sashes of red or black, presumably to emphasize their Spanish heritage. A lot of the Anglo women—the blondes, primarily—were wearing dresses of bright summery white or yellow. Presumably to emphasize their blondhood.

I climbed up the steps into the bumble-bee rumble of conversation and spotted, among the crowd, a few people I knew. Two Santa Fe artists, Doug Higgins and Bobbi Kitsman, were sitting on the portico rail, talking to each other over plastic wineglasses. I nodded to them, and then nodded to a filmmaker friend, Sally Jackson, who was standing a few feet away. At the front door, I stopped for a minute to talk to Claudia Jessup and Jon Richards, both writers, who introduced a friend of theirs visiting from New York, someone named Meredith Rich. Jon asked me about the bruise on my cheek, and I told him I'd cut myself shaving. He asked me if I shaved with a bowling ball.

Inside the gallery I moved through thickets of chatter and streamers of scent. Lauren, Giorgio, Opium, Clinique, Chanel—the Chanel reminding me, with the immediacy that only the sense of smell can give, of my visit to Silvia Griego's house.

As I eased around one formally dressed cluster of talking heads, I bumped elbows with a man in a white sportscoat. A few drops of wine sloshed from his plastic cup, and he turned toward me, the annoyed glare already beginning. He took in the bruise on my cheek and he blinked and turned back to his friends. Even if you have the right of way, you don't pull out in front of a '65 Ford with a crumpled fender.

Without trying to, without really wanting to, I caught snatches of the conversation buzzing around me. It seemed to be divided equally between Griego's death and the art on display.

"...horrible, I heard she was *raped*...is delicious, and he's got such a *supple* feel for line...police haven't any idea at all who...lacking a certain subtlety of texture, and...I mean, *Silvia*, for God's sake, who would've *thought*...I only wish he'd chosen colors that were less *honest*..."

The artwork under discussion was a series of paintings hanging on the walls of both rooms of the gallery. They were all very much alike, splashy abstracts with a few recognizable symbols—leather moccasins and deer antlers and bison heads—floating across the muddle. They had titles like *The Medicine Man Has Passed Away and the Sun Dance is Dead*. Meaty stuff.

Someone tapped me on the shoulder and I turned. Denim work shirt, pale blond hair, delicate young male features, a grin that displayed a lot of teeth. Kevin Leighton. "Hey, Mr. Croft. How you doin'?"

"Fine, Kevin. But the name is Joshua."

There was a girl standing at his side, and it wasn't until she smiled, showing two rows of painful-looking silvery braces, that I realized it was his sister, Miranda. She wore a dark plaid skirt and a yellow sweater and she seemed more comfortable with her body tonight; and, with a figure that showed a lot of promise, she had every reason to be. She wasn't wearing her glasses and her eyes seemed bright and shiny with excitement. Without the smile, without the braces, I wouldn't have recognized her. It was as though by leaving her home, leaving her parents, she was able to fill out, ease up, become a different person.

Kevin asked me, "What happened to your face?"

"I was eating a burrito," I told him, "and it blew up. How are you, Miranda?"

"Oh, okay, I guess," she said, abstracted, her glance skittering around the room. She turned to me, smiled with pleasure, "It's a nice opening, though, isn't it? I mean, even if most of these paintings are sort of bogus."

"It's swell," I said. "Your mother didn't come?"

The girl's face went tight and guarded, and I realized that I'd asked the wrong question.

Kevin showed a nice quick sense of diplomacy and interjected, "My mother wasn't feeling too well. She and Mrs. Griego were pretty close, I guess."

Miranda brightened suddenly, waving off to the left, then turning to her brother to say in a rush: "It's Janice, Kevin, I'm going over to say hello." And then she was gone.

Kevin watched her weave through the crowd, then turned to me and confided, "They had a big fight tonight."

"Your mother and Miranda?"

He nodded.

"What about?" I asked him.

He shrugged. "Nothing. They never fight about anything *real*, do you know what I mean? Sometimes it just seems that my mother thinks Miranda can't do anything right."

I nodded. Felice, super-competent as she was, would be a difficult mother. She'd be difficult, probably, in any capacity.

"So what brings you here?" Kevin asked me. He grinned. "You think maybe you'll spot somebody wearing my mother's necklace?"

I smiled. "Nope. Looking for someone. What about you? I wouldn't have pictured this as your idea of a good time."

"My father thought someone should go. My mother didn't want to—like I said, she was pretty tight with Mrs. Griego."

"You're representing the family. You and Miranda."

"Yeah. Miranda likes all this stuff." He looked around him with the weary cynicism that only an eighteen-year-old boy can achieve. Or a thirty-eight-year-old private detective.

Not looking at me, he put his hands in his pockets and said, "You know, I was kind of a jerk the other night. When I came to your office."

"Don't let it bother you, Kevin. I've spent years at a time being kind of a jerk."

"Well, anyway," turning to me, "I apologize."

"No need to. I appreciate your help."

"Yeah, well," a shrug, "if I can help you any more, let me know, okay?"

It was an offer of friendship, and I would have been a boor not to accept it. I smiled, held out my hand to shake his, and said, "I appreciate it, Kevin. I'll do that. You take care now."

He grinned and nodded.

"I'll see you later," I told him. "I've got to find someone."

And, like Miranda, I moved off through the crowd.

In the narrow room leading to the gallery's office, the Santa Clara pottery and all but one of the kachinas had been carted off to make room for two trestle tables, one loaded with hors d'oeuvres and cold cuts, the other with bottles of liquor and California champagne. Naturally, it was in here that most of the deadbeats—a friend of mine calls them The Cake-Eaters—were hanging out, after having made a quick obligatory pass around the gallery. These are the people who've never been seen buying groceries or eating in restaurants. They move from opening to opening like chimps swinging from branch to branch for bananas.

And it was in here that I found the person I was looking for.

Talking with animation to a big man dressed like an honorary Indian in a headband and a buckskin shirt, her pert head cocked, her tight blond curls agleam, she was wearing a clinging black long-sleeved top, scoop-necked, and another black miniskirt, this one made of leather. As mourning clothes went, they weren't bad at all. Unfortunately she was also wearing a pair of those patterned gray pantyhose that make women look as if they're suffering from impetigo.

I tapped her on the shoulder. When she turned to face me, all the Pepsi-Cola brightness fizzled away from her wholesome face. I seemed to be having that effect on a lot of people lately.

Her features stony, she said, "What are you doing here?"

"I came for the canapés," I said. The guy in the buckskin shirt was glowering at me from beneath a single dark Neanderthal eyebrow. He didn't look like he avoided '65 Fords with crumpled fenders. He looked as if he drove one.

The Pepsi-Cola girl said, "I gave the police your name. They know that Silvia was upset after she talked to you."

"Good," I said. I reached into the inside pocket of my blazer, slipping out the Polaroid print, and showed it to her, holding it so Buckskin couldn't see it. "I don't suppose you mentioned this to them?"

Instinctively, she reached for it. I snatched it away, tucked it back into my pocket.

Her mouth was set in a tight frown, her lower lip curled. "What do you want?"

"Let's talk. In the office."

She took a deep breath, let it out, nodded once crisply. She turned to Buckskin. "I'll be back in a few minutes, Carl."

Carl glanced at me, said to her, "You okay, Linda?"

"It's nothing," she said, touching him lightly on the arm. "Business. Be back in a minute."

The door to the office was only a few feet away. She opened it, and I followed her inside. Neither of the two television screens was on. Apparently, whoever was in charge had decided that no one would try to walk off with any of the paintings hanging outside. I agreed.

She flicked the light switch and turned to face me. "That photograph," she said. "You got it from Silvia."

"Yeah."

Her mouth parted and her eyes widened as she realized, or thought she did, what that meant.

I shook my head. "I didn't kill her. Sit down." I closed the door.

She sat down behind the desk and crossed her arms protectively over her breasts, exactly as Silvia Griego had done in that same chair only the day before. It seemed to me like a week ago.

I sat in the white padded chair opposite her. "Your name is Linda?" I said.

She nodded. "Linda Sorenson." Her voice was small and guarded. Huddled against herself like that, wary, uncertain, she looked about sixteen years old.

"Linda," I said, "I didn't kill Silvia and I'm not going to hurt you. I'm a licensed private investigator and I'm looking for a necklace that was stolen sometime last year. Your friend Silvia knew at least one of the people who could've been involved in the theft. When I spoke with her yesterday, she denied any knowledge of the necklace. That may or may not be true, but I think Silvia Griego was involved in something that got her killed. I want to know what it was."

"What—" it came out scratchy, and she cleared her throat, "—what are you going to do with the photograph?" She winced suddenly, remembering. "There's more than one," she said. "Isn't there?"

"There are three of them," I said, "that you'd be interested in. If you cooperate with me, I'll hold them until this thing is cleared up. Then I'll destroy them or mail them to you, whichever you want."

"You could've made copies."

"I didn't. All I want is any information you can give me about Silvia Griego."

"I've never done anything like that before," she said, unlocking her arms, leaning forward. "With a woman, I mean. I'm engaged. He's a really good man, and we're getting married in September. I've never seen that woman again, either. I mean, not that way." She actually fluttered her eyelashes and blushed. I hadn't witnessed anyone doing that for a long time, and I thought it was fairly fetching. "Honestly," she said. "I was drunk and coked up, and I didn't know what I was doing."

"I believe you," I said. I didn't, not really, despite the blush. In the photographs she seemed to be displaying a lot more expertise than she was giving herself credit for now. But at the moment, my belief in her was less important than her belief in me. "And I don't have any reason to hurt you. I only want to know about Silvia."

She frowned. "What do you want to know?"

"How long had she known Frank Biddle?"

She shrugged. "For four years, at least. He was hanging around as long as I can remember, and I started here four years ago, as assistant director. Silvia made me the director two years ago." Adding this last bit because she was rattled, I think, and wanting to reestablish her importance to herself.

"What was her relationship with Biddle?"

"They used to sleep together. Not all the time. Occasionally."

"How occasionally?"

She shrugged. "I dunno. Once a month, maybe. Sometimes Silvia liked to do scenes."

"Scenes?"

The eyelashes fluttered and she blushed again. It was slightly less fetching this time. "You know. Sex stuff. Fantasies. Sometimes she'd call him up and he'd come over in a pick-up truck and they'd do it in the back. Things like that."

"How do you know?"

"She told me. She was proud of it." She frowned again, bemused, and gave a small shrug. "Like that was a big deal, making it in a pick-up truck."

"This was here at the gallery?"

She shook her head emphatically. "No, no, Silvia was always really straight at the gallery. Prim and proper, you know? No, she did all this at home, at her house. Sometimes she organized parties there, too, and once in a while she'd ask Biddle to come."

Her face crinkled slightly when she mentioned his name.

I said, "You didn't like Biddle."

She shook her head. "I thought he was creepy. He was always coming on to me, staring at my breasts."

Involuntarily, my own glance dipped in that direction.

She fluttered her eyelashes again, but left out the blush. Maybe she forgot it. She did remember, though, to reach up and run her fingers through her short blond curls, which tightened the material of her low-cut top against the breasts in question.

"Had she been seeing Biddle recently?" I asked.

"No. Not since last year, in the fall."

"Do you know why she stopped seeing him?"

She shrugged. "I never asked."

"These parties," I said. "They were the ones in the Polaroids?"

She nodded. She was more relaxed now. She had decided that she knew how to handle me.

"How often did you go to them?" I asked her.

"Only that one time. Honestly." She held up her right hand, two fingers raised. Scout's Honor.

"Then how do you know whether Biddle went?"

"Like I said, Silvia was always telling me about her sex life. I mean, sometimes, that was all she talked about. She'd say, 'Listen, Linda, you'll never believe what I did last night, I had Frank over and we did blah blah blah.' She really thought it was fascinating."

"Why listen to her?"

She looked at me as though the question were senseless. "She was the owner here."

"Right." I had a sudden image of the two women, the older one confiding her sexual adventures with a kind of excited, almost frantic pride; the younger one listening, nodding and smiling with a feigned interest that masked boredom and, apparently, contempt. It occurred to me that although the older had been dead for almost twenty-four hours, the contempt was still alive. I said, "How often did she have these parties?"

"Not very often. Once or twice a year. She hasn't had one for over a year—that one, the photograph you've got, was the last one." Another shrug. "I think the AIDS thing, all the stories about people dying, I think that sort of scared her."

"Did Stacey Killebrew ever come to these parties?"

"Stacey who?" Frowning, puzzled.

"Big guy, works out with weights. Light brown hair, light brown mustache. Yellow teeth."

She shook her head. "No, I never—wait, was he a friend of Frank Biddle's? I mean, like a long time ago? Two years, maybe?"

"Yeah."

"Uh-huh, yeah. I saw him here with Biddle once or twice. Then I didn't see him for a long time, and then he came by here again a couple of months ago. It was in the morning, I was coming to work, and he was leaving. I asked Silvia about it and she said he was delivering something."

"Do you know what it was?"

She shook her head. "No. I mean, I didn't know it was important. Was it?"

"Maybe. Who handled the accounts for the gallery?"

"I did. I signed all the checks, kept the records, and Silvia and I went over everything together at the end of the month."

"Do you know anything about a company called Liebman and Sons in Germany?"

"Sure, in Munich. We do a lot of business with them. The Germans are crazy about Indian art, especially the old stuff, the artifacts. Silvia told me there's this German writer, Karl May, Its M—A—Y, but they pronounce it *my*. Anyway, he writes these crazy Westerns, and the Germans love him. They all want to be cowboys."

"How long has the gallery been dealing with Liebman and Sons?"

"Since before I came to work here."

"And how much business have you done with them?"

"Money-wise? Altogether? Well…over the whole time, I mean the four years I know about . . . maybe sixty thousand dollars. Maybe seventy, I don't have the exact figures. But that's pretty close." She raised her eyebrows, made herself look helpful, open, trustworthy. "I could look them up if you want."

I shook my head. "What happened to the money?"

She frowned, as though wondering why I'd want to know, and then shrugged, as though deciding motives didn't matter. "Some of it went to pay outstanding bills. The rest went into the corporation account."

But none of it, evidently, had gone into a numbered account in Berne. I said, "The gallery was doing well?"

"Sure, really well. Of course," her face going slightly sour, her voice slightly weary, "we never did well enough for Silvia."

"Silvia was greedy."

"Well, no. I wouldn't put it that way, exactly." She raised her eyebrows again. "I mean, after all, I don't want to speak ill of the dead or anything. It's just that Silvia was sort of an anxious person. Insecure, I mean. You know how women can be sometimes, when they get older? And money was like a security blanket for her. Profits were down a little bit this year, not much, nothing to worry about, you know? But Silvia was all bent out of shape. I mean, she was practically living on Valium."

I was glad I'd never been around the girl when she did want to speak ill of the dead.

"What sort of things did you sell to Liebman and Sons?" I asked.

"Artifacts, mostly. Hopi pottery and ceremonial stuff from Awatovi. That's the ancestral Hopi city. The new stuff was all kachinas."

"Who made the kachinas?"

"John Lucero. He's the only kachina artist we carry."

"Do Liebman and Sons handle jewelry?"

She shook her head. "As far as I know, they only do art."

"Have the police asked you yet about the gallery accounts?"

"No, not really. I talked to one of them this morning, and he mostly wanted to know whether or not Silvia had any enemies."

"Did she?"

A shrug. "Not that I knew of. I mean, honestly, she was okay and all, but I don't think she was interesting enough to have any enemies."

And with employees like this one, who needed them?

I said, "The police'll be back." I knew that if they hadn't already found the strongbox in Griego's closet, they would, soon enough.

She said, "I won't tell them I talked to you. Honest." She smiled and showed me her Boy Scout hand again.

"Tell them anything you want. But if I were you, I'd probably forget about mentioning the Polaroids."

"Oh God, yes. What a mistake." Her face went earnest and she said, "Look, could I at least have that one, the one you're carrying? I mean, I've been straight with you, haven't I?"

I reached into the blazer, took out the print, tossed it to the desk. She picked it up, grinning happily, and leaned back to study it. Without bothering to flutter her lashes, still grinning, she looked at me. "At least you can't say I take a bad photograph."

"Nope."

She opened a drawer, tossed the print inside, closed the drawer. The grin became a smile, and there was a hint in it of self-satisfaction, of a job well-done. "When can I have the others?"

"In a few days. Soon as all this is cleared up."

She plucked a card from a silver salver on the desk and leaned forward, offering it. "Here. It's got my home phone number, too." I think that manipulating me, which she clearly thought she had done, wasn't enough for her. She wanted to neutralize me, and the only way she knew how to do that was sexually. I took the card, stood up.

"Call me," she said, smiling as her glance slid up and down me. "Maybe we could have lunch or something."

"Sure," I said. I wondered which one of us was supposed to be the entrée.

# FIFTEEN

WHEN I CALLED RITA from my house that night and told her what had happened at the gallery, she asked me what I thought of Linda Sorenson.

I said, "I don't think she's going to become one of my favorite people."

"As I recall," she said, "you don't have too many favorite people. How many at last count?"

"Besides you and Tina Turner?"

"Yes."

"None. And to tell you the truth, I'm starting to worry about Tina. She's not returning my calls."

"So what is it, exactly, that's wrong with Linda Sorenson?"

" I wouldn't want her working for me. I wouldn't want her to be standing behind me with a knife, either."

"Could she have killed Griego?"

"Not that way. She wouldn't want to mess up her miniskirt. But if it were in her best interest, I think she could've poisoned her without losing too much sleep."

"But do you think she was telling the truth?"

"For the most part, yeah. Like I said, I think she was exaggerating the little girl number. From the Polaroids, I doubt she was the novice she's claiming she was. But about the other stuff, I think she was telling me what she believes is the truth. When I mentioned Liebman and Sons, she didn't even blink. Unless she's a much better actress than I think she is, she doesn't know anything about that account in Switzerland."

"And she says that Griego hadn't seen Biddle since last fall."

"Yeah."

"All right. What do we have so far? Biddle came to Santa Fe five years ago. For four years he and Griego are sometimes lovers. That relationship ends, if Sorenson is right, in the fall of last year. We don't know why. Griego has been dealing with Liebman and Sons for at least five years, and it looks as though she's been keeping two separate accounts with them, one legal, the other not. For at least two years, Biddle has been working for the Leightons. Last year, in the fall, the Leightons fire him. We don't know why. A few weeks later, the necklace is stolen. According to Sergeant Nolan, the M.O. matches that of Stacey Killebrew. But according to your good friend Montoya, Killebrew hasn't fenced the necklace. No one has. Again, we don't know why. According to Carla Chavez, Killebrew and Biddle had a falling out after Biddle came back from Amarillo in November."

"At about the same time Biddle stopped seeing Griego."

"Yes. And once again—"

"—We don't know why. Are you reading this out of a book?"

"Six days ago," she said, "Biddle comes to you with an offer to return a piece of jewelry to an insurance company. The next day, he's dead."

"And we don't know why. And we don't know what Montoya meant about 'birds of a feather.' Personally, I think all that staring at empty walls has affected the guy's brain. Turned him into a road company version of The Inscrutable Oriental."

"You're going to have to talk to the kachina artist, Lucero."

"Hey, I knew that already."

"Aaron called tonight from the bank with some information about Leighton."

"Yeah?"

"Apparently, Peter Ricard was right. Leighton was in financial trouble last year. In order to cover his note, he had to unload some stocks. They were down at the time, and he took quite a loss."

"This was when?"

"September. A month before the necklace was reported stolen."

"So maybe he got pissed off and decided to recoup the loss by faking the theft."

"I don't think so. A week later, he sold a piece of property to some developers from Dallas, and according to Aaron, he made a tidy little profit on the deal."

"If he had the property to sell, why unload the stocks?"

"Aaron says he'd had the property for over a year. The sale to the Dallas people was unexpected."

"So he wasn't hurting for money when the necklace disappeared."

"He was tight, Aaron said. He'd had to cut back on a few of his projects, but no, he wasn't really hurting. And Joshua, I spoke again to Romero, at Atco. He's convinced there was no fraud involved."

"He okayed an insurance payment of a hundred thousand bucks, Rita. He's not going to start saying, 'Holy cow, maybe I screwed up.'"

"You just don't like Derek Leighton."

"I like him fine. I think he's swell. But if Killebrew took that necklace, why didn't he fence it?"

"I don't know. I don't know that Killebrew took it. You're talking to Hector tomorrow?"

"Yeah. Making my statement."

"After you do, talk to Nolan again. See if he'll let you look at the reports of the other burglaries, the ones he knows Killebrew committed."

"What am I looking for?"

"Whatever you find."

"Shit," I said, "you're not going Zen on me too, are you?"

"Maybe he missed something."

"I doubt it."

"Humor me."

"Yes, dear."

She hesitated for a moment, and then said, "Joshua, how are you doing?"

"I'm okay."

"You're sure? Do you want to come over for a drink?"

"No thanks. I'm not drinking tonight, Rita. I'm going to hang out here and try to get some sleep."

"All right. But don't be more stoic than you have to be. If you need to talk to someone, call me."

"I will. Thanks, Rita. I'll talk to you tomorrow."

I brought a book to bed with me, a mystery by K. C. Constantine. It was a good book, canny and wise, but after the day I'd had, no book would've been good enough to keep me awake longer than ten minutes.

I WAS BACK in Norman Montoya's house in Las Mujeres, standing before the broad wall of glass in the living room, looking down at the clouds as they swirled through the dark towering pines. *The Four Seasons* was floating from the stereo speakers, and I was feeling secure and protected, isolated and detached, in my hilltop fortress with the world spread out like a Japanese painting beneath me. But suddenly there was movement out there, off to my right, a tiny faraway figure sliding through the mist.

I saw that it was Rita, and that she was running. She looked back over her shoulder at the unknown thing that was chasing her, and even from this distance I could see that her face was twisted with terror. She was running along a narrow path that wound down through the trees toward the ribbon of river at the valley bottom. Somehow I knew that this was the wrong direction, that the thing she was trying to escape had circled around and that it was waiting for her there, where the cold gray water tumbled over the cold gray rocks.

And then I was out there, in the mist, running downhill after her, calling out her name. Clammy branches smacked against me, drenched me with water so chill it burned like acid. The mist had grown thicker, billowing from between the trees, and I couldn't see her, but I could hear her ahead of me, her quick terrified breath, her feet against the rocky ground. I could hear the water now, too, drumming relentlessly along the ragged riverbed.

And then I heard her scream. A long sustained shriek that knifed through the whirling fog and pierced my heart.

I tore through the black brambles at the waterside, and she was lying there, facedown in the river, her long red skirt fluttering at her ankles like a pennant in the gray current, and I felt a sense of grief stronger than any I had ever felt. It was as though all the losses of a lifetime, all the failures, all the regrets for missed opportunities and for vanished friends and lovers, had melded together in one moment of overwhelming, infinite despair.

The river no longer drummed; sound had stopped. I fell to my knees beside her, the icy water piling up against my thigh, and I bent down and gently turned her over.

Her face was the face of Silvia Griego and bright red blood was spilling from the wicked wound at her temple. And as I knelt there holding her, immobile, paralyzed, her

eyes opened and she smiled up at me, a wide red trium-
phant smile.

I woke up, my skin oily with sweat, my heart slapping at
my chest. It took me a moment or two to realize where I
was. And even after I did, even after I understood that it
had all been a dream, I couldn't shake the sense of dread,
or the feeling of total, irredeemable loss.

I glanced at the clock. Two o'clock. Too late to call Rita.
Particularly to whimper about a bad dream. I turned on
the light, staggered out into the kitchen, poured myself a
drink, staggered back to bed. Lay there for a while wondering why on earth I did the kind of work I did.

It was a question I usually asked myself only on those
long nights when I sat stakeout in the Subaru, surrounded
by cellophane wrappers torn from 7-Eleven sandwiches,
and waiting for something, anything, to happen.

You sit there in the car and you look at the windows
along the street, some of them lit by the shifting flickering
blue light of a television, some of them bright with snugly
ordered living rooms or cozy pine-paneled dens; all of
them, it seems, opening onto a security, a protected
warmth, that you yourself have never known, not even in
memory. And you stare at those blank black walls and you
wish that, magically, you could turn them all into glass,
transparent, so you could see what really goes on in there,
the reality beyond the seeming.

And you ask yourself, why? Why the desire, why the
need, to poke and pry and peer into these other lives?

And the answer, simply, is that it's what you do, and
that you do it well. Maybe it's the only thing you do well.
Maybe it's the only thing you *can* do well.

You can't see inside the minds of other people. But if
you do this job well, you can discover what goes on inside
their lives, inside their houses. You can turn those shelter-

ing protective walls into walls of glass, and sometimes that amounts to the same thing.

I picked my book up off the floor and, for an hour or so, I followed Mario Balzic around the bars of Rocksburg, Pennsylvania. At last, around three-thirty, I was able to fall asleep again.

WHEN THE ALARM went off at seven o'clock on Thursday morning, I woke up feeling better than I had any right to feel. I'd been avoiding the thought of Griego's death, been keeping from my mind's eye the image of her lying, brutalized, in that bathtub. The night before last I'd used bourbon to help with the process. Yesterday I'd used movement. But the dream had brought the image back to me, more real even than I remembered it, and somehow, by making me confront it, had burned at least some of the horror away.

Psychology 101. Puttering about the bathroom, trying not to mistake the athlete's foot cream for the toothpaste, I wondered what a good analyst would make of the thing. Rita hadn't only been up on her feet, she'd been running. With me running after her. And talk about your sexual symbolism. Brambles by the waterside indeed.

Whatever the reason, I felt good. I felt lightened. I felt that Something Important would happen today.

I put on jeans, boots, a pale yellow oxford buttondown, a red V-neck sweater. Preppie Goes to the Rodeo.

Out in the kitchen, I took an English muffin and a couple of chorizos from the freezer. I zapped the muffin in the microwave for a minute, until it was thawed, then took it out, split it with a fork, and slipped the halves into the toaster, ready to go. I wrapped the chorizos in paper towels, thunked them onto a plate, opened up the microwave again, lay them inside, set the phaser on Kill and the timer on six minutes, and hit the button. I cracked three eggs into a bowl, went into the living room, and slid a Willie Nelson tape, *Always on my Mind*, into the stereo. I hit the play button and went back into the kitchen.

While Willie was singing about Do Right Women and Do Right Men, I turned the toaster on, turned the microwave off, rotated the chorizos, turned the microwave back on. Opened the refrigerator and got out butter, a jar of Scottish lemon curd, and a plastic container of apple cider that looked like sewage but tasted exactly like apple cider. Clearly, in this day and age, a flawed product. I poured myself a glass, carried it out into the kitchen, set it on the coffee table, and came back just as the muffins popped up in the toaster. Buttered them, spread them with lemon curd. The microwave chimed. I took out the chorizos.

Chorizos are Mexican sausages whose main ingredients are red dye number two, trinitroglycerin, and parts of the pig that even its mother wouldn't recognize. I sliced these two open, scraped the meat from the casings, which are made of the same material that goes into bullet-proof vests, and dumped the meat into the bowl with the eggs.

I slapped some butter into a frying pan, turned the gas up to max, waited until the butter bubbled up and began to scent the room, then dropped in the eggs and meat. Stirred quickly with a wooden spoon. After a minute, when the eggs had set, eased everything onto a plate, next to the English muffins. Grabbed a clean fork from the dish drainer beside the sink, carried the plate into the living room, set it on the coffee table, sat down. Willie was asking someone to Let It Be Him. I took a bite of breakfast. Perfect.

The doorbell rang.

At a quarter to eight?

When I was eating?

I got up, crossed the living room, opened the door. Derek Leighton stood outside, looking bigger and broader than I remembered him. Over a nicely tailored dark gray three-piece suit, he was wearing a fawn colored topcoat, open, that had to be either camel hair or cashmere. I would've bet cashmere. His hands in its pockets, he bobbed his head abruptly once and said, "Croft."

I bobbed my head back and said, "Leighton." I could keep that up as long as he could.

"I've only got a few minutes," he said. "I've got to get down to Albuquerque to catch a Dallas flight." He moved forward, inviting himself in.

I sighed. "Right," I said, backing away from the door. "Come in."

He stepped in and I shut the door. He glanced around the room, not quite managing to conceal his disdain. He noticed the breakfast plate and turned to me. "You're eating," he said.

"Yeah," I said. "I'm trying to quit, but now and then I backslide."

He frowned, tightening his dewlaps. "All right," he said. "We got off to a bad start the other day, Croft. I admit that. But I see no reason why both of us can't behave like adults today."

I knew that this was as close as men like Leighton ever came to an apology. I nodded to him. "Have a seat." I circled the coffee table and sat down myself.

Without taking off his coat, he hiked his trousers up a bit, just above the knees, and sat down in the chair that had held his wife's jacket and scarf last Sunday, when she was the one interrupting my meal. Maybe this was a conspiracy: the two of them trying to starve me to death. He crossed his legs, right ankle over left knee, and I saw that today's boots were ostrich, gun-metal blue. I didn't think they went all that well with the business suit, but he was headed for Dallas, after all, and down there they wear cowboy boots when they're doing the backstroke.

He waved grandly at my eggs and sausages. "Don't let me stop you eating."

In a way I felt sorry for the man. Even when he was trying to be pleasant, he came off like a finalist in the Asshole Olympics.

"Can I get you something?" I said. "Juice? Tea?"

He shook his head curtly. I said, "What can I do for you?" and took a bite of eggs. They had tasted better before Leighton showed up.

"You know, of course," he said, "about the death of Silvia Griego?"

I nodded, chewing a chunk of chorizo.

"My wife tells me that Silvia phoned her earlier this week. Apparently you'd spoken to Silvia about the necklace."

I nodded, drank some cider.

He said, "I wouldn't want to think that the necklace had anything to do with Silvia's death."

"Then don't."

He shook his head. "Silvia couldn't have been involved in something like that."

"Are you asking me or telling me?" I ate some more eggs.

He frowned again. He took a breath, his stomach swelling against the vest. "I'd like your assurance, Croft, that your investigation and Silvia's death are unrelated."

"I can't give you that."

"Now look here—"

Any second now he was going to start jabbing a finger at me again. I said, "I can't give it to you because I don't know. I don't know who killed Silvia Griego, and I don't know why."

He sat back with another frown, and took another deep breath. "Mr. Croft," he said. He was trying to be pleasant again, and the effort showed. "Mr. Croft, Silvia was one of my wife's closest friends. They've known each other since high school. And naturally Felice is...extremely upset about all this. She's afraid that somehow your questioning Silvia may've had something to do with this..." he searched for a word, found it, "tragedy. I explained to her that this was nonsense, that in all probability the person who killed her was some sneakthief, some burglar, that Silvia happened upon accidentally. But she's distraught, of course, and she won't really listen to reason."

"So you came over here," I said, "hoping that I could ease your wife's mind." Maybe he wasn't a complete loss after all.

He nodded. "She feels somehow responsible. She feels..." he shrugged unhappily, not very comfortable with the word, "guilty."

"She shouldn't," I said.

He nodded briskly. "Exactly what I told her. It was some sneakthief. Some drunken Mexican. And poor Silvia was in the wrong place at the wrong time."

I shook my head. "I don't think so."

He frowned. "But you said—"

"I said your wife shouldn't feel guilty. And she shouldn't. I don't think Silvia Griego even knew the necklace had been stolen. But she was involved in something, probably something illegal, and I think her involvement was somehow responsible for her death."

He shook his head again. "Impossible. My wife and I have known Silvia for over twenty years. There's no way she could've been involved in anything illegal."

I shrugged. "Okay. It's impossible." I took a bite of English muffin.

He crossed his arms over his chest and put his head back, atilt, the better to look down his nose at me. He said, "And just what was it, according to you, that Silvia was involved in?"

"I'm not sure." I drank some cider.

"But obviously you've got *some* idea. And dammit, Croft, I have a right to know what it is. I'm not just some bozo who wandered in off the street."

As far as I was concerned, that was exactly what he was. I picked up my fork, and discovered that I'd lost my appetite. I set it back down. "Look," I said. "Mr. Leighton." If he could make an effort, so could I. "I understand that you have a vested interest in this. It's your necklace, you're the one paying the finder's fee for Atco, and Silvia Griego was a friend of yours. I understand all that. But *you* have to understand that my only responsibility here, assuming I locate the necklace, is to return the thing to Atco. Anything else I might stumble into is my business, and it has to stay that way. If I find clear evidence of a felony, then by law I'm required to report it to the proper authorities. But I don't have to report anything else to anybody else. Are we clear on that?"

Still frowning, he said. "I've made some inquiries about you around town. People I know."

"Yeah?"

"The consensus seems to be that you're an arrogant bastard, but fundamentally honest."

I nodded. "I see it as a serious character flaw. The honesty, I mean."

"All right," he said, nodding as though he'd suddenly made a decision. "All right. I'll hire you. Personally. To investigate the death of Silvia Griego." He lifted his ankle from his knee, put both feet on the ground, and reached into his suitcoat pocket for a wallet. "What sort of retainer would make you happy?"

I shook my head. "It's an open case. The cops wouldn't let me near it. They tend to think they're better at murder investigations than anybody else, and they're usually right. Besides, I'm already working."

He tapped the wallet against the arm of the chair. "On a speculation contract. You said so yourself. I'm prepared to offer you cash. Up front."

"For what?"

"I told you. For investigating Silvia's death."

"Why?"

"Let's say I'm not happy with the way the police are handling this."

"The police haven't even begun to handle it yet."

"Silvia was a friend. I only want to make sure that whoever did this is brought to justice. You have contacts in the police department. You can keep me apprised of what they learn."

"Ah," I said.

He scowled at me. "And what is that supposed to mean?"

"Just for curiosity's sake," I said, "is your wife really upset about Griego's death? Or did you only come over here to see if I could find out whether the cops picked up the Polaroids?"

He opened his mouth and blinked at me. "Polaroids?" He might've been a successful contractor, but he would've made a lousy poker player.

I went around the corner, down the hall, into the bedroom, and took the photographs from the place where I'd hidden them. I shuffled through the stack, found the ones that showed either Leighton or his wife, or both, and put the others back. I carried the Leighton photographs back to the living room and flipped them into Leighton's lap. "They didn't," I said, and sat down.

He had clapped his knees together when I tossed the Polaroids at him, but one of the prints had fluttered past his legs to the floor. He bent down, picked it up, put it with the others. He sorted through them quickly, tapped the stack back into shape, and slipped it into his suit coat pocket. He opened his wallet and looked at me. "How much?"

The man was impossible.

I shook my head. "All I need from you are the answers to a couple of questions."

He stared at me for a moment. At last he said, "I want to make one thing clear to you, Croft. I'm not ashamed of what I do, and I'm not ashamed of who I am. I have a good marriage, a viable partnership, that's probably more stable then eighty percent of the relationships in the country."

I nodded. "Good for you."

"But I have my children to think of. If these had come out—" he tapped his left breast "—the children are the ones who would've suffered."

I nodded. Maybe he believed this. Maybe he had to. I didn't. I knew that in this town, a business like Leighton's could survive anything but ridicule.

"I won't ask you," he said, "how you got these. But I want you to know I'm grateful." He shot his wrist, glanced at his Rolex, looked up at me, and said, "What would you like to know?"

"Why'd you fire Frank Biddle?" I said.

# SIXTEEN

DEREK LEIGHTON crossed his legs again, frowned at me from the chair, and said, "I can't see how that's relevant. I had my reasons."

"I'm sure you did. But I'd like to know what they were."

A small, quick shake of his head. "They were personal."

"Look," I said. "You want that necklace back, am I right?"

"Of course I do. But I don't see that the two things are related."

"The police think they're related. What was the reason you gave them for firing Biddle?"

"I told them it was a personality conflict. It was no more their business than it is yours."

"Nolan, in Burglary, thinks that Biddle planned the robbery to spite you for firing him, and that Stacey Killebrew carried it out."

He nodded. "Sergeant Nolan apprised me of his theory at the time. I didn't think much of it then, and I don't think much of it now."

"Why not?"

"I had a long talk with Frank when I let him go. I also paid him a sizable cash settlement in lieu of notice. I don't believe he held a grudge, and I don't believe he'd steal the necklace in order to spite me."

"So why'd you fire him?"

He shook his head, as stubborn as a child.

"Look," I said. "I don't know how that necklace of yours figures in all this, but I'm convinced that Biddle had access to it last week. And this week, two people are dead. One of them, Biddle, was a man who worked for you. The other, Silvia Griego, was a friend of yours. That doesn't mean anything to you?"

Frowning again, he said, "I thought it was your contention that Silvia knew nothing the necklace."

"So far as I know," I said. "And that's the problem. I don't know very far. And all the people I talk to suddenly turn up dead. I'd like to avoid any more of that. Why'd you fire Biddle?"

He was looking down his nose at me again, as though he smelled something offensive in the room. Maybe my scrambled eggs were beginning to rot. "You're trying to browbeat me," he said. "Trying to make *me* feel responsible for these deaths."

I said, "What I'm trying to do is get your cooperation. Look at it this way. Whatever personal reasons you had for firing Biddle, they couldn't have been more personal than those Polaroids. And those Polaroids could be lying on some desk over at the police station right now." Not without Hector putting me through the wringer they couldn't; but Leighton didn't need to know that.

He crossed his arms over his chest, lips pursed in thought. I let him think. It would've been rude to interrupt a process that took so much energy. After a moment he said, "Do I have your word that this will remain confidential?"

I nodded. "You have my word."

He narrowed his eyes, doubtful. People who don't put much stock in their own word don't put much in the word of someone else.

I shrugged. "I'm honest, remember? Ask anyone."

"It had come to my attention," he said abruptly, "that Biddle was selling drugs."

"What do you mean 'come to your attention'? You knew he was selling drugs. Wasn't he supplying coke for those parties at Griego's house?"

He nodded. "That was one thing, providing it for us, for adults. We could weigh all the factors involved, the risks and benefits. We could make an intelligent decision."

Ignoring my doubts about that, I said, "Kevin. You found out he was dealing coke to Kevin."

He blinked, surprised, then frowned, as though irritated at my stealing his punch line.

"I talked to Kevin earlier this week," I said. "He told me Biddle had sold him coke."

Leighton nodded curtly. "I spoke with Frank. I told him I knew he was . . . distributing it in my home. I overheard him once when he made the arrangements. I told him I couldn't allow him to stay on there. As I said, I gave him a month's pay in lieu of notice. He understood the reasons for my decision, and I think he respected them."

I said, "You never told Kevin you knew about the coke."

"No."

I nodded.

He uncrossed his arms, putting them along the arms of the chair, and said, "I've talked about drugs before with both my children. Explained all the dangers involved, legal and otherwise. I'm a responsible adult, and I want my children to grow up to be responsible adults. And sometimes that means allowing them to make decisions for themselves." His voice was growing louder; an attack is the best defense. "What would I accomplish with a confrontation, besides anger and resentment? I did the proper thing, the only thing, and removed the threat from my house."

I nodded some more.

"And Frank," he said, "Frank understood my motives. He thought the cash settlement was more than generous."

"You liked Biddle," I said.

He shrugged. "He was a likeable sort. A picaresque character."

A guy sleeps with your wife and sells coke to your kid, he'd better be a picaresque character. I said, "How come you were so angry at him then, when he came by your house a week, two weeks ago?"

He frowned again. "Kevin told you that."

"Yeah."

"I wish you'd leave my family alone." It was said more with regret than anger.

"I'll be happy to, soon as I find the necklace. Why were you so angry?"

"The man had given me his word he wouldn't come back to my house."

Code of the West. Biddle had violated it.

"But I want to tell you one thing," he said. "I've never accepted Nolan's theory," he said, "that Frank was involved in the theft of the necklace."

"He had it last week. I'm sure of it."

"If he did, he got it from that Killebrew person."

"Did you ever meet Killebrew?"

"No."

"He never came around the house when Biddle was working there?"

"Not that I know of." According to Kevin, Killebrew had been by. Didn't mean Leighton was lying; maybe he just hadn't been there when Killebrew had.

"One more question," I said.

He glanced again at his watch, nodded. "One more. I've got a ten o'clock flight."

"When I talked to Allan Romero, at Atco, he said you were in Albuquerque the day of the burglary. Your wife called down there at eleven o'clock, but you didn't get back here until two. You flew up in a private plane. What took you so long?"

He pursed his lips, shrugged, and said, "I have a friend down there."

I nodded. "You mean a woman."

He got defensive again. "Felice knows about her. We don't have any secrets from each other."

I nodded.

"As I said, we've got a better relationship than most couples ever dream of."

I nodded again.

He eyed me for a moment, as though expecting me to contradict him, then he said, "In any event, it took John— I was staying with John and Emily Dupree—it took John a while to locate me. As soon as he did, I drove over to the airport. He met me there and flew me back to town." He looked at his watch. "Speaking of airports. If I don't leave now, I'll miss my plane." He stood up, held out his hand.

I stood, took it.

"I'm glad we had this little talk," he said.

AFTER LEIGHTON LEFT, I drove down to the police station to see Hector. I signed my second statement, the one I'd made after someone had shot at me and Felice Leighton, and then dictated a third, this one about my visit to Griego's gallery. Hector was right; I *had* been making more statements lately than a politician. And I'd made this last one about as honestly. There'd been no outright lies in it, at least none I could get called on; but there'd been a fair amount of equivocation. Had I seen the decedent at any time following the incident at her gallery? No. Telling myself that what I'd seen that night, lying in the bathtub, had not been Silvia Griego. And reminding myself that mentioning the visit to her house would only complicate life for everyone involved: the Leightons, Linda Sorenson, Peter Ricard. And, of course, me. It's a rare altruism that doesn't hide some self-concern.

Anyway, I had a few days grace before I actually had to sign it. Maybe I could get this whole thing cleared up before then, and I could tell Hector the truth.

Sure I could. I'd been making terrific progress so far.

After he turned off the tape recorder, Hector sat back away from his desk and linked his hands behind his neck, the light gray tattersall shirt tautening against his biceps. "I wish you'd tell me, Josh, who gave you the information about Biddle and Griego."

"Sorry, Hector. But if it helps your conscience any, it was just someone who happened to see them together."

"We got confirmation this morning," he said, "from the girl who works in Griego's gallery. She says they were a number, off and on, for three or four years. She didn't mention it yesterday, she says, because they hadn't seen each other for a long time, and she didn't think it was important."

"And you didn't ask her because you didn't know that Biddle and Griego were an item."

He nodded. "She also says you talked to her last night."

"Yeah. I was out and about last night, taking in the culture and art that Santa Fe offers us all. She tell you that Griego knew Killebrew?"

"She said he made a delivery to the gallery, a couple months ago."

"Same thing she told me. You talked to Killebrew?"

"Not yet. He's not at his apartment, and he hasn't been hanging around that garage he owns over on Cerillos. No one's seen him for two or three days."

"You figure him for Griego? You think the two killings are related?"

He nodded glumly. "I got two dead people in less than a week, and it turns out they both knew each other. Yeah, Sherlock, I'd have to say I think they're related."

"Different M.O.," I pointed out.

He shrugged. "I'd bet that Stacey's capable of a little variety now and then."

"If it actually was Stacey. And where's the motive? I don't think that Griego knew anything about the necklace."

He shrugged. "You're the one has to worry about the necklace. Maybe the necklace doesn't have anything to do with this. Maybe Biddle got killed for something else."

"I've been told that the thing hasn't been fenced."

"Oh yeah? And who was it, exactly, told you that?"

"A reliable source."

He snorted. He was still good at snorting, and this was one of his better efforts. "These sources of yours, they're so reliable, how come they don't have any names?"

"They're like the people who donate anonymously to the United Way. They're self-effacing."

He snorted again.

I said, "You find anything at her house?"

He shook his head. "Nothing to let us know who killed her. And nothing connecting her to Killebrew. There were some financial records in a strongbox, hidden in her closet. She was working some kind of tax fiddle, looks like."

"What kind of tax fiddle?"

He shrugged. "Don't know yet. The Fraud people are on it now, and the I.R.S. is sending someone up from Albuquerque to look over the stuff."

I nodded. "Good. They're a great group, the I.R.S. Probably clear the whole thing right up for you."

"Yeah. Maybe in our lifetime, too." He unclasped his hands and leaned forward, stroked his mustache with finger and thumb. "You're not holding anything back on me, are you, Josh?"

"After all we've meant to each other?"

"I'm giving you a lot of rope here, and I'd hate to see you hang yourself with it."

"So would I, Hector."

He nodded. "You find anything more about Griego, you let me know."

"I'll do that."

"And give my regards to Rita."

DOWN THE HALL, in Burglary, Sergeant Nolan was out, but I knew the uniformed cop manning the desk, Larry Baca, and after a call to Hector for approval, he used the computer to pull up the reports on the Killebrew burglaries.

There had been six of them, three art galleries and three private homes. As Nolan had told me, the phone wires had been cut in each case. The wires to the exterior siren had been bypassed at all three galleries, but not at the two houses which'd had sirens, the Garcias' and the Hammonds'.

I asked Baca if there had been any other burglaries since Killebrew left prison that matched his M.O. He said there'd been one possible—phone wires cut at a burglary out in La Tierra, an expensive subdivision on the west side—but that Killebrew had apparently been out of town when it occurred. Which, he said, had very seriously pissed off Sergeant Nolan, who'd been trying to get Killebrew back in jail since the day he got out.

I copied the reports into my notebook, then went across the street to the Public Library and called Rita. Maria answered and told me that Rita was in the pool. I said I'd call back later. I checked the phone book for John Lucero. He was listed, and I called the number. No answer.

LUCERO LIVED ON Camino Don Miguel, a dirt road on the east side of town. The yard was hedged in and the house was hidden, which suited my purposes just fine. I drove the Subaru about seventy-five yards past the driveway and parked it. I didn't know how long I'd be in there, and if Lucero or anyone else came along while I was occupied, I didn't want him blocking my way. Or getting my license number.

I walked back to the house, a clipboard tucked under my arm. The clipboard was supposed to make me invisible—anybody carrying one is clearly on the up-and-up. But there was no one fussing around in the yards or peering from the windows, and my cunning, as usual, went unnoticed.

At the entrance to the driveway, I checked Lucero's mailbox. Empty. Which meant that someone was picking up the mail, or that he wasn't getting any. But this was an election year, and political circulars were flooding the post office. I threw away at least three or four of the things every week.

I crunched up the gravel driveway. The air was warm and the smell of fresh-cut grass ran through it like fine silver wires. But the smell wasn't coming from Lucero's grass; his lawn was rocky and untended, overgrown with weeds. The house was a single story weather-beaten adobe, limp lilac bushes standing forlornly on either side of the entrance. I knocked on the front door. John Lucero didn't open it, hand me a diamond necklace, and tell me who had killed Frank Biddle and Silvia Griego. No one opened it.

I tried the handle. Locked. With a Medeco lock, a nasty piece of hardware to pick. There are people who can do it, but I'm not one of them. I went around to the back.

The back porch was screened in. The metal latch on the rickety wooden door was no match for my credit card, and neither was the slam-lock bolt on the door to the house. I've seen it before. People invest good money in a heavy-duty lock for the main entrance, and they ignore the rear. Hoping, apparently, that thieves will do the same. Or maybe there's a chain lock, and they figure that's enough, and, naturally, they forget to use it.

I was in the kitchen, and there was a chain lock; and, obviously, Lucero had forgotten to use it. Not a real careful guy, it seemed.

He was certainly a whole lot less finicky about housekeeping than Silvia Griego had been. He was one of those people who waited till all the dishes and silverware in the house are in the sink, dirty, before deciding to wash them. A decision that, in this particular cycle, hadn't yet been reached. The counters were littered with empty cans, torn wrappers, and discarded TV dinner cartons, and the floor beside the single brown paper garbage bag was strewn with still more junk. Which meant he probably lived alone; two people would be unlikely to share the same appreciation for squalor.

I started looking in there. Fifteen minutes later, hidden back toward the corner on the top shelf in one of the cabinets, I found a round red metal fruitcake tin. I opened it. The fruitcake had been replaced by a neat pile of hundred dollar bills. Forty-two of them. Four thousand, two hundred dollars. I put the bills back in the can, put the can back on the shelf.

I moved through the house. None of the other rooms were any neater than the kitchen. There was a living room, a bedroom, and a second bedroom that was being used as a studio. Smell of cut wood in the studio, and the sharp odor of turpentine, then two identical kachinas, unpainted, standing atop a stained drafting table covered with carving knives and paint brushes.

Now that I'd found his stash, I wasn't sure what I was looking for, and didn't know if I'd recognize it if I found it. Whatever it was, I didn't. Not in the studio, not in the bedroom.

In the living room, a phone answering machine sat on one of the end tables. I rewound the tape and played it back.

The first voice was a woman's. *"John. We've got to talk. Call me."* A click and then a dial tone.

I rewound it, played it once more to make sure.

It was Silvia Griego, and there was an urgency in her tone that might have been fear.

I also recognized the next voice on the tape, the flat west Texas accent, the lack of emphasis in the words that somehow made them sound more threatening. Only one sentence. *"Just keep your mouth shut and stay outta sight."*

Killebrew.

The next message was a woman, her voice unfamiliar and brittle with anger: *"Thanks a lot, Johnny. I waited there for an hour. Do me a favor and go fuck yourself."*

The last message was the same voice, the anger gone, a pleading tone taking its place: *"Johnny, this is Bev again. Call me when you get a chance?"*

The last three messages on the tape were empty, each only a click and a dial tone as someone hung up. Bev, still trying to locate Lucero?

All right. Assume that the message from Griego came on the day I'd talked to her, Tuesday, two days ago. That meant that the next message, from Killebrew, could've come that night. After he'd killed her?

Killebrew tells Lucero to lie low. And Lucero does, even missing his date with Bev, whoever she is.

It fit, but only the assumption that Griego's call had come in on Tuesday. For all I knew, it could've been there on the tape, waiting, for a week.

I went back to searching.

Finally, under the sofa and pushed back all the way to the wall, I found a large blue-and-yellow beach towel, folded into a long flat rectangle. I tugged it out and opened it up.

Inside were a pair of wings. Bird wings.

They were big. I fanned them open, side by side. The feathers were dark brown streaked with stripes of lighter brown. The undersides were a still lighter brown, with stripes of creamy white. The longest feathers, at the wing-tip, were over two feet long. The wings had apparently come from the same bird, which meant that the thing had possessed a wingspread of over four feet. An eagle?

Was this what Montoya had meant up in Las Mujeres? Birds of a feather?

# SEVENTEEN

"YOU WANNA KNOW about eagle feathers, huh?" Winnifred Gail was in her mid-fifties, a big woman maybe six feet tall who needed that height to carry her weight, which had to be at least two hundred and fifty pounds. She was sitting back in her office chair, behind an eight-foot-wide slab of four-inch glass that served as her desk, and she was wearing a bright yellow dress printed with big bright red carnations. Her lipstick was the same color as the carnations, and her hair, piled up in a 1940's bouffant, was the color of steamed carrots. The one thing that kept her from looking like a cartoon was the intelligence, shrewd and hard, that glinted in her small eyes.

I nodded to her. "Rita said she'd call you."

"Oh she did, she did. Talked to her a little over an hour ago." She nodded, eyeing me. There was the hint of prairie in her voice, Oklahoma or Texas. "So you're the Croft fella works with her," she said.

I nodded.

"Heard a lot about you," she said. "You carryin' a torch for Rita, like they say?"

"We work together."

She barked at me. *Arf, arf, arf,* like Little Orphan Annie's Sandy. It took me a moment to realize that she was laughing. "I like that," she said. "No denials, right? And no admissions neither. Slippery, but honest." She nodded approval. "We'll get along, Croft. Just what is it you wanna know about eagle feathers?"

"First of all," I said, "is possession of them illegal?"

"Depends," she said. "Depends on who you are. If you're an Indian, a Native American with your name on the census polls, and you got a warehouse full of the things, the Fish and Wildlife people might stew about it some, but there isn't a whole lot they'd be able to do. See, you could find yourself maybe eighteen thousand reasons why you needed those things for religious reasons, and Fish and Wildlife, they know that the courts all say you got a right to practice your religion, even if it uses raptor feathers."

"Raptor feathers?" I said.

"Raptors, birds of prey. Eagles, hawks, owls, vultures. They're all protected, see, by the federal government. Most of them since nineteen-eighteen, when the Migratory Wildlife Treaty Act went into law. The Indians are allowed to own the feathers, but they can't sell 'em, and even the Indians aren't allowed to kill the birds."

"If they can't kill the birds, then how do they get the feathers?"

She grinned. "There's the rub, huh? Tell you a story. I was on a buying trip once, up to Chinle on the Navajo reservation, and this ol' boy, frenna mine for years, comes up to me with an eagle claw, right? 'Bout so big, size of my hand, ugly as sin but it had some nice silver work on it, he's good with silver. I say to him, 'Harold, you know damn well I put that in my gallery, the Federales'll be all over me like warts on a horny toad, and besides, where'd an ole fart like you get that sucker anyway?' He tells me, this is with a straight face now, he tells me he was just walkin' out along the hills and this big ol' eagle keels over out of the sky and plops down at his feet." She barked. "Tells me it was probably sick." She barked again.

I smiled. "So an Indian," I said, "is allowed to own the feathers. What about someone who isn't an Indian?"

"Then," she said, "Fish and Wildlife can bust your ass good. They think you're selling the things, you're lookin' at a five thousand dollar fine and five years in the pokey."

"The eagle feathers," I said. "They were once used in kachinas."

"Right," she nodded. "You still see some of the old ones hangin' around, eagle feathers all over. Worth a pretty penny. And legal, too, long as they're pre-nineteen-eighteen. But you gotta have *certification*, see, something that proves the kachina is old enough. Last year, frenna mine on the Plaza, 'nother dealer, he had one in his window, and I *know* the damn thing was a hunnerd years old if it was a day, and Fish and Wildlife came and carted it off anyway. Confiscated the thing, just like that." She shrugged her heavy shoulders. "Guy didn't have any proof."

"Would it be illegal for an Indian to sell a kachina made with eagle feathers, one that wasn't certified?"

"Sure would. Get the same penalty as a white guy."

"You buy all your kachinas, the ones in your gallery, directly from the Indians?"

She nodded. "For thirty years now."

"Have any of them ever offered you kachinas, new ones, that had eagle feathers?"

"When I started up, sure they did. And ever so often one of the ol' guys like Harold tries to sniff me out, but that's a game with 'em now, mostly. They all know I wouldn't touch the things."

"Have you heard of any dealers here in town who might be selling eagle feather kachinas?"

Her eyes narrowed, nearly disappearing between folds of skin. "Everyone in town knows the score. Don't make any sense to sell something for a thousand bucks that'll cost you five thousand in fines and maybe some time in the pen.''

"But what about overseas sales? Wouldn't it be possible for a dealer to sell eagle feather kachinas somewhere overseas—to Germany, let's say—without much risk?"

"You know," she said, her eyes still narrowed. "I'm startin' to get kind of a weird feeling about all this. Couple days ago Silvia Griego dies, and I know for a fact that Silvia's a heavy dealer to Germany, probably the heaviest in town. And suddenly you show up here asking questions about dealing kachinas to Germany."

"Would it be possible?"

"Sure it would. Even if the things are checked at customs here in the States, no one's gonna know the difference. A feather's a feather, right? And once they're in Germany, Fish and Wildlife can't do a whole hell of a lot about 'em.''

"The eagle feathers make the kachinas more valuable over there?"

"'Course they do. More authentic, right? You think the kachinas the Indians use on reservation land, the Hopis and the Pueblos, you think those suckers are put together with dyed goose feathers? Or turkey feathers? And the Krauts, see, they're ape-shit about Indian stuff. Only it's gotta be *authentic*, know what I mean?"

"What do you think of John Lucero's work?"

Eyes narrowed again, she said, "You wanna tell me what this is all about?"

"Would it surprise you if I told you that I think Silvia Griego was dealing eagle feather kachinas to Germany?"

She looked at me for a moment. At last she said. "Surprise me? No. I gotta admit it wouldn't surprise me much. Depress me some, maybe. I liked Silvia." She frowned. "Well, no, that's puttin' it too strong. You gotta respect somebody, I guess, before you can like her. I felt sorry for her, is what it was, probably. She was a widow, see. Husband died ten years ago. She bought the gallery with the insurance money and she's been runnin' hard ever since, tryin' to prove something. And the way she proved it, see, was with sex and money. Now you gotta figure sex and money, they're at the bottom of most'a what folks do, right? And Lord knows I don't mind makin' a buck or two myself, or slippin' into the sack for a quickie now and then—'' grinning, she winked at me ''—we could talk about that a little later, if you got the time—but with Silvia, both of 'em had become almost like obsessions. New men and more money. New kicks, new tricks. And more money.''

"Would John Lucero make kachinas using eagle feathers?"

"The thing you gotta remember here, about Johnny Lucero, is that he's good. I mean he's real good. *Too* good."

"How so?"

"Well now, most of the artists who do kachinas they're gonna sell, they leave stuff out. Little details, you know? Maybe some paint here and there, or some beadwork. Nothing major, nothing an Anglo buyer might spot. But always *something*, you get me? And makes sense, too, you think about it. I mean, these things are *religious*, they represent the important spirits, and they're *connected*, see, to the spirits they represent. And the more accurate the image is, the stronger the connection is. So no Indian's gonna want a real accurate image of one of the spirits sitting on some Anglo's coffee table, right next to the empty beer bottles. It's like blasphemy, right?"

"And you're saying that Lucero's kachinas are too authentic."

She nodded briskly. "Too authentic, right. Lot of the other artists hereabouts, they don't care much for Johnny. What it is, they think he's selling out their religion. Some people, seems to me, are born with some important parts missing, and Johnny's one of 'em."

"So Lucero is capable of making the kachinas with eagle feathers."

She frowned at me. "Didn't I just get through sayin' that?"

"What would an eagle feather kachina be worth in Germany?"

"Depends on the quality. A good piece, one of Johnny's, could bring in maybe five thousand."

I frowned at her.

"'Smatter?" she said. "Sound like too much? You gotta remember, like I said, those Krauts go bonkers over this stuff."

"No," I said. "It sounds like too little. How long do you think it takes Lucero to make one of these things?"

She shrugged. "Start to finish, carving the wood, painting it, decorating it, embroidering the cloth, maybe a month."

"So in four years, if he made only the illegal kachinas, he could put out forty-eight of them. At five thousand a piece, that comes to—" I looked away, calculating.

"Two hunnerd and forty thousand," she said immediately.

I nodded. "Right. So let's suppose that Silvia Griego had some money tucked away in a Swiss account. And let's suppose that it was over four hundred thousand dollars."

She eyed me. "We're talkin' hypothetical here, huh?"

"Right. Now if she had it hidden away, then the money probably came from illicit sales—why hide it otherwise? But let's say she's been putting it into the account for a period of five years. Even if Lucero worked faster than you say he does, he couldn't have put out enough kachinas to bring in that much cash. And besides, in order to show where his income was coming from, he had to make legitimate sales, too. Legitimate kachinas. And I know he was, because I've seen them. So where did the extra money come from?''

Winnifred Gail picked up a ball-point pen, stared down at it, clicked it a few times. "Over four hundred thousand, huh?"

"Four hundred and twenty. Hypothetically."

Frowning, still looking down at the pen, she shook her head sadly. "Poor Silvia."

"What do you mean?"

She looked up at me, took a deep breath, and said, "Well, I shouldn't be sayin' this, probably, no proof of anything, but if Silvia was selling contraband kachinas, she coulda been selling other kinds of contraband, too."

"Like what?"

"Artifacts. Ceremonials."

"How would they be contraband? All the dealers sold those, I thought."

"They'd be contraband if they were robbed from graves on federal land, and the Indian reservations are all on federal land. And in the past ten, fifteen years, people been robbing graves on the reservations like crazy. See, what happened is, back in nineteen seventy-one the Parke-Bernet Galleries in New York, they held the first big auction of American Indian art ever, and they got prices on some of the stuff, big money, that knocked the socks off a lotta people. Now once you got a market that's ready for goods, you're gonna find people who'll supply the goods, and a lot of them aren't gonna care where they get 'em."

"Looters."

"Looters, yeah. Things got so bad in the seventies, the guv'mint passed the Archeological Resource Protection Act in seventy-nine. Didn't stop 'em, though. Prices keep going up—especially in Germany, like I say. Problem is, you got three agencies involved—National Park Service, Bureau of Land Management, and the Forest Service—but all three of them put together don't have enough people to keep these scumbags away from ceremonial gravesites. Too much area for them to cover. Too much money for the scumbags to make."

"What kind of money?"

"Guy I know at B.L.M. figures twenty-five million a year in black-market sales."

I must've looked surprised, because she smiled sadly and said. "Yeah. Lotta people can't believe it. You talk about gravesites and they figure you're talkin' arrowheads, maybe a feather or two. Well listen, last year in Munich, a single Hopi ceremonial basket went for a hunnerd and fifty thousand. One single solitary basket. And the scumbags don't stick to baskets and bowls, neither. The Anasazi—that's the Navajo name for the Old Ones, the Indians who lived here before the Navajo and the Hopi showed up—they used to mummify their dead. Men, women, children. What the scumbags are doin' is diggin' up the mummies of the dead children, and then castin' 'em in acrylic blocks. Just the right size, see, for a mantelpiece. Look real good next to that lamp shade from Buchenwald. Real conversation piece. Germans are paying five to ten grand for one. I tell you, on a scale of ethics or morals, these guys, these looters, are a couple steps below maggot puke."

"What'd be the most valuable kind of contraband that Griego might've had access to?"

"Be your Hopi and Anasazi stuff. Krauts like 'em both."

"What would she need to get it?"

"All she'd need," she said, "would be someone who knew where the stuff was, which'd be one of the Hopis, naturally, and then a couple of strong backs to dig it up."

A couple of strong backs. Killebrew and Biddle?

"John Lucero," I said. "He's Hopi."

She nodded. "Sure is."

AFTER I LEFT Winnifred Gail's gallery on West San Francisco street, I drove over to the house of Carla Chavez, Biddle's girlfriend. She was home, and by now she'd gotten used to answering my questions. Yes, she said, when Frank had gone on hunting trips, Stacey Killebrew had gone along. Just the two of them? Yes. Had they ever actually bagged any deer? No. And where, exactly, had they gone hunting? Arizona. Where in Arizona? She wasn't sure, she said, but she knew that it was somewhere on the Navajo Reservation.

The Hopi Reservation is on the Navajo Reservation.

When was the last time Biddle had gone hunting? Last year, in the spring. Did Killebrew go with him? Yes.

I gave her another twenty before I left.

Since it seemed to be a day for tying up loose ends, when I got back to my office I called Peter Ricard at his. The secretary put me through.

Peter sounded tired, and I told him so.

"Yeah," he said. "A tough night. Some married lady I barely know showed up on my doorstep at two in the morning and told me she wanted to have an affair."

"Your reputation precedes you, Peter."

"I sat her down and explained to her, very rationally, that I don't do married ladies. There are too many problems, moral, legal, and logistical. So she took off her blouse."

"Doesn't sound like you were very persuasive."

"I'm only human." He laughed. "The lady wasn't Felice Leighton, was it?"

"Felice? Jesus, no. Why Felice?"

"It's just that I remember you telling me you'd never been involved with Felice. And recently, I've been hearing about a party at Silvia Griego's."

There was a moment's pause. "Oh yeah?"

"I saw a couple of interesting Polaroids. You photograph well, Peter."

He laughed. "Yeah, well, I don't really count that, Josh."

"Count it? Like on a score card?"

"Yeah, right. It was a group endeavor. Everyone was a little bit nuts. Sex and drugs and rock 'n' roll. You know how those things work, Josh."

I said nothing.

"She was a helluva girl, Silvia," he said, the words coming out a shade too quickly. "A bitch, isn't it, her dying like that. Is that what you're calling about?"

"No. Just trying to get the stories straight."

"Well, glad to help. Listen, Josh, I've gotta run. You going to the pool today?"

"Probably."

"I'll be over there at five. How about some racquetball?"

"I don't think so, Peter. Not today."

"Maybe next week."

"Maybe," I said, but I didn't think I'd be playing racquetball with Peter next week either.

IT WAS DARK that night by seven-thirty, and by eight o'clock I was sitting in John Lucero's unlit living room.

The pile of hundreds was still in the fruitcake tin in the kitchen; I'd checked with a pencil flash when I came in.

I knew that the money gave me no guarantee that Lucero would be back, tonight or any other night. He could have more cash stashed in a safe-deposit box somewhere. If he had a bank card, he could use one of the automatic teller machines scattered around town. But people who hide money away for emergencies tend to use it in emergencies, and, as I'd told Rita, it seemed to me that Lucero was smack in the middle of one.

It seemed to me, I'd told her, that Lucero had taken Killebrew's advice, or orders, and gone to ground. If he had, he wouldn't want to be seen at all. Which meant the banks, and even the automatic tellers, were out.

Rita hadn't been over-enthusiastic about my plan. "If you're right about him hiding," she said, "he's been doing it for a day or two now. He's going to be jumpy."

"I won't give him a chance to jump."

"Call me," she said. "On the hour. Let the phone ring three times. I won't answer it. But if I don't hear from you, I'll call Hector and ask him to send in the troops."

"Yes, dear."

So I called her at eight, let the phone ring three times, and hung up. I called her again at nine, and at ten and eleven and twelve. In between calls I just sat there. Sometimes I thought about Silvia Griego. Sometimes I thought about John Lucero, and wondered whether anything would've been different if I'd talked to him earlier this week. Phil, at the Lone Star, had told me he was a friend of Killebrew's—I could've questioned him then about the necklace. And maybe Griego would still be alive.

And then again, maybe she wouldn't.

At ten minutes after twelve, he showed up at the front door.

HE MOVED VERY WELL. I didn't notice anything, not a sound, until I heard the key slip into the lock. I picked the gun up from my lap with my right hand and reached with my left for the switch to the lamp beside me, on the end table.

He came in, pushing the door quietly shut behind him, then padding silently across the carpet. For a moment he was silhouetted against the pale moonlight spilling into the room from the front window. I pushed the light switch and the room lit up.

He wheeled about, his long hair flying, his face twisted with fear.

"Take it easy, John," I told him.

Still in a crouch, ready to spring, he glanced quickly around the room as though expecting someone else to be there. Killebrew, maybe. He looked as Phil had described him, tall and slender, with loose black hair that reached nearly to his waist. A red cotton windbreaker, a plaid flannel shirt, faded jeans, cowboy boots.

"Who are you?" he demanded.

"My name is Croft. I'm an investigator. Sit down."

His glance flicked toward the hallway to the kitchen, and I knew that he was measuring the distance, calculating the time it would take.

I said, "No way, John. I could put a bullet in your leg before you got halfway there." Assuming I could actually hit the leg.

He straightened up and glared at me. Ready to brazen it out. "What the fuck you doin' here?"

"I want some information. Sit down and we'll talk."

His eyes narrowed. "This is *my* house, man. You don't fuckin' tell me what to do in my own fuckin' house."

I thumbed back the hammer of the .38.

"Yeah?" he sneered. "You gonna shoot me, man? The neighbors hear that, cops'll be all over the place."

I pulled the trigger. The slug went nowhere near him—I was aiming at the chair to his right—but the gun made a very satisfying boom in the enclosed space of the living room. Yet from the street, from the houses nearby, the shot probably wasn't even audible.

Lucero had jumped, his eyes wide. "Jesus *Christ*!" he shouted. "You're fuckin' *crazy*!"

"Sit down, John." My ears were still ringing, my voice sounded muffled.

He swallowed, moved to the chair, looked at the small round hole in the upholstery. "Jesus Christ, man."

"Sit down," I said.

He sat down, hands between his thighs, eyes on my gun.

"Here's how it's going to work," I said. "First I'll tell you what I know. And then you'll tell me what you know. A fair trade. Got it?"

He nodded, looking up from the gun. "Sure. Sure, man. Whatever."

"All right. First off, I know that you were using eagle feathers to make kachinas for Silvia Griego."

"Hey, that's bullshit, man. I never—"

"It's not your turn, John."

"I never used no fuckin' eagle feathers, man."

"Shut up and listen. I know that you helped Stacey Killebrew and Frank Biddle move illegal ceremonials from the Hopi reservation. I know they brought them to Silvia Griego."

He tried to frown, but it didn't quite come off. "I don't know what you're talkin' about."

"I know that Griego sold the stuff to Leibman and Sons, in Munich. The same people who bought your kachinas."

"Hey, man—"

"Now here's the situation, John. The cops've got Griego's financial records. Everything. They know about the sales to Liebman and Sons. They know about the numbered account in Switzerland. The I.R.S. is already involved, and pretty soon the rest of the Feds will be, too. The B.L.M., the Parks Service, Fish and Game, everybody, including the F.B.I. All someone has to do, all anyone has to do, is locate one of your kachinas over in Germany, just one of them, John, and you're looking at five years in a federal penitentiary. That'll give you plenty of time to talk to the feds about moving contraband goods off the Hopi Reservation. And plenty of time to talk to the I.R.S. about the four grand you've got stashed in the kitchen. And plenty of time to talk to the local cops about being an accessory to the murder of Silvia Griego."

He leaned quickly forward, nearly coming out of the chair. "Jesus Christ, man, I didn't have anything to do with that!"

"But you know who did."

He sat back, lips compressed, eyes narrowed and wary.

"The only way out of this, John, that I can see, is your turning state's evidence. You give yourself up, you give what you know. I'm no lawyer, but I'd guess you'd get a suspended sentence on the kachinas. The other charges would probably be dropped."

He nodded. "Yeah, man, sure. And that'll do me a lot of good if I'm dead."

"Killebrew," I said.

"Hey, man, he's crazy. I mean he's fuckin' nuts. Why d'you think I'm sneakin' into my own house like this? And you think I *like* hiding out in my car all day?"

"You can put Killebrew away," I told him.

"Yeah, sure. And then he gets out on bail and he comes by one night and he wastes me." He pointed his finger like a gun. *"Bang!"*

"The cops'll protect you. And if they won't, the Feds will."

He put his arms along the arm of the chair and shook his head as though trying to clear it. "Shit, man."

"Did Killebrew kill Silvia Griego?"

He put his head back against the chair and rolled it slowly, left to right. *"Shit,"* he said, the word protracted into a single long sorrowful sigh.

"Did he?"

Looking up at the ceiling, he took a deep ragged breath. He let it slowly out. "Yeah," he said, and his voice was flat, empty, emotionless. "He killed her."

"Tell me about it."

He did. It took him a while, but by one o'clock I had everything he knew. There were still some questions left unanswered, but I was convinced that Lucero didn't know any more than he'd told me.

Lucero was sitting slumped in the chair, drained and pale.

I stood up and holstered the gun. "Come on, John," I said. "Let's go talk to the cops."

Wearily, he pushed himself up out of the chair. He stood for a minute, looking a little shaky on his feet.

I blame myself for what happened. I knew, after all, that Killebrew was roaming around somewhere, and certainly I knew that he was capable of killing. Less than a week ago someone had shot at me through a window, and here I was, standing in another brightly lit room, in front of another window, with the only person who could tie Killebrew to Griego's death.

Simultaneously, or so it seemed, the window burst apart and John Lucero shrieked, spinning off to the right as blood sprayed through the air.

# EIGHTEEN

I WENT FOR THE LAMP first, grabbing it with my left hand and wrenching it off the end table as I dove for the floor. The wire tautened, the plug popped from the outlet, the room went abruptly dark. I heard a loud flat crack come from outside and—once again, the two things seemed to happen simultaneously—a dull smack as the slug hammered into the floor. My hands were against the carpet now and I felt the vibration as it hit. It sounded like a hunting rifle out there, a big one.

I got up onto my knees, tugged out the .38 and fired blindly out the window, not really hoping to hit anything, but trying to give Killebrew something to think about. Then I tucked in my shoulder and rolled across the room, toward where Lucero had gone down. A split second later, another slug ploughed into the floor, exactly where I'd been kneeling.

My eyes hadn't adjusted yet to the darkness, and the muzzle flash of the revolver had left a bright green afterimage. I had to feel around with my hands, slapping at the carpet before I found Lucero's leg.

Two more loud cracks from outside, two more slugs slamming into the floor. Lying on his back, Lucero was breathing, but he was out cold. Shock; the energy expended on impact by the slug from a hunting cartridge is vicious. His right arm flopped loosely inside the windbreaker and the material was sopping wet. The bone had been shattered, an artery hit.

I ripped off my belt, wrapped it around his arm above the wound, tied it. Tourniquets are tricky, tie them too tightly or leave them on too long and you kill body tissues. But at the moment the most important thing was stopping that blood.

Another slug pounded into the floor, only a few feet away. How much longer could he keep that up before someone called the cops? I glanced at my watch. Ten after one. I hadn't checked in with Rita. Had she phoned for help?

I slipped the revolver into the holster and wrapped my arms around Lucero's back. He groaned. Awkwardly, shuffling along on my knees, I tugged him across the carpet, toward the hallway to the kitchen, out of the line of fire.

When I thought he was safe, I moved into a squat, my back against the wall. I took out the gun again and cocked it. I didn't think he'd rush the house—he knew I was armed, and here inside, a handgun had the advantage over a rifle—but I was ready for him if he tried.

And then I heard the sirens. Faint at first, and faraway, they grew louder and more strident as I listened. I think it was the sweetest sound I've ever heard.

"GRIEGO WAS COMING APART," I said. "Even before Biddle was killed. You remember that Valium prescription I found in her medicine chest?"

Rita nodded. We were sitting out on her patio by the balustrade and the day was beautiful and warm, taut blue polished sky overhead, sunlight spilling down the hills around us and splashing across the town beneath. I had condescended to accept a glass of lemonade; the temperature was in the upper seventies. It was Friday, one week to the day since Frank Biddle had come to my office.

Rita said, "How did it all start?" She was wearing a pale yellow blouse and a white skirt. At her neck a thin gold chain held a small golden cross that caught the light and sparkled just below the hollow of her throat.

"Griego and Lucero started selling the eagle feather kachinas to Germany six years ago. They made a couple thousand dollars more on each kachina than they would've made if the kachinas hadn't been made with the eagle feathers."

"Not a lot of money," Rita said, "to risk a term in jail."

"Neither one of them saw it as much of a risk. Griego knew the people at Liebman and Sons, knew they'd take all the illegal kachinas she could send them. And like Winnifred Gail said, even if the packages had been opened at Customs, no one there would be able to tell whether the feathers were eagle or turkey or Red Red Robin. And, remember, Griego was apparently a little bit money crazy."

"Whose idea was it to move up from kachinas to sell the contraband artifacts?"

"Lucero says it was Biddle's. According to him, Griego told Biddle four years ago about the eagle feather deal, told him about the European market for Indian art. According to Lucero, Biddle pointed out to Griego that she could make even more money if she didn't limit herself to kachinas. She already had herself a willing dealer who was depositing her funds in a Swiss account. And she already had a Hopi hanging around, Lucero, who could help them locate the stuff."

"And Lucero went along with it."

"He says he didn't have any choice. He said that Biddle told him—not really threatening, just putting out hints here and there—that Lucero was already too involved in the sale of contraband to turn down the idea."

"You think that's true?"

"That Lucero was coerced?"

She nodded.

"Hard to tell. Maybe. But like Winnifred Gail says, he's one of those people who've got important parts missing."

"There's a lot of that going around," Rita said.

"And from what she tells me, by doing the kind of kachinas he did, he was already selling out his religion and his people. Helping Biddle locate a couple of old bowls maybe didn't seem like all that big a deal. The whole thing may even have been his idea. Maybe he went to Griego with it, and she brought in Biddle. Biddle and Griego aren't around to tell their side."

Rita sipped at her lemonade. "When did Biddle bring in Killebrew?"

"From the start. According to Lucero, Biddle saw it all as a lark, and he wanted Killebrew to share the fun. They'd known each other for years, liked the same things—according to Lucero, young girls, old whiskey, and fast times. Lucero says Griego never really paid them all that much, a couple of thousand apiece for each shipment they brought in. That makes sense. Griego wouldn't pay them any more than she had to, and Biddle would've probably done it for free. He was getting a chance to play Cowboys and Indians."

"And then Killebrew was arrested on the burglary charge here in town. That was the eighteen months when there were only two deposits to the account in Berne."

I nodded. "Yeah. Killebrew's arrest slowed the operation down some. Lucero was willing to spot the stuff for Biddle, tell him where the graves were located and how to get to them, but he refused to go along on the trips. People knew him there, and he couldn't afford to be recognized. So Biddle had to work it on his own. Which made it more difficult and more dangerous. He made only two trips up there the whole time.''

Rita nodded.

"And then," I said, "Killebrew got out of the slammer, and last spring the two of them went back to the Hopi reservation. Only this time, they were almost caught. An old man stumbled onto them while they were digging up a grave. Killebrew killed him.''

She frowned, nodded again.

"That was Biddle's last trip, according to Lucero," I told her. "He didn't mind making a few quick bucks robbing graves, but he didn't want to be involved in murder.''

"Murder One," said Rita.

She was right. The grave robbing was a felony, and any homicide committed during a felony automatically becomes first-degree murder.

I said, "Neither one of them, Biddle or Killebrew, told Griego about the killing. But the old man's body was found, and because he'd obviously been killed during a looting expedition, the F.B.I. came in. It also made the papers, even here in Santa Fe. Griego spotted it. It was only a tiny little article, Lucero says, almost a filler, but naturally Griego knew what it meant. She told Killebrew that was the end.''

"Killebrew had other ideas.''

"Yeah." He let it alone for a while, and then came back at the end of the summer and told her he was going to start making the trips again.''

"Why?"

"Two reasons. First, the guy who'd been fencing the stuff he'd gotten on the burglaries here in town—some guy in New York, Lucero doesn't know his name—he refused to deal with Killebrew after he got busted. So Killebrew needed cash. And second, he'd learned—in prison, I think—how much money Griego had probably been getting for the stuff he'd provided. He felt she owed him. So he went to her, told her that if she wasn't prepared to come across with cash, and more of it, for whatever he brought back, he'd make a few telephone calls. To the F.B.I., to Customs, to the Fish and Game people. Griego was trapped.''

"Biddle wasn't in on this?"

"No. Griego told him about it later. It was the reason he was so pissed off at Killebrew. He couldn't do anything about it, though, because if Killebrew got caught, and talked, tried to plea-bargain, Biddle would've gone down the tubes with him."

"So if Biddle hadn't died," Rita said, "Killebrew might have kept on looting indefinitely."

"Right."

Rita sat back, sipped her lemonade. "It doesn't sound as though Killebrew killed him, does it?"

"No," I said. "Lucero says Killebrew was furious when he heard that Biddle was dead. The cops knew of the connection between the two of them, and Biddle's death brought a lot of pressure down on him."

"It brought a lot of pressure down on Silvia Griego as well, I imagine."

I nodded again. "Like I said, she was already cracking. Biddle's death nearly pushed her over the edge. The old man at the reservation had been bad enough, but this was someone she knew, someone she'd slept with. And she thought Killebrew had killed him."

Rita sipped her lemonade.

"And then," I said, "I showed up. I spooked her, Lucero says. She called him after I left the gallery, and she was talking about ending it, going to the cops before Killebrew killed her, too."

"And Lucero called Killebrew."

I nodded. "He says all he wanted to do was persuade Killebrew to talk to Griego, convince her he didn't off Biddle. I think that's probably true. I don't think he wanted Griego dead."

"But Killebrew did."

"Killebrew had more to lose. He had a couple of federal offenses hanging over him, *and* a murder charge—the old man on the reservation. He'd already done time, and he didn't want to do any more."

"So he went to Griego's house that night and killed her."

"And then I showed up and he clubbed me."

"You're lucky that's all he did, Joshua."

"I know. He was in a hurry to get out of there. If he'd had the time to think about it, he probably would've decided to finish me off."

"He almost did last night."

I shook my head. "He was after Lucero. I'm sure I would've been a nice bonus, but it was Lucero he wanted. And Lucero knew it. That's why he'd been hiding out since Tuesday, the day he learned Griego was dead. Lucero was the one person left who knew what had happened, and with Griego dead, sooner or later the cops would get to him. Killebrew didn't trust him to keep his mouth shut."

"How is Lucero doing?"

"Hector says he'll live. But the slug turned his right arm into Jell-O. He won't be carving any more kachinas for a while. Maybe not ever."

"He's told everything to the police."

"Yeah. It looks like this thing is pretty much over."

"Except for Killebrew," she said.

"They'll get him. Everyone in the world is after him right now, including the Feds. But I'll tell you, Rita, I don't think we're ever going to see that necklace of the Leightons.''

"Why not?"

"If Killebrew stole it, if he actually had it in his possession, he's probably dumped it by now. He's already got enough shit to worry about, without worrying about a hot necklace.''

She sipped her lemonade. "I don't think Killebrew stole it," she said.

I looked at her. "You don't, huh? Well if Killebrew didn't, then who did?"

"The same person who killed Frank Biddle."

"And who might that be?"

"I'm not sure," she said. "But I have an idea or two."

"And would you care to share them with me?"

She shook her head. "Not just yet. I want to make a few phone calls over the weekend. I should know for sure by Monday.''

"Rita," I said, "I hate it when you do this."

She laughed.

"What do you know," I said, "that I don't?"

"Nothing," she smiled. "Didn't you read the reports you brought me? Killebrew's burglaries two years ago?"

"Yeah, I read them. What was in them that was so important?''

"It wasn't what was in them," she said. "It was what *wasn't* in them."

I frowned. "Are we talking here about the curious incident of the dog in the nighttime?"

She nodded. "We are, Dr. Watson."

"Rita."

She smiled again. "Monday. In the meantime, Joshua, I think you should be very careful. Killebrew is still out there somewhere, and he has no reason to like you. Maybe you should leave town for a while, go up to Taos and get a room in one of the hotels.''

"I don't like Taos.''

"Are you carrying the gun?''

"Yes.''

She nodded. "Good.''

WHEN THE OFFICE PHONE rang at ten o'clock on Monday morning, I thought it might be Rita, calling to wrap everything up for me. It was Derek Leighton.

"Croft,'' he said, and his voice was harsh and coarse, fraying at the edges. "Croft, you've got to get out here! He's got her! He's got my daughter!''

"Slow down,'' I said. "Who's got your daughter?''

"*Killebrew*, goddamit! He's got *Miranda*; he's kidnapped her. There's a note and he wants money, a hundred thousand dollars, and he wants you to deliver it.''

"You're at home?''

"What? Yes, yes of course I'm at home.''

"I'll be right there.''

LEIGHTON MUST'VE BEEN standing just behind the door, because he swung it open only a second or two after I rang the bell. Jeans, boots, a denim work shirt with the tails hanging outside the pants. His face was blotched with red and his curly hair was tangled, as though he'd been raking it with his fingers. Breathing quickly through his mouth, he said, "Come in, come in.''

"Where's the note?'' I asked him.

"Living room,'' he said, and I followed him down the red tile steps. The note was on the sofa. He picked it up and handed it to me, his hands shaking.

I held it carefully, by the edges, but Leighton had obviously been worrying the thing, handling it again and again as he reread it. I didn't think it would show any prints but his. It was a half sheet of lined yellow legal paper, torn from the larger sheet, not cut. The writing was in neat block letters that had probably been done with a ruler.

IVE GOT YOUR KID. I WANT ONE HUNDRED THOUSAND IN USED BILLS READY BY FOUR OCLOCK. HAVE CROFT THERE TO GET INSTRUCTIONS FOR DELIVERY. NO GUNS AND NO COPS OR I SWEAR TO GOD THE GIRL DIES.

"Will you do it?" Leighton asked me, urgency making the words tumble out. "Will you carry the money? I'll pay you whatever you want."

"Mr. Leighton, sit down for a minute."

"Don't bloody tell me what to do!" A vein pulsed at his temple. He ran his hand back along his scalp, swallowed, took a deep breath. Trying to level out. "If you won't carry it, I'll carry it myself."

"Everything will be all right," I told him. I didn't really believe that, but the man was working himself into a coronary. "Let's sit down and see what we've got here."

He frowned, but sat down in the padded white chair. Still breathing heavily through his mouth, he leaned forward and rested his arms along his thighs, letting his hands dangle. I sat down on the sofa and held up the note. "When did this come?"

"Twenty minutes ago." He looked at his Rolex. "Twenty-five minutes, a half an hour. Five minutes or so before I called you."

"And how did it come?"

He took another deep breath, let it slowly out. "The doorbell rang. When I answered it, there was no one there." He nodded to the note. "That was lying on the mat."

"You didn't see or hear anyone?"

"I thought I heard a car driving away. But by the time I read that and got out to the gate, it was gone."

"Your wife's not home?"

"She spent the night down in Albuquerque with the Duprees."

"Have you called her?"

He pursed his lips, looked away. "She has a friend down there." I knew from the way he said it that friend meant lover. "I can't reach her, and she won't be back until tonight." He shook his head, ran his hand through his hair again. "This will kill her."

I asked him, "Are you normally home on Monday?"

He looked up. "Yes, but what's that got to do with anything? My God, man, we're sitting here talking and that bastard Killebrew has got my daughter."

"First of all," I said, "we don't know that Killebrew sent the note."

"Of course it was Killebrew!" He pointed to the note. "He knows your bloody name, for godsakes! He's trying to get away, that's what the newspaper said. He needs money, and so the sonofabitch has taken my daughter to get it."

"Mr Leighton, if it is Killebrew, and I think you're probably right, it is, you've got to remember that the man's not stupid. He knows that his best chance of getting away with this is to keep her alive and well." I hoped that was true. I said, "You've got to call the police."

"Are you *insane*? Didn't you read what he said. He'll *kill* her."

"Kidnapping is a federal offense, Mr. Leighton. Any evidence of it and the F.B.I. can come in right away. They've got equipment, resources—"

He sat up. "Absolutely not. I forbid it, Croft, do you hear me? This is my daughter we're talking about, and I've got the right to make the decision. If you won't carry the bloody money, I'll carry it myself."

"Nothing's going to get accomplished here if we don't stay calm. Are you positive that Miranda is actually missing? When was the last time you saw her?"

Another deep breath. "Last night. She went over to a friend's house, Nancy Garcia, over on Gonzalez. I called there after I called you. Miranda left there this morning to go to school."

"This friend of hers, Nancy. She and Miranda went to school together?"

"No. They both have their own cars. And I called the school right after I called you. Miranda never showed up for classes."

"We'll have to talk to Nancy."

"I did, I insisted on it. She said that the last time she saw Miranda was when the two of them left her house this morning."

I sighed. None of it looked very good.

"Well, Croft," said Leighton. "Are you going to help me? Are you going to carry the money?"

"Can you raise that much by four o'clock?"

"Of course."

Of course.

I thought about Killebrew. As Rita had said, the man had no reason right now to like me. And he was running scared. I thought about the note; it's telling me no guns. I thought about the girl. Just another adolescent girl, a bit gawky, a bit awkward, just another pair of pale gray eyes blinking behind thick horn-rim glasses.

I sighed again. "I'll carry it," I said.

LEIGHTON WENT OFF to talk to bankers and brokers. I went off to talk to Rita. She had some ideas, and she made some suggestions.

By three o'clock I was back at Leighton's house. He had the money, one hundred thousand dollars, mostly in small bills, neatly piled inside a Lufthansa flight bag.

He waited. Neither one of us said much. The call came exactly at four, and Leighton answered it.

"Hello?" His voice was ragged and his knuckles were white as his hand gripped the receiver. His face lit up. "*Miranda!* Miranda baby are you okay?" He canted his torso to the right, leaning into the phone. "Okay baby, it's going to be okay, I promise. Okay, okay, baby. He's right here. I'll put him on." He held out the receiver to me, his lips compressed, his brow furrowed.

I took the receiver, put it to my ear. "Hello."

"Mr. Croft?" The voice was thin and frail.

"Yes, Miranda."

"He says to bring the money to the Cerillos turn-off on Route Fourteen. At six-thirty. He says no policemen, Mr. Croft. He says he'll kill me."

"Is Killebrew there, Miranda?"

"Yes, he—" And the line went dead.

# NINETEEN

THE CERILLOS TURN-OFF had been a good choice. South of Santa Fe on Route 14, it stood on a rise of land with a view for miles in every direction. There was no traffic this time of day, and if you saw more than one car coming to the drop, or spotted a helicopter clattering in your direction, you could simply drive away and give it a shot some other time.

It was high desert country all around, rocky and gullied, crisscrossed by narrow arroyos, barren except for the occasional piñon or mesquite. Far off to my right as I approached, the sun was setting behind the Jemez Mountains and a bright red stain was spreading across the pale blue sky.

At the top of the incline, on the far side of the dirt road that led to the small town of Cerillos, was a ragged jumble of rock maybe fifty feet high. I saw no car parked nearby, but if people were waiting for me, they were waiting in there, hidden.

I swung the Subaru off the road and parked it. I lifted the Lufthansa bag from the seat and got out, closed the door.

A narrow passageway led between the rocks into thickening shadow. The rocks were boulders, all piled helter-skelter atop one another, each big enough to hide someone with a gun.

I shifted the flight bag into my left hand and took a step into the the passageway.

And stopped. And called out: "Killebrew." Playing it according to the script. And hoping that Rita had been right about it.

There was a sound up ahead, a click and rattle of stone, and then suddenly, as though she'd been pushed, the girl lurched out from behind one of the rocks. Fifteen feet away. She wore running shoes, khaki slacks, a silver Porsche racing jacket.

She adjusted her glasses and I could see a movement in her throat as she swallowed. She said, "He has a gun, Mr Croft."

I reached into my windbreaker and slid the .38 free and held it out. "So do I."

Her voice went higher. "Mr. Croft, he'll shoot you."

"I don't think so, Miranda."

She pleaded. "Mr. *Croft*."

"Forget it, Miranda. I know what happened."

She shook her head, her arms pointed straight down, her hands balled into fists at her sides. Confusion twisted her features. "What are you talking about?"

"Did Biddle figure out that you stole the necklace? Or did you tell him?"

She shook her head, pale brown hair flying, "Mr. Croft, honestly, I don't know what you're talking about."

"Where's Killebrew, Miranda? How come he hasn't shot me yet?"

Abruptly she straightened up, crossed her arms over her breasts. She said nothing. The light was fading more quickly now, all the color in the world moving toward gray.

When Rita had laid it all out for me this afternoon, my first reaction had been disbelief. The girl had seemed, the two times I saw her, too young and too vulnerable. Too innocent. And maybe those of us who see so little of it are the ones who most want to believe in innocence.

But the indications, the signposts, had been there all along. The clothes on the mother's floor, the earlier robberies, the necklace never turning up, the fact of Biddle's—and Killebrew's—fondness for young girls.

I asked her, "Did you know it was the real necklace when you took it? Or didn't you care? Were you just trying to hurt your mother?"

She spoke, and her voice was petulant. "I think you're going crazy, Mr. Croft."

"The clothes, Miranda. Your mother's lingerie. Tossed all over the room. Killebrew wouldn't have done that. No professional burglar would." There had been no vandalism at any of the houses Killebrew had actually robbed. That had been what Rita meant, that had been the thing that wasn't in the reports. Nolan hadn't noticed it, or hadn't cared; he had wanted to nail Killebrew.

She said nothing.

"Your friend Nancy Garcia," I said. "Her family's house was robbed two years ago. It was in the police reports, and a friend of mine talked to her mother today. You knew what a real burglary was like; you knew the details. You knew how to fake one."

She merely stood there, watching me.

"You came back to the house, punched in the right sequence for the alarm—your brother *had* set it, hadn't he."

Still nothing from the girl.

"You knocked out the window in the living room, to make the burglary look real, and then you went upstairs and went through your mother's room."

She said, and her lip was curled in a sneer, "You can't prove any of this."

"I don't know why you were so angry at your mother—"

"You saw the way she treats me." She spat the words at me, fast and vicious. Then, as though regaining control of herself, she began to speak calmly, deliberately. "She hates me. She orders me around. She makes me feel stupid and ugly and clumsy." Suddenly the girl cocked her head and said, "Why does she do that, Mr. Croft?" Asking me with genuine curiosity in her voice, as though there were actually an answer, and I knew what it was.

"I don't know, Miranda. She's afraid, probably. Most of us are afraid of something. Of growing old. Of losing her control, maybe. Of losing her looks."

I could hear the disbelief in her voice. "But she's *beautiful*."

"But that won't last forever."

I saw that she didn't really accept it. When you're sixteen, everything lasts forever.

"She sent Frank away," she said.

"You and Frank were..." I hesitated, looking for the right word. There really wasn't one.

"He liked me," she said. "He said he liked me a lot. He gave me cocaine. We had a lot of good times."

It had been Miranda and Biddle talking about cocaine that her father had overheard, not Kevin and Biddle. And that had been, as Leighton admitted later, the reason he had fired Biddle.

"Your mother didn't send Frank away, Miranda."

"Yes she did. She used him, she had an affair with him, and then she threw him away."

"Did Frank tell you that?"

"He didn't have to. I've got *eyes*, you know."

"Miranda, when did Frank find out about the necklace?"

"Two weeks ago. I told him."

"You were seeing him again."

"He came to the house and asked me to meet him. He said he still liked me."

Had Biddle suspected all along that the girl had taken it? Possibly. He'd worked there, almost lived there for a long time. He must've seen how things were with the mother and the daughter.

"Why'd you kill him, Miranda?"

"I didn't mean to. I really didn't. He said he talked to you and found out we could get money for the necklace. He was going to sell the necklace back to the insurance company. He said we could go away together."

I nodded. Although the air had grown cold, my hand was beginning to sweat along the grip of the revolver.

"But I didn't want to. The necklace is mine now. It belongs to me. I didn't want to sell it."

"He threatened to let people know that you'd stolen it."

"That was when I knew he was lying. About liking me. He only wanted the necklace. He wanted the money."

"You had him meet you at the arroyo."

"I wanted to frighten him away. I thought if I showed him the gun, he could see that I was serious and he'd leave me alone. But he only laughed at me, and then he kept coming at me. I really didn't mean to kill him. I swear I didn't."

"What about Killebrew?" I said. "Did you really mean to kill him?"

She pursed her lips and shook her head, suddenly stubborn. "I don't have to answer any of your questions."

"He has to be dead, Miranda. It's the only way you could make this work. Did you know him before this? Was he somebody else who gave you cocaine?"

"I've got to get away," she said, and there was a frantic edge to her voice. "You don't understand. Nobody does. Nothing's right anymore. It's like, since it happened, since

I shot him, it's like there's this glass wall between me and everything else, you know? Like I reach out to touch things, or be with people, and I can't get to them. I'm trapped inside there, and I don't want it to be that way anymore. I've got to go *away*, Mr. Croft. I've got to get *out*, and I need that money."

She didn't understand yet, she might never understand, that no matter where she went, the wall of glass would be there, separating her from the rest of the world. It's the human condition—we're all of us separated, one from another, by those same walls. Miranda had just run up against hers earlier than most of us do.

I shook my head. "I'm sorry, Miranda."

She frowned. "What's going to happen to me?"

"I think we've got to talk to the police. The two of us."

"They'll tell my parents," she said. "And then they'll send me away."

"I think your parents will help you, Miranda."

"Not *her*. She'll say it's what I deserve." She uncrossed her arms and her hands moved toward the pockets of the racing jacket.

I knew what she was going to try. There was one other person who had to be out of the way before this thing would work. I raised the gun. "Don't, Miranda."

"I'm cold, is all," she said. She shrugged, and then she smiled. In the twilight, for a moment then, she looked the way she would in a year or two, still young, but tall and poised and very beautiful. "You're not going to shoot me just because I'm *cold*." She put her hands in her pockets.

I pulled the trigger.

The slug couldn't have come closer to her than three feet. But she'd never been shot at before. Her hands jerked from her pockets, empty, and her mouth fell open. When I reached her, she was shaking. I took the pistol from her jacket pocket and slipped it into the pocket of my windbreaker. I put my hand on her shoulder. "Come on, Miranda. Everything will be all right."

It was the second time I'd said that today, and both times it had been a lie.

BUT FOR A WHILE THERE, it seemed as though perhaps I hadn't lied, that everything might, in fact, turn out all right. At least for Miranda.

Because the girl was sixteen years old, the state had the option of charging her either as an adult or as a juvenile. If charged as an adult, and convicted, she faced a mandatory life sentence in the penitentiary, with no parole for thirty years. If charged as a juvenile, she faced a year in the New Mexico Girls School, in Albuquerque.

Derek Leighton got her the best lawyer in the state, a former governor with a lot of flash and dazzle. From what I understand, Miranda's testimony to the police and to the courts was impressive. She seemed open, honest, and sincerely repentant. She admitted shooting Biddle, but claimed it was an accident. She admitted stealing the necklace and the gun, and keeping them, but claimed she was sorry. She admitted shooting through my living-room window, but claimed that she hadn't meant to hurt anyone, only to scare her mother and me, and to stop me from looking for the necklace. That last part, at least, I believe.

She claimed she knew nothing about Killebrew or his disappearance, and that part the police believed. The official theory was that after shooting at John Lucero and me, he had left the town, left the state, left the country.

Rita didn't agree. She was convinced that the girl had gotten in touch with him somehow, had lured him off somewhere and killed him. I was inclined to agree with her;

I'd seen Miranda reach into that windbreaker for the gun, and I'm certain that she intended to use it.

The court chose to try her as a juvenile. She was indicted for second-degree homicide, and she was convicted and sentenced to a year in the Girls School. She was due to be released in about three months.

Two weeks ago, a pair of hikers found a man's decomposed body in a shallow grave in the forest up by the ski basin. The police investigation established that the man had been killed there, on or near the spot where he was buried, that he'd been buried almost immediately after having been shot, and that this had all occurred approximately a year ago, last spring. The run-off of winter's meltwater, and the foraging animals, had exposed the body. Dental records from the penitentiary helped identify it as Killebrew's, and the forensic lab of the state police had no trouble, even after all this time, matching the slug found in the body with the others fired from Miranda's gun.

Her trial is set for next month. And the betting is that everything, this time, will not turn out all right.

I found the necklace, that day last year at the Cerillos turn-off, in the glove compartment of her Jeep Renegade, which she'd parked on the other side of the mound of boulders. Atco paid the finder's fee to the Mondragón agency, but Allan Romero told Rita that Derek Leighton never reimbursed them for it. He didn't want the necklace back.

A DEB RALSTON MYSTERY

# HACKER

*First Time in Paperback*

 LEE MARTIN

### OVERKILL

Hovering perilously near burnout with the demands of police duty and family life—specifically toddler, husband, teenager and a friend comatose from a hit-and-run—Fort Worth detective Deb Ralston now adds a grisly ax murder to her twenty-five-hour days.

A man and his computer are hacked to pieces. Eric Huffman had no enemies, no reason to be so violently murdered. The evidence is thin, but disturbing...since the pattern seems poised to repeat itself in Deb's own household.

"Martin continues the fine work begun in the earlier *Deficit Ending* and *The Mensa Murders*..."  —*Booklist*

**Available in January at your favorite retail stores.**

## LAST REMAINS

Had sweet, fragile, silver-haired Jane Engle, school librarian and churchgoer, murdered someone and put the victim's skull in her window seat? Did Aurora Teagarden, fellow librarian and astonished beneficiary of Jane's estate—including house, cat and half a million dollars—want to expose her friend as a murderess?

An intruder's careful search alerts Aurora to the unsettling fact that somebody else knows about the skull. Where is the rest of the body?

"Harris provides some genuinely funny scenes..."
—*Publishers Weekly*

**Available in January at your favorite retail stores.**

# A BONE TO PICK

AN AURORA TEAGARDEN MYSTERY

## Charlaine Harris

# FLASHBACK

**First Time in Paperback**

## TED WOOD

### DISTURBING THE PEACE

As chief of the one-man police force in a small Canadian summer resort town, Reid Bennett and his police dog, Sam, lead a quiet life. But things change overnight. A teen gang is threatening Reid's town. A bank robber who has sworn vengeance on him is on the loose. Worst of all, though, is the body. A stolen car, its radio missing and seats slashed, has sunk in the lake. It might have been just a routine case of vandalism—until a woman's body is discovered in the locked trunk.

Just as Reid begins to follow his hunch that the link between Marcia Tracy—an ambitious movie producer summering nearby—the gang leader and the body in the trunk is more than coincidental, another corpse and a stash of drugs point to a conspiracy that's getting too big for a small town.

"Wood's books are charactertized by clearcut plots, lots of action and backwoods adventure..."

—*Alfred Hitchcock Mystery Magazine*

**Available in February at your favorite retail stores.**

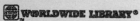

# Caught in the Shadows

## C. A. Haddad

**STRANGER THAN FICTION**

Hacking may be borderline legal, but the profit is there, big-time, especially in a high-profile divorce case such as the one Chicago computer "researcher" Becky Belski has just been handed.

Arrest record? Bank statement? Charges? If it's in a computer network, Becky can find it. What she didn't expect to find was a link to her own murky half-forgotten past…and the murder of her stepfather.

An open-and-shut case convicted Becky's mother more than twenty years ago. Now Becky is certain that the wrong person went to jail. Between hacking away at the past and juggling two men, she finally discovers the shocking truth.

"The hallmark of the C. A. Haddad mysteries…is that they're sassy, sexy and very funny."—*Publishers Weekly*

**Available in February at your favorite retail stores.**

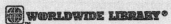

# COFFIN AND THE PAPER MAN

First Time in Paperback

## Gwendoline Butler

A
JOHN
COFFIN
MYSTERY